ELIZABETH REED ADEN/EUNICE MAYS BOYD

MURDER WEARS MUKLUKS

An Alaska Vintage Mystery

Bonanza Road and its seven houses, as well as
all the characters and events in this book, are
entirely fictitious

Contents

Acknowledgments

This book was republished by Eunice Mays Boyd's goddaughter, Elizabeth Reed Aden. Many thanks go to her nephew Harry Mays and her grand-nephews, Kirk Rademaker and John Rademaker, and her grandniece, Erica Rademaker each of whom granted their consent to make the republication of the book possible. Many thanks as well to Verena Rose for accepting the book for republication.

Praise for Murder Wears Mukluks

I read the charming MURDER WEARS MUKLUKS many years ago, I am delighted that it is being republished and still wish you'd selected Mysterious Press to publish it. —Otto Penzler, President & CEO, Mysterious Press (2025)

She [Eunice Mays Boyd] wrote only three mysteries, all set in Alaska, the first mystery writer I believe who used that state for the primary setting. Her detective character is F. Millard Smyth, a "little mild-mannered grocer." —J.F. Norris, Pretty Sinister Books (2012)

Who's going to resist a murder mystery about *mukluks*? I mean, **really** ? Fabulous—-detailed, colorful, set it a very specific time and place—-Fairbanks, Alaska, in living memory of the great prospecting days, even though the ghost could only be one person, and even though the heroine's love interest is a scary control freak whom she very much wants out of her life (before she suddenly realizes she just loves being dominated by a scary control freak!), this is still one humdinger of a novel. Read it to learn what's fun about high tension. —Victoria Mixon, fiction editor and author *The Art and Craft of Fiction: A Practitioners' Manual*

CHAPTER ONE

For the first time in his life F. Millard Smyth wished for a full-length mirror. But the foot-square shaving glass was the only mirror in his cabin. He'd have to view his newly fur-clad figure in sections.

Clumsy in white fur mittens, he set the shaving mirror on the floor and admired the feet of his white reindeer mukluks and the crossed and tied leather thongs, admired all he could see of the leg.

He propped the glass on a chair and beamed at the furry checked band of black and white and fluffy fringe of gray-tan wolf on the top of the mukluks and bottom of the parka.

Stacking an armful of magazines on the chair raised the mirror enough to show, by judicious tipping, the knee-to-neck expanse of white reindeer parka body and around his neck the childish harness of varicolored yarn attached to the mittens.

Back on its nail above the washstand, the glass reflected the hood and the spectacled face inside it. Turning his head like a girl with a new hair-do, F. Millard's mild blue eyes caressed the tan wolverine face-frame and met their own reflection in a delighted, sheepish grin that tucked his chin down, prickling, into the coarse wolverine hairs.

"My gracious!" he said aloud. These clothes weren't made for house wear. Fumbling for a handkerchief to wipe his forehead he pushed back his parka hood.

As it fell away from his ears he heard the deep-throated, drawn-out wail of scores of dogs howling in concert. And not even the warmth of his furs could stop a little shiver. What his sourdough neighbors called the "Malemute Chorus" might be only further, and possibly delightful, proof that he lived in Alaska; but every time a lone dog's howl set off the others, F. Millard's flesh crept.

The chorus died and silence settled over Fairbanks. In the hush came a sharp report.

His slight body stiffened under the parka and his eyes leaped to the stack of magazines on the chair. From the cover on top, beneath the word *Flatfoot* in red, the pictured eyes and gun muzzle of Flatfoot Flannagan fixed him.

F. Millard told himself he'd been reading too many detective stories; that report hadn't sounded quite like a shot. Surely not a shot. Only the dogs' mournful howling had given it significance.

He crossed the room and jerked the door open.

Outside, Bonanza Road was as quiet as his cabin. Both street lights were out again, he saw with surprise. They had gone out last night too, but were on when he came home from the store this evening. A short circuit, perhaps, as there were lights in two of the three cabins across the street, and the windows next door spilled light on the snow in cheerful yellow oblongs.

Snow kept the night from utter blackness. But it was black enough to make a hazard of the jagged stack of polewood unloaded today in front of his house. He must have it sawed and piled, though Bonanza Road was a dead-end street, and no one lived between him and the river. He wouldn't want to fall over the wood pile himself on his frequent trips to the warehouse.

He turned toward the frozen Chena and the building on his right, looming big and dark beside his small cabin. Only a prosaic warehouse now, included in the grocery deal with Tom Blaine, it had once been a dance hall. F. Millard never could move about among the cases of canned goods piled there without peopling the long ground-floor room with clamorous miners and spangled-dressed girls, dancing, gambling, at the bar. In fancy, gay girls in gayer costume swished along the balcony or down the open stairway.

Merely looking at the old Bonanza whisked him back to the years before dance halls were outmoded and it had been floated downriver from the center of town. Here it gave this block-long street its name and settled back in tattered finery to the dull state of warehousehood.

F. Millard had been just too young for the Klondike and Nome stampedes and, after his father's death, too firmly bound to the family grocery to leave home till his mother died. In his wistful imagination the old Bonanza was still uptown and doing a roaring business. For him the dog teams he had missed still panted outside its double doors, where townsmen, shapeless in fur, shouldered miners who went in with full pokes and sometimes came out with them flat. The other door, too, had its patrons, leading up the outside covered stairs to the balcony booths where a man could dine and drink less publicly with a special girl.

F. Millard sighed and came back from 1905 to the present. That covered stairway, once flush with the walk, still clung to the river side of the building; the three or four broken-off bottom steps left space for his ash can to stand on the ground under shelter. Only one of the double doors was used now when F. Millard twice a day banked the fire that kept his canned goods from freezing. He'd wait till after lodge meeting to bank it tonight.

His eyes came back to the logs in the street. What was that? Had a shadow moved at the warehouse end of the pile? Craning his neck above the fur of his folded-back hood he peered nearsightedly into the dark.

The wood made a long black blot on the nearly black snow. Beyond, the warehouse loomed black and tall against the sky. All the shadows in a street of shadows were still now—if any had ever moved. That was probably the answer: he'd peopled Bonanza Road so thickly with ghosts that his eyes had begun to play tricks.

A moon would have helped him sort out shadows, but there was no moon tonight. Across the speckling of stars above the warehouse a finger of northern lights flickered and withdrew. A dog raised a mournful howl in the distance, and from all over town the Malemute Chorus chimed in.

F. Millard shivered in his parka. Anything unmoved by that spine-chilling performance must be inanimate. And if he didn't hurry up he was going to be late to lodge meeting.

He stepped back in and closed the door. A clean handkerchief and the store keys. . . . Too bad he'd lost the key to the warehouse. But this was a little-used street, and for the benefit of imported construction workers and soldiers, he'd been putting on a show of turning an imaginary key every time he entered in the daylight—not much of that in a Fairbanks January.

Now a quick slick at his mouse-colored hair just sprinkled with gray, and he'd be ready to pull up his parka hood and go. His lodge brothers ought to think he was prospering when they saw his handsome new furs. Or should he tell them he'd let a native family turn them in on their bill? But good gracious, the whole town didn't know he was having money trouble, did it?

Clunk! A solid, wood-ringing sound came in from outdoors, a thump he wouldn't have noticed on a street less quiet, through air less crisply clear. Someone must have missed F. Millard's path in the dark and bumped into an outthrust log. But the wood was stacked on the river side, and Bonanza Road ended at the river; Front Street wasn't cut through.

He hurried to the door. In the light yellowing the snow he saw a figure in another white parka by the wood pile. The hooded head turned, and he recognized Tom Blaine.

"Why, Mr. Blaine—why, Tom," the little grocer stammered, "you're the last person in Fairbanks I'd expect to *miss* this path. Even a year and a half in California—" He interrupted his own forced jocularity in surprise. "Aren't you going to come in?"

The other man hesitated, then turned abruptly up F. Millard's path, and the yellow patch on the snow narrowed and vanished as the door closed behind both white parkas.

In the cabin F. Millard placed a second chair beside the stove. Funny to think of being too warm just a few minutes ago. Now he was cold. And the other man's face was cold in a way that had nothing to do with thirty below zero weather. The hard chill in his eyes beneath jutting brows where outdoor frost still clung was harder and chillier than yesterday when he had looked up F. Millard at the store. It was almost impossible now to think back a year and a half to the time Tom Blaine had sold him the store and that face had been all one genial grin and that hand in the fisted mitten always out to shake F. Millard's or clap him on the back.

The straight line of Blaine's lips divided. "I wasn't kidding yesterday,

Smyth. I can't wait for those back payments any longer. You'll have to arrange to make them somehow—right away."

And this was the man who had lowered the price of the store and told F. Millard to take his time, the man who had offered his cabin at the lake and asked F. Millard to call him Tom—a year and a half ago. Six months ago Blaine had written that a few overdue payments made no difference, and even a month ago intimated that F. Millard could let them run a little longer.

"I—I'll see what I can do," F. Millard croaked.

"See fast," the other rumbled. "I've been too damn easy with you. Guess that's what comes of doing business with the sort of Outside trash that takes advantage of kindness."

The little man straightened indignantly in his parka. "Why, I never— You know I'm not like that! Ask anyone in town. Ask your nephew across the street. Ask your friend Beulah Raymond next door."

"My nephew!" snorted Blaine. "Beulah Raymond! All you've got to do is get the money, to show me what you are."

"You know very well what the war's done to the grocery business," F. Millard exclaimed with a sharpness he was too indignant to be surprised at. "And here in Alaska with all the freight coming by boat—"

"The war was on when you bought the place," grunted Blaine.

"But I didn't know the man who bought my Nebraska grocery was going to die, or his widow have an auto accident and spend five months in the hospital. I was counting on those Nebraska payments to swing this. I told you all about it, and you said—"

Blaine stood up. "What I say now is get that money. I've got every right to demand it, and I'll expect you to have it tomorrow."

F. Millard stood up too and tried to make himself as tall as Blaine. "I'll go to the bank tomorrow," he said stiffly, "and see if they'll accommodate me." And do the best he could, he thought, with his mental chin up, about the doubled rate of interest.

"If the bank won't let you have it, get it somewhere else," Blaine commanded. "I've got to have it right away." He paused, and a slight thaw warmed his voice though not his eyes. "Don't let me keep you from lodge meeting. Now I won't have to see you later."

F. Millard watched the door shut, heard the catch fall in place, and moved closer to the stove. He should never have let his longing to live in Alaska get ahead of his business sense. A store that cost twice as much as his own was no store for him. And war conditions—borrowing to make his down payment—installments not coming from the store he'd sold in Nebraska. . . . Funny that Tom Blaine had been so lenient at first, even right up to yesterday when he and his bride came in on the Seattle plane. . . . Three thousand dollars. If Blaine hadn't been so lenient F. Millard might have managed some way to do more than meet the interest, and not let so many payments slide. Funny to think of a man Blaine's age, older than himself, with a bride. Three thousand dollars. . . .

At last F. Millard sighed and looked at his watch. Eight-twenty. The meeting began at eight-fifteen; anyone more than five minutes late had a five-dollar fine slapped on him. He couldn't afford five-dollar fines now. Besides, after seeing Blaine, he was out of the mood for lodge.

Then F. Millard jumped to his feet. A man only got his first parka and mukluks once. By gracious, he wasn't going to let Shylock Blaine spoil everything! He'd christen these new clothes if he did no more than walk up and down the block!

Drawing the parka hood over his head he pulled the light cord and found the door in the dark by long practice.

With the light behind him gone, the snow-wrapped night looked only gray. But not light enough to see the hard thing his toe sent spinning against the wood pile. If the street light by the warehouse had been burning he wouldn't need to grope by hand to identify what he'd kicked: an eight or ten inch chunk of icicle as big around as his wrist. Funny place to find it. His own house was nearest, with a roof too tight to drip an icicle that big. And there was just enough fire in the warehouse to keep the canned goods from freezing. Canned goods—grocery —Blaine—three thousand dollars.

He jerked his mind back to the icicle. *Keep it there*, he told himself; *don't think of anything else.* The two oldest cabins across the street, the Malones' and the Hawleys', were heavily fringed with ice, and icicle fighting was a favorite sport of the local young. But there weren't any young on Bonanza Road, unless he counted dainty, gray-eyed Klondike Malone who was just out of high school and worked at the drugstore soda fountain. Or Whit Hawley, the bombardier whose crew had been given a furlough. Or the young man named Valentine Voss who lived in Whit's house and worked on the local paper.

Across the street, as F. Millard turned left toward Second Avenue, the Malones' and Hawleys' lighted windows eclipsed the faint, starlit glimmer of the icicles trimming their eaves. The newer, tighter-roofed Trent house on the corner next to Hawleys' had no more icicles than F. Millard's. Mae Trent couldn't have set her watch by the grocer tonight, even if she'd been home, and the street light burning on the corner. Tonight the Trent house was dark and the street light out and F. Millard nearly half an hour late—and not on his way to lodge meeting as he always was on Tuesday nights.

The single block of Bonanza Road ended. On Second Avenue, both upstream toward town and downstream past more cabins, widely spaced bulbs with feeble reflectors twinkled their brash challenge to the stars. There was nothing wrong with the street lights on Second. What a relief it was to be rid of the blue headlights and sunset-to-sunrise blackouts of the months that followed Pearl Harbor, to have bright windows and street lights again.

His eyes lifted to the bulb that wasn't burning. Above it, the yellow finger of northern lights that he'd seen a while ago was bolder, quicker, stronger, knotting scarfs of green and red into its contortions. Telephone wires sang in the cold. He felt the presence of the wilderness beyond the town—the miles of forest and tundra.

All alone in the dark F. Millard smiled. Fur mittens stroked his fur parka. In spite of the war and financial troubles he was glad he had bought Blaine's grocery. Now he held the rank he had longed for. Watching the freeze-up and break-up of the Chena—whose waters flowed into the Tanana and through its bed to the Yukon—had bestowed on the little grocer the cherished title of Sourdough.

A malemute howled, and F. Millard's eyes returned to Bonanza Road with its few squares of bright windows. They made the street even darker by contrast. He couldn't see the pile of logs by his cabin. Or could he? Was that a shadow? He blinked, and the shadow was gone. But after all, with the Aurora writhing overhead, anything could happen to a shadow.

He shifted his weight from one mukluk to the other. His new clothes were tested now and there was nothing to be done about his money troubles till morning. Might as well bank the warehouse fire and go to bed.

Even the Fairbanks winter custom of using the street for a sidewalk was endearing, thought F. Millard as he started back. In Frank Ord's cabin on the corner of his own block, light showed at the edge of drawn shades. If Beulah Raymond hadn't shared her neighborly attentions equally with Frank on her left and F. Millard on her right, the little grocer might have liked the younger man better—big and careless and easy-muscled as he was.

Beulah's place, from this side too, oozed light at every window. The bedroom and kitchen shades were down, but the front windows still made yellow oblongs on the snow. Since Frank's place was lighted, he probably wasn't at Beulah's, but she might have other company. Anyway, F. Millard didn't feel like trying to keep up with her kidding tonight or struggling with a new dance step. It was nice of her—so much younger, and popular and all—to bother with a shy, middle-aged duffer like himself, but he wouldn't stop in tonight.

The bulky warehouse beyond his cabin looked dark and almost forbidding. He could make out the wood pile now well enough to skirt it, and just as he kicked the broken icicle again, or another like it, a stray dog began to howl in F. Millard's own back yard. That ought to explain the chunks of ice. He'd throw a few, himself, to stop those howls.

Again his head turned in its cozy hood toward the ice-fringed cabins across the way. In the Malone house, nearest the river, the shades were crooked, as usual. But what wispy young girl with a full-time job and an invalid mother, with dances and movies and boy friends, could be expected to straighten shades? Wasn't it just like an ex-dance-hall girl to name her daughter Klondike? After what had happened tonight F. Millard could understand for the first time something of Mrs. Malone's bitterness toward Tom Blaine. It dated back to dance-hall days and the injury on which she blamed her present partial paralysis. In those days people called her Silver Star for her pre-Jean-Harlow platinum hair and her maiden name of Starr. The old-timers called her that yet. She used to dance in the Bonanza while it was still uptown. And here they both were, woman and building together once more, growing old on the same back street.

The dog howled again, and F. Millard hurried up the shoveled path to the warehouse. This was one time he wouldn't have to make a show of unlocking the door. Too bad he didn't have his flashlight in his pocket when he pulled the parka on over his suit. With the door shut and post-Pearl Harbor blackout shields still on the windows, the building was black—cold, too, but warm enough to fog his glasses and make him doubly glad of the aisle of boxes to lead him to the light cord in the dark.

One mittened hand sliding along the cartons he reached for the light cord, and stubbed his toe on a box out of line. Straightening, he reached up again, but couldn't find the string attached to the chain. That stumble must have thrown him off. He took a step backward and batted air, another forward and batted air. Step. Bat. Step. Bat. He began to fight reasonless panic.

Involuntarily he rubbed a mitten over his steamed glasses. How silly, he scolded himself, with that clutch of panic still at his throat, inside a completely dark room.

But it was not completely dark. With the steam rubbed away and his eyes uncovered he saw faint light beyond the edge of the balcony.

The clutch at his throat tightened. It must be just a stray prowler—a soldier hunting non-G.I. rations. . . .

Cautiously he made his way between boxes toward the pale gleam. Then he was far enough out in the room to see what made it. On the balcony along the left wall two candles burned on a table. Staring up, astonished, he caught a stir of movement among the shadowy booths that lined the wall. The movement took on form and sparkle, and a woman stepped from darkness into dim light.

Even in the flicker of two candles he could see the spangles on her red dress, the fullness of the skirt, the low-cut neck and white bosom above it, the outline of a gracious bust and hips and a tiny waist, the young round of her face, and the shining white pompadour of hair.

This was no old woman's face or figure, no old woman's walk. All he had ever seen of her was untidy white hair and a pain-racked face staring up from a pillow. But as surely, he felt, as she had once danced on the floor where he stood, that was Silver Star on the balcony above him— in the flesh of 1905.

CHAPTER TWO

The woman in the spangled dress peered over the balcony railing—right at him, F. Millard felt, shrinking into his parka. Her hair gleamed pale as a patch of moonlight above the flickering candles. Slowly one bare arm drew back, and between himself and the two tiny flames something made an arc through the air.

He tried to jump aside, and couldn't. All he could move was his shoulders. He jerked back as a shadow like a small bird passed with a faint, elusive perfume. He heard no sound of its fall and couldn't pull his eyes away from the girl to see what she had thrown.

The figure above bent farther forward, smiled, waved; then stepping back, broke into a gay little dance step. He couldn't see her feet, but the red skirt swirled and the spangles twinkled—and he heard no sound of steps.

The whirling stopped in an arm-raised pirouette like a Spanish senorita's, and the girl came nearer the railing. Her lips moved, but he heard no sound. Her smile widened into what must have been laughter, but still F. Millard heard no sound. Clapping one hand over her mouth, she rocked with noiseless mirth and beckoned to the man below. Then the beckoning finger pointed toward something past the candles.

F. Millard pried away his glance to probe the shadows. Dim booths behind the candles with deeper shadows in the corners, and on beyond the feeble range of mothlike flames nothing but the dark.

His eyes came back to the girl with hair like moonlight. She was laughing again—without sound—and her hands went through some fluttery routine meaningless to him. Suddenly she sobered, leaning toward him again above the railing. Her lips parted, not in a smile, and her mouth opened as if to form one syllable. One syllable that sent no sound to the watcher below, yet she looked as if she were calling. Both lips came together, then parted again, and the soundless call was repeated.

Once more she beckoned. Clammily wet under his parka, F. Millard started for the stairs at the back of the room. The girl shook her head, pointing with an outthrust arm to the balcony opposite above the shadowed bar. His eyes searched the gloom, and as they searched, the gloom turned into deep darkness. His head jerked back. The candles and woman were gone.

Stumbling wildly over boxes in the dark F. Millard rushed for the door. When he finally found it, clawed it open, and slammed it to behind him, he made no stop till he had also slammed the door of his cabin. For the first time since he'd been in Fairbanks, he locked his cabin door. Then, by the eerie aid of the Aurora outside the windows, made more eerie by renewed steam on his glasses, he found his own light cord and sat down in the heartening glare.

For a minute he only tried to stop shaking, and after that tried to think. The fact that he'd never seen a ghost —before—that his mother had told him there were no ghosts when he used to be frightened of the dark, actually *proved* nothing. One argument kept sticking in his mind: in the stories he'd read, ghosts appeared only after death or when their flesh-and-blood originals were dying, just passing over the divide. And only yesterday, when he ran in with some tomatoes just off the train, F. Millard had seen Silver Star Malone propped up on her pillows, looking the same as always, no more fragile, no more pale. Her voice had been as strong as ever, and as acid.

He must look at this levelheadedly, he told himself, with teeth down hard on his lower lip. Perhaps if he slipped his hands out of his mittens and held the palms near the stove they'd be warm and dry—perhaps.

There might be some practical explanation. There must be, of course. And that would mean the ghost hadn't been a ghost but a real live woman. He cleared his throat and sat straighter. But could Silver Star Malone, whose legs were paralyzed, walk across the street and up those balcony stairs, make that swirling-skirted pirouette? According to one school of writing, a bedridden invalid in Chapter One only paved the way for nocturnal expeditions in Chapter Two and a secret active life all through the book. If it was a murder story the bedridden invalid would be the murderer. But this wasn't a question of murder.

Let him yield a point. Suppose Silver Star Malone had been faking paralysis for years. Even if she could walk and climb stairs and dance, how in the name of goodness could she recover the curves and motion of youth? The bosom and hips might be managed, but how about the facial contour and shapely, firm-looking bare arms? Silver Star's face was ravaged and haggard, her arms on the blankets flabby. In their late fifties, with the right makeup, some women might have managed such a comeback, but he couldn't believe it of this one.

There was only one other answer on the practical side of the ledger: a younger woman impersonating the former dance-hall girl. Never mind why, for the moment. The figure on the balcony had been as buxom of breast and hip as Beulah Raymond, as tiny-waisted as Klondike Malone. The hair might be accounted for by a wig—a bit unlikely in a town the size of Fairbanks. Anyone could borrow an old dress of Silver Star's or make one like it. Klondike's hair was brown, and Beulah's, this year, red. Last year it had been yellow. Beulah Raymond had a beauty operator's license. She still took care of a few customers' hair in her home. If she could change the color of her own at will, why not tonight have made it platinum?

But, gracious—F. Millard jammed on a mental foot brake—whatever Beulah might do with her hair, she couldn't make her waist as hourglass small as that girl's had been tonight. That waistline let Beulah out, and didn't the face let out Klondike? Padding might account for the curves of the body on slim young Klondike Malone, but how could a slender face like hers bloom into the doll-roundness of the face of the girl he had seen? Could even eyebrow pencil turn the sharp slant of Klondike's brows —like bird wings at half stretch—into the nearly level line of her mother's—and that girl's?

Of course there were other women in Fairbanks, but why would anyone want to impersonate Silver Star?

Outside he heard the pat of running feet on packed snow. Hands beat a frantic tattoo on his door, and the knob rattled roughly. Nothing ghostly about those sounds. F. Millard jumped up and fumbled over the lock.

"Hurry, hurry," a girl's voice called, "I've got to—"

He jerked the door open and Klondike Malone tumbled in. Her hair was turbaned in a green bath towel. Her small face, usually so vivid, was white and frightened. A dark sweater hung crookedly over her shoulders. Her teeth chattered, and her whole slim body shook.

Leaning anxiously close to make sense of the words that came out in gasps, F. Millard saw something move on her forehead at the edge of the towel. A drop of water slid down into one upslanting brown eyebrow—eyebrows that held no trace of make-up.

Blinking he put out an involuntary hand to the towel.

"Why, Klondike," he cried, "your head's all wet and cold as ice! You'll catch pneu—"

"Oh, what's the difference now? What if I do? Mother —Mother . . ." She burst into tears.

F. Millard caught his breath. "Sh-sh-she—Silver Star— you mean she . . . What's happened, Klondike?"

"If I just hadn't been washing my hair! Oh, Mr. Smyth, if I hadn't left her so long. I was out in the kitchen—I had to heat the water—and when I went in her room, she looked so— Oh, Mr. Smyth, I've got to use your phone I"

"But what—?"

"I've got to call the doctor!" "D-doctor?"

"Mother's heart's been bad so long. And when I saw— I knew she couldn't—"

"Couldn't what, Klondike?" His breath was as short as her own.

"Oh, I'm afraid it's too late. Right while I was looking at her she . . . Oh, I've got to get the doctor. I'm afraid Mother—oh, I know Mother's—gone."

CHAPTER THREE

Gone! Silver Star Malone was dead. Or dying. And fifteen or twenty minutes ago . . .

He hardly heard Klondike's broken stammering on the telephone. When someone lay dying—reaching out—groping. . . . To return to a place she'd been happy in . . . .

He forced himself, when the girl hung up, to offer to go back with her across the street. Did she know, when she said she'd rather be alone, why he reached out so suddenly for a chair?

The door had closed and the last sound of her steps died away before F. Millard realized that he hadn't banked the warehouse fire.

Again moisture wet the palms of his hands. Go over there again where Silver Star had danced? Step beneath the very balcony where he had seen her? Seen her while she was dying.

But what about the canned goods? With the mercury at thirty below, if he let the fire die down overnight all his cases of canned goods would freeze. Tom Blaine was expecting three thousand dollars in the morning.

He had to fix that fire. But he couldn't go back to the warehouse tonight. If the light was still on at Hawley's . . .

He jumped up. It was. He hadn't taken off his parka and mukluks. Jerking off the light, he hurried out.

Whit's parents had left Alaska years ago. The two boys lived alone. F. Millard hoped it would be the reporter he'd find at home. Not that he knew Valentine Voss any better than Whit Hawley, already in the Air Force before

F. Millard came to Bonanza Road, but a name like Valentine must be as hard to bear as F. Millard's, and young Voss, too, wore glasses. He was a newcomer, a Cheechako, like F. Millard two years ago, with a meticulous neatness somewhat like his own.

But it was the furloughing bombardier instead of the reporter who opened the door.

"H-hello, sergeant," F. Millard stammered. "Is M-Mr. Voss in? I—I wondered if he'd do something for me."

Whit Hawley grinned down at the little man from his towheaded six-feet-two. Contrasted with such light hair and eyes and teeth, his skin looked Eskimo-brown. "Anything a Voss can do, a Hawley can do better."

"I—I—" Hadn't Beulah Raymond said Whit was crazy about Klondike? Perhaps F. Millard ought to tell him the girl's mother— But Beulah had also said Klondike couldn't bear Whit because his mother was Tom Blaine's sister. The poor child wouldn't welcome Blaine's nephew now. Anyway, F. Millard wasn't the town crier. Anybody's nephew could fix a fire, and wouldn't necessarily see ghosts. "I got a hurry call to come down to the store," the grocer mumbled. He had never learned to lie glibly. "Have to go right away, and I may be gone for hours, and if the fire in the warehouse isn't fixed—I was going to ask Mr. Voss—"

Whit grinned again. "Brother, I know that warehouse like the palm of my hand. Just leave me your key."

"Th-thank you, sergeant. I didn't lock the door. You don't know how I appreciate this." Not a fraction of how he appreciated it, F. Millard thought as he hurried up the street at a sort of squaw shuffle in his stiff-soled mukluks.

⁎⁎

It was after midnight when he returned, with more than six hours to go before the warehouse stove must be replenished. Those hours, long and dragged-out as they seemed toward morning, went altogether too fast.

At seven he cooked breakfast. He couldn't put off banking the fire much longer and reach the store before opening time. The two fried eggs on his plate looked revolting. He gulped a cup of coffee. Then a burst of second-cup inspiration sent him after his coat.

Not parka and mukluks today, but the old overcoat from Nebraska and the cap with a long flap that covered both ears. Feeling for the flashlight he always kept in his overcoat pocket, he opened the door. Without dragging in impersonations there was still one sane explanation—the only one left to grasp at—for the figure he'd seen last night. Klondike said she'd been washing her hair in the kitchen. The Malones had no rain-water tank in the house as many families without plumbing did, and F. Millard knew how long it took to melt snow or ice for soft water. If Silver Star's heart was bad . . . Suppose her legs weren't completely useless. From what he'd heard, the paralysis had been gradual. Suppose, in a burst of longing for the gay, active past, she'd put on the red dress she'd saved through the years and crossed the street to the old dance hall. Then, all keyed up, she had somehow accomplished that little scene he had witnessed. Perhaps his own presence had inspired her. She'd certainly seen him; she'd thrown something at him. And perhaps, when she felt her strength ebbing, she'd pointed across the room to distract him, put out the candles, and waited for him to leave so she could drag herself home. Perhaps she'd had just enough strength to put away her old finery and get back to bed before her overstrained heart played out, and Klondike had come in with a towel around her dripping head just in time to see the end.

But the look of youth, the feeling of youth given off by that skirt-swirling figure! He faltered by the wood pile. Could his own imagination have glamorized what he saw? He'd been picturing that very dance hall in its heyday. But what about that business of hearing no sounds?

Shaking his head till his ear flap wiggled, he marched on. No use dwelling on the breaks in his line of defense, just throw in more men and ammunition. This fire had to be kept up, and he couldn't call for help every time.

At the warehouse door he tucked the flashlight under one arm and took a deep breath before turning the knob. Inside, he kept one wool-mittened hand on the knob while he wiped his glasses with the other. This time there was no dim radiance beyond the balcony's edge. The room was utterly black. With a sigh in which apprehension still gnawed at relief he switched on the flashlight and followed its reassuring path the few yards to the out-of-place tier of boxes he had stubbed his toe on last night. Above it the light bulb hung from its cord where it had always hung, where he couldn't find it last night.

He pulled the string attached to the chain, and the big room flashed into sight. The balcony made a rectangular half-ceiling all the way around it. Near the light, packages, cases, and sacks of groceries stood out clearly. Farther on they blended into shadow. The stove was in the center, out past the shelter of the balcony in full view of the left-hand wall where last night he had seen lighted candles and a girl in spangled red.

Unfortunately the stove was his objective. Face tilted left, he watched that stretch of balcony come in sight as he emerged from under the length across the front. No candle flames now. No girl. In the shadows past the spindles of the railing he could only see more shadows.

F. Millard picked up the full coal scuttle and glanced quickly over his shoulder. Then he paused. The stairs cascading down from the rear balcony, breaking the line of spindles in the center—they hadn't been swept since he owned the building, and goodness knew when before that. The shadow of the stove sprawled halfway up; the straight, dark line of the pipe mingled at the top with other shadows. He had heard no sounds last night. Would feet that danced in silence leave prints?

As coal rattled into the stove he reminded himself of the outside stairs still clinging to the building. But the door at the top was bolted inside. The inner stairs would have to be climbed to unlock it.

He refilled the scuttle from an open sack, tossing it on a pile of empties flung over a case of canned grapefruit. He couldn't see the hatchet he always kept there to open cases and cut kindling and break up lumps of coal. Well, he could put off looking for it a day or two. Perhaps in time he'd get used to feeling the warehouse was haunted, and go on about his business unperturbed—providing the scene on the balcony wasn't repeated.

It was just about here where he'd stood last night and watched that eerie performance. His glance moved on to the stairs. If he walked past the stove and played his flashlight on them . . .

But he whirled and started for the door much faster than he'd left it. He wasn't ready yet to put things to a test. Suppose there were no footprints. . .

There was also that thing the girl had thrown. If he looked around he might find it—providing it was real; after all, he hadn't heard it land. Never mind it now either.

One hand flew up to pull out the light. He clicked on the flash with the other, again stubbing his toe on the tier of boxes out of line. He gave it a nudge with one hip, thinking vaguely that the torch beam made a funny shadow along the edge, and hurried out into the welcome fresh air.

* * *

Gus Ingersoll, one of the deputy marshals, was the first customer at the store. He asked the clerk for a carton of cigarettes and came down the aisle toward F. Millard, leaning his two hundred pounds on the counter till the tails on top of his dark mink hat almost brushed the grocer's nose. When he spoke his lips parted barely enough to show gold crowns. "You seen anything of Tom Blaine, Smyth?"

"T-Tom Blaine?" F. Millard stammered.

Gus nodded. "Wife says he didn't come back to the hotel last night."

The little man gripped the edge of the counter. "Wh-why are you asking me?"

"Why not?" The deputy's eyes were a cold hard blue. "Got anything to hide?"

"My g-gracious, no. As a matter of fact he did come down to my place last night. But that was early in the evening and he only stayed a few minutes. I just wondered— I just wondered—"

19

Gus Ingersoll grinned and his gold crowns flashed. "Yeah. And I just wondered if -you'd claim you hadn't seen him since he was in the store here yesterday. Matter of fact, someone saw him turn down Bonanza last night. That's why I asked you about him."

"Oh," said F. Millard weakly. "Well, he did stop by. Don't know where he went after that. What—what time did his wife see him last?"

"Said he left the hotel around quarter of eight and hasn't been back. She phoned before I got up this morning." The deputy leaned closer, and F. Millard drew back from the dangling mink tails. The eyes beneath the lustrous fur were as hard and cold as before, but now the gold crowns showed full length. "You seen Mrs. Tom Blaine yet, Smyth?"

The little grocer shook his head.

"Well, it's my opinion Tom'll show up when he gets good and ready. I don't blame him for stepping out. Not that she ain't good-looking—handsome as one of those blue-green icebergs splitting off Columbia Glacier. Hell, a woman like that . . . ."

The door behind him opened, and the deputy's voice dropped. He said something across the counter in a whisper. F. Millard blushed.

The clerk came out of the back room and Gus straightened, resuming his normal tone. "Thin but not skinny, if you know what I mean, and clothes that I don't go for but I'd sure hate to have my wife see. Bet a whole month of my salary wouldn't pay for the suit she had on. Anyway, she's positive something's happened to him, and I got to spend my time checking up. We're short-handed in the office too, with one deputy in Circle and one on his way Outside, and Jeff Peters in Nenana. Well, let me know if you run across Tom.'" The big man's eyes held the grocer's. "Providing everything's O.K., he'll sure be seeing you again, even if he don't his wife."

F. Millard watched the glass door close on Gus Ingersoll's bulky shoulders. Did that mean the marshal's office knew he was behind in his payments, or was it just Gus's way of referring to ordinary business?

But what could have happened to Blaine? With scores of old friends to see and a handsome young wife to show off, with last night only their second in town, he must have been prevented from returning by something over which he had no control. A street accident would have been discovered, and this time of year no one could fall in the river without first cutting a hole in the ice. Kidnaping would be out in a town like Fairbanks. And that left only—

"I asked for canned tomatoes," a customer objected; "that's pears."

Tomatoes, F. Millard's mind repeated. Wasn't that a case of tomatoes he'd been stumbling over in the warehouse? When he'd shoved at it this morning, there'd been some sort of shadow or smudge at the edge. One of those cans might be leaking. He'd better have lunch at home today instead of at a restaurant.

Why hadn't Blaine stopped in about that money? He'd been so insistent last night. F. Millard hadn't seen the banker yet. Somehow—after Gus Ingersoll's visit . . .

Someone asked for a pound of rice and F. Millard measured out five. Another voice asked for beans, and he opened the next bin.

If he saw—*when* he saw Blaine coming he could start for the bank. He must really check up on that case of tomatoes, and wasn't there something else? The hatchet. He'd mislaid his hatchet. . . .

The bag he was closing slipped from his hands, and beans shot all over the floor. But instead of going for a broom F. Millard stood still. Suppose the ghost hadn't been a ghost. Silver Star Malone had more reason than anyone in town to hate Tom Blaine. Beans cleaned up at last, the little man exchanged grocer's apron for overcoat. He'd take an early lunch hour today, he told the clerk, at home.

In spite of sunlight and the rate at which F. Millard's short legs worked, the walk down Second Avenue had never seemed so long. He felt as if all the log cabins and small frame houses peered after him as he passed, and the low white arc of hills—ahead, behind, and to the right—peered too. This near the river he couldn't see the jagged Alaska Range on his left, but he felt it craning at him, watching every move. The river paralleling his course a block to the right—ice-covered, snow-covered, smooth and white, waiting at each intersection—seemed to be following under the ice.

Too bad, he thought, when Bonanza Road finally came in sight, that he couldn't take any of this sunshine, almost blinding on the snow, inside the cavernous warehouse. He passed his own cabin as if it didn't exist, and once more went through the routine of pretending to unlock the warehouse door.

A box to prop it open—at least he'd have something to steer by if the power went off or his flashlight battery failed.

Now what? Hunt the hatchet first—or something larger than a hatchet? Perversely F. Millard decided to examine the case of tomatoes.

He hurried down the now fairly well-lighted aisle of boxes and reached up to add the extra brilliance of the light bulb. Then he lifted off the top box of the tier still outthrust in the aisle. No leak in the bottom of this one.

Another grunting heave. . . . The second case of tomatoes was tight.

One left to be upended. It fell back with a thud. Beneath it was a large red-brown stain. One glance was enough to tell F. Millard it wasn't tomato juice. Another to tell it was blood.

CHAPTER FOUR

T hrough two thicknesses of wool mitten F. Millard's fingernails scored his palms. Somewhere in this building . . .

Even if he couldn't find a body there must be other traces. If only he had more light! But with the aid of the light he had, augmented by his flashlight, he caught the first gleam of white.

He played his torch beam on it. In the left-hand front corner of the room, thrust out from behind a fat stack of powdery sacks of flour, he saw a white-mukluk-covered leg, its mate beside it, toes in, heels leaning outward. So even before walking around the flour sacks and squatting down he knew the body would be lying on its face, and the rest of its outer clothing must be a white parka. His flashlight showed the parka strangely twisted, and, almost hidden in the hood, the blunt end of his missing hatchet.

For an instant F. Millard shuddered away from imagining the vicious strength behind a blow that could sink a hatchet nearly out of sight in a human skull. Then he realized the significance of the twisted parka. Someone must have crouched in the dark behind a tier of boxes just where Blaine, even if he carried a flashlight, would stop to pull the light cord. The hatchet would be swung—probably down only an inch or two in the skull— and the pool of blood spilled that the murderer had covered with boxes. The parka would be shifted to keep the bleeding inside the leather, the body dragged, face down, to the dim spot where he had found it.

F. Millard unbent quivering knees and rose. It wasn't for him to test out his theory by examining the body; that would be for the authorities, and he must notify them. In the faint light he paused and looked up.

From here all he could see of the balcony was the floor— a ceiling to him. And the same was true of the spot beneath the light bulb where he had found the blood. No one on the balcony could have thrown the hatchet that killed Tom Blaine, even if the grocer hadn't already been convinced it was a close-up job.

But the way that girl had beckoned last night, leaned forward, and seemed to be calling. Each time she made one of those soundless calls her mouth had opened only once, as it would in a one-syllable word—as it would in "Tom!" "Tom!"

F. Millard shivered.

There was one thing he was going to do before calling the marshal, the thing he should have had nerve enough to do this morning—look for steps in the dust on the stairs.

His flashlight made a last yellow-white streak along the parka on the body whose face he hadn't seen, whose face he didn't need to see, before he clicked the switch off and made his way among the boxed and sacked groceries toward the center of the room. Now he passed the stove that had been his deadline this morning and slowly, stubbornly approached the stairs.

At their foot he stopped, gulped, and clicked on the light. As he had known it would be, the dust of years was thick upon them. And it was undisturbed.

F. Millard broke for the door. That oblong of sun-and-snow dazzle with the lighted electric bulb feeble before it was his only safe world—away from ghosts and dead men.

He shot through the door, down the warehouse path, around the logs still unsawed in the street, and up the path to his cabin. The telephone receiver clattered in his hand.

"Watch the warehouse," Gus Ingersoll roared after F. Millard got the marshal's office and had stuttered out his story. "Watch the door and don't let anyone inside! Don't go in yourself!"

That last command, the little grocer thought as he fumbled for the hook, was unnecessary. The receiver finally fell into place, and he staggered back out the front door. For a minute he just leaned against it, wishing his cabin hadn't been built even with the ground, so there'd be steps for him to sit on.

A door banged across the street, and Whit Hawley came down his walk. "What you trying to do," he yelled at F. Millard, "take a sun bath? Say"— he crossed over and lowered his voice—"I sure hated to leave the warehouse unlocked last night with all that stuff inside, but you didn't give me the key."

"Oh—uh . . ." F. Millard roused himself. "It was mighty nice of you to look after the fire. I—uh—thought about locking up, all right." That was no lie. He'd thought about locking the warehouse, and wished he could, every day for a week.

Whit turned toward the Malones'. "Guess I'll see if Klondike'll have lunch with us. s Voss told me about her mother. Hate to think of the poor kid. . . . Don't suppose she'll touch any food of mine, though."

F. Millard watched the younger man swing up to the Malones' door in his broad-shouldered, slim-waisted uniform. The sound of his knock was gentle for such big hands, but carried clearly across the street to the little man on sentry duty.

The door flew open and Klondike Malone appeared just long enough to say something F. Millard couldn't hear, and bang it shut again, with Whit still on the outside.

He came away looking more like an overgrown, tow-headed ten-year-old than a seasoned bombardier. "Don't know why," he flung across at F. Millard, "I thought a death in the family'd make any difference to the way that gal feels about anyone half Blaine. Just sort of a chilblain, I guess. Now she says my uncle hounded her mother to her grave."

F. Millard started. What would Whit say if he learned it might be the other way round?

"If you don't go inside, fella," the younger man added, "you're liable to get frostbit—like me."

The Hawley door slammed, and the little grocer was left alone in a glittering world with the door to the warehouse open and a still form waiting inside. In the silent street, the two old cabins across the way, with their white lines of plaster chinking, stood at the bibulous slant of age and rotting logs. The heavy icicles fringing their eaves sparkled in the sun.

Once F. Millard saw Klondike's face at a window; and once, while he peered up the street for Gus Ingersoll, Beulah Raymond, in a short-sleeved cotton dress, came out of the trim log house next door to shake a dust cloth. She waved it at him, hugging her rounded shoulders in an exaggerated shiver, and hurried back inside.

The grocer made a mental note that now three neighbors had seen him. Funny that Mae Trent hadn't come bouncing out of her modern cabin next to Hawley's with a fur coat over a house dress or one of those trailing hostess gowns that made her look shorter and wider than ever, to find out what was going on. There wasn't much she missed as a rule behind those plant-filled windows.

At last someone turned down Bonanza from Second— three men and a woman on foot. None of *Flatfoot's* squad cars with wailing sirens. Gus Ingersoll was in the lead, then the man they called the "office deputy," whose name F. Millard couldn't remember, then Valentine Voss. He might have neatness, poor eyes, and a sissy name in common with F. Millard, but the reporter was only an inch or two shorter than Gus. All three men looked enormous.

The woman was a stranger—tallish, with a smart coat and hat, and beneath the smart hat coin-cut, coin-still brunette features.

Mae Trent's door and Beulah Raymond's opened simultaneously. Both women came out bareheaded. Mae's hair looked as if it hadn't been combed, and the bottom of a hostess gown trailed below her muskrat coat. Beulah was as neat as ever, the fresh house dress under her otter coat worn with as much assurance as the elegant stranger's mink and tweeds. Beulah's 1944 hair curled in the sun with hennaed defiance.

The little man's shivering started again as they all bore down upon him.

"In there?" Gus demanded, pointing at the warehouse.

F. Millard's eyes sought the smartly dressed woman's. "I don't think—if that's Mrs. Blaine—I don't think she'd better go in."

A door banged across the street and Whit Hawley loped over as Valentine Voss took social charge. "This is Smyth, Mrs. Blaine. And Mrs. Raymond and Mrs. Trent."

The stranger gave a barely perceptible nod.

"Hey, what is this—a convention?" Whit demanded. "If Aunt Natalie's receiving the local yokels count me in too."

"Cut the comedy, Whit. If you've never met your uncle's wife, you chose a poor time for it now." The reporter turned trim broad shoulders on his housemate and said to F. Millard, "She was in the marshal's office when you phoned, and insisted on coming with us."

Natalie Blaine stood without speaking—waiting and controlled.

Gus was halfway up the warehouse path. "Come on, Smyth," he called over his shoulder. "Show me where you found him."

The others all started forward, Mae and Beulah gabbling excitedly, Whit Hawley suddenly silent.

"You folks wait here at the door," directed Gus. "Come inside and shut it. O.K., Smyth, which way?"

F. Millard led the two deputies and the reporter through the big shadowy room. In the left-hand front corner his flashlight found the yellow-white mukluks, pigeon-toed, and then the parka.

Gus and the other deputy bent close. They did what F. Millard had wanted to do: pulled back the slit in the parka hood till it stuck, and peered inside with the flashlight.

Gus straightened, casting the beam around the boxes. "Ought to be some blood on the floor."

"Guess I didn't make much sense on the phone," F. Millard fluttered. "I found blood under one of those boxes by the light. And the hatchet—That's what made me start. . . ." He realized suddenly that his voice had stopped, and finished with a rush, "Finding that blood's what made me start hunting for him." Trying to explain a hunch and a tier of boxes out of line, missing a hatchet and meeting a ghost would be too complicated.

He blinked to find the three regarding him closely: speculation in the deputies' eyes, behind the rimless glasses of the newspaperman keen interest.

Gus Ingersoll's voice was cold. "Your hatchet, Smyth?"

F. Millard gulped, and nodded. "

What'd you come down here for," the deputy asked, "at eleven in the morning?"

"Why, I—I wanted an early lunch, and I—I thought I'd fix it at home."

"When'd you have that notion last—a year ago?"

"Oh, I—I had lunch at home several times last summer."

"Yeah," said Gus. His lips barely opened. "That's what I thought."

The little man's hand went involuntarily to his hip where the tightly rolled current copy of *Flatfoot*, thrust into a trouser pocket, made a bulge in his overcoat. Gus Ingersoll was talking the way Flatfoot Flannagan talked to suspects; not witnesses—but suspects. F. Millard stood blinking and trying to swallow.

Valentine Voss stirred restlessly. "You haven't identified the body, have you, Gus? I've got to get back and do a story."

"Be a hell of a note," said the nameless deputy, grimly waggish, "if it's not Blaine."

"Take his feet, boys," directed Gus. "We'll heave him over."

Urged by three pairs of hands, while F. Millard still blinked, the body rose stiffly and was laid on its back. The feet still toed in, the arms were still straight—but now they weren't flat on the floor.

The grocer's first thought was for his canned goods. If he'd left that door open too long . . .

The lid was off a near-by case of peaches. He clawed out a can and shook it, heard the liquid slosh.

"Think he was froze?" Gus grunted. "Ever hear of rigor mortis?" He bent to pull the twisted parka hood from the face, found it stuck, and again peered inside with the flashlight.

"It's him, all right." He straightened and clicked off the light.

From the group by the door Natalie Blaine started forward. "Is it …? Mr. Ingersoll, what's happened?"

Gus waved her back. "Don't come, Mrs. Blaine. It's your husband, all right. He's dead."

"You mean—" a slim, gloved hand touched her throat —"was he—?"

"I'm sorry, Mrs. Blaine. He's been killed. No, don't come." Again he waved her back. "Beulah, you got an extra sheet at your house? Run home and bring it over till Doc gets here with a stretcher."

The door opened and closed. Natalie Blaine stood waiting. The hand remained at her throat. Her face was still.

"O.K., Smyth," said Gus. "Show us the blood."

F. Millard brought them back to the light and the overturned case of tomatoes. In silence they examined the stain.

Gus turned toward the door. "You may as well go back to the hotel, Mrs. Blaine. There's nothing you can do here."

The smart hat quivered as the woman between Whit Hawley and chubby Mae Trent took another uncertain step forward. "Was he—was my husband—murdered?"

"No doubt about it." The mink tails on Gus Ingersoll's hat bobbed with vigor. "But there's nothing you can do now," he repeated. "Want to wait at Beulah's or Mae's till I can take you back?"

"I—no, I can find my way—thank you." Taller than F. Millard in her high-heeled galoshes Natalie Blaine reached for the door knob.

With the widow gone and the brief outdoor dazzle cut off again, Gus said to F. Millard, "You stay with Mae and Whit while we have a look around."

Beulah Raymond came back with a sheet, the office deputy spread it over the corpse, then his flashlight joined those of Gus and the reporter flitting about the big room.

The group at the door by turns chattered feverishly or waited in an almost breathless silence.

Valentine Voss gave up first. "Anybody find anything?" he shouted. "I've got to get that story out."

"Found a broken flashlight," grunted Gus.

In the back of the room the office deputy's torch beam played on the balcony steps. "Haven't found a thing," he called. "No one's been upstairs."

Something taut in the grocer's chest relaxed at another's confirmation of that lack of prints. The room briefly brightened as the reporter opened the door. Then F. Millard heard the latch click, and a voice beside him murmured, "I'd sure hate to be in your shoes, Smitty."

His head jerked left. Mae Trent's round, blue eyes in her cookie-round face were as full of wonder as a child's. To make the illusion almost complete—here where the light was dim enough to hide lines and sags and the hair-edges that needed retouching—she began to bat her thick, short lashes and bite her thumb.

"Why, Mae? What's the matter with my shoes?" The voice F. Millard tried to make light came out hoarse.

Her lashes batted faster. "With the body in your warehouse and you owing Tom Blaine all that money? If it's your hatchet he was killed with . . ."

Had they talked so loudly over the body that their voices carried to the door? *My warehouse*, F. Millard's mind kept repeating, *my hatchet; the man I'm head over heels in debt to.* No wonder Gus Ingersoll had treated him the way Flatfoot Flannagan treated suspects.

Gus was striding toward them. "Hey, Smyth! Any other way into this joint?"

F. Millard tried to make his voice steady and matter-of-fact. "The back door was boarded up when they took off the kitchen wing and moved the building. The door at the top of the outside stairs is bolted inside."

"What's up there, anyway—just the balcony and dining booths?"

F. Millard nodded, catching back one addition—a ghost.

"Don't make any difference," said Gus. "No one came down the stairs. Blaine was killed over there by the light, and the guy that did it was standing right behind him. No windows disturbed. Anyone got a key but you?"

The grocer's head started to shake, then words tumbled over each other: "I haven't had the key for a week! 1 don't know where it is. I've just been pretending to lock the door so no one would know I couldn't."

The office deputy came up and the two exchanged glances. Then Gus turned back to the others. "Any of you neighbors know about it?"

For a moment the group around the door in the dim outer fringe of light was silent. Then Beulah Raymond gave a little laugh that sounded forced. "May as well admit I knew it. Bet most of us did. Smitty forgot to put on his act one day till he had the door half open. Silver Star saw him from her window across the street and told me about it. I thought it was so funny I told Frank Ord, and I told you, too, didn't I, Mae?"

The other woman nodded. "And I thought it was so funny—aren't we goofy, Beulah?—that I told Valentine Voss."

"No one told me," said Whit Hawley. His tone was emphatic.

Mae Trent was biting her thumb again. "The old man spent last night at Gulkana."

The old man? Oh, yes, F. Millard told himself, that was what Mae called her husband.

"He's gone back to freighting, you know, Gus," she went on. "And I was hardly home all evening, myself. Know what time Tom was killed?"

"Can't tell till Doc does the autopsy. If the door was unlocked and you folks all knew it . . ." Gus hesitated. "Guess you better all come down to the office."

F. Millard's sigh was flavored with relief. Losing the warehouse key had really been a lucky break. Now the possibilities were more spread around. Of course the best break would have been for Blaine to have got himself killed on someone else's property. How, he wondered suddenly, would this murder affect the matter of his debts?

"You'll have to pick up Klondike Malone too, won't you, Gus?" the office deputy asked. "If Silver Star knew about the key—"

"Can't you leave the kid alone?" Whit objected gruffly. "Her mother's not buried yet."

Gus looked stubborn. "Whoever killed Blaine should have thought of that. You know, it's a funny thing that those two who hated each other so died the very same night."

Unconsciously F. Millard's eyes lifted to the floor of the balcony above them.

"I remember when the Malones bought that house across the street," volunteered the office deputy. "God, it made Blaine mad!"

"Let's get going," said Gus. "Be pretty slick if I can get this straightened out before Jeff gets back. He always claims just sitting chinning with the suspects does more good than any amount of leg work. I'd sure laugh to see leg work come out on top while he's away."

F. Millard felt sorry he wasn't to see Jeff Peters in action. He'd heard so much about the old marshal's apparently aimless ramblings that almost always got results. But he had little time for regrets. Mae Trent broke in firmly:

"Listen, Gus Ingersoll, I was getting my hair done from before seven-thirty till after nine, and from ten o'clock on I was dancing at Moose Hall. I'd like to know when I had time for murder!"

Whit Hawley grinned.

"Give me your alibis after we get to the office," Gus directed. "And listen, folks. I don't want you deciding among yourselves what they're going to be, either. Maybe the guy that did the killing already has his, and maybe not. If anything's slipped up, I'm not giving him a chance to fix it now. So don't talk about it. See?"

The two deputies herded the others outdoors. As each separate breath rose like smoke from separate fires, F. Millard thought each face took on stillness, a sort of guarded waiting.

A car turned down Bonanza.

"Here's the ambulance," Gus said to the stoop-shouldered deputy. "I'll take Doc in and you stay and see these folks don't pool alibis."

Two men got out of the ambulance, one with a doctor's bag and the other a folded stretcher. Gus waved them into the warehouse.

"Want to get more clothes on, girls? It's a cold walk to the Federal Building." The office deputy's voice was friendly. "You go up to your place, Mae, and when you get there Beulah can go to hers, then Gus'll be satisfied you're not putting your heads together."

Mae bustled up the street in a series of bounces, her long house coat sweeping the snow. As she turned in at her shoveled path, the deputy nudged Beulah. "Your turn now. I'll see you get your sheet back."

Beulah moved off, and F. Millard watched sunshine play in the warm-looking hair that gave the town a fresh shock every year. He remembered a phrase from the novels his mother used to keep in the golden-oak bookcase with glass doors—"queenly carriage." That was the way Beulah walked, as if, indulgently, she owned the earth and the snow she put her feet on—nice feet too, even if they didn't make as tiny tracks as Mae's. Near one of Mae

Trent's doll-size prints ice glistened in the sun. Another of those big broken chunks of icicle.

Suddenly F. Millard's eyes went to the street light above him—and he saw why it hadn't been burning last night. The lights were of the type that had no globe, just a bulb below a reflector. The bulb had been shattered.

So he'd guessed wrong about what that chunk of ice had been thrown at. And that report, the sharp pop in the hush last night after the dogs had stopped howling! He'd heard a light bulb burst before; no wonder he'd confused it with a shot.

Then how about the woman on the balcony, the woman who had danced and laughed and called without a sound? Now there were too many tangibles to deal with—the street lights had been put out with a solid chunk of ice, a man killed with a solid hatchet. Even if there were no footprints in the dust of the balcony stairs, the outside stairs were still intact except for a few bottom steps. Suppose the woman (no ghost now in F. Millard's mind) had substituted the ash can for the first few missing steps? The bolt on the upper door was flimsy, with half the screws gone when he bought the place. Judicious prying and a few determined shoves should have let her in. Suppose she'd lighted her candles and waited for Blaine whom she had somehow arranged to meet? In that dim light she could easily have mistaken F. Millard for him; they both had worn white parkas. She must have had some reason for going through that eerie little act in utter silence. Whatever the reason, she could have counted on getting down the outside stairs and into the front of the building while her victim still stood bemused, or hunting for the light cord. Perhaps she had finally recognized F. Millard and that was why she had put out the candles, waiting till he had left, for her real victim. Perhaps only the fact that he'd scrambled so madly to get out of a place already familiar to him had saved F. Millard from being further mistaken for Blaine—mistaken with a hatchet. And Blaine had not been quick enough.

As he stood waiting with the stoop-shouldered deputy and the bombardier, F. Millard's gaze turned toward the river and the building's fungoid protuberance with an oblong hole where there had once been a door at the foot of the covered stairs. That door had long since gone the way of the three or four bottom steps. Sunshine slanting in made a geometric figure on the wall and just touched the edge of the ash can.

His eyes came back to the closed front door. Beside it stood a bucket of ashes.

Whit Hawley must have been watching. He said quickly, "I left that bucket there. Stove was so full of ashes I shook them down and couldn't find where to dump them in the dark. If you'll tell me—"

"Please don't bother." F. Millard darted forward. "I'll empty it while we're waiting."

His eyes flew from side to side of the path to the covered stairs, shoveled just wide enough for himself and the bucket. No marks here of women's heels like those left by Beulah and Mae and Mrs. Blaine on the path from the street. All distinguishable prints had been made by mukluks or men's galoshes.

He made a show of setting down the bucket in the doorway, of clattering the lid to the ash can which he laid, top up, in the light beside the pail. No print showed on the lid. The roof protected it from snow and the whole ash can was new this fall, bought after the summer's dust had settled. The stairs would be free of snow too, but not of dust.

His back to the men by the other door, F. Millard clattered the bucket bail with one hand and slid the flashlight from his overcoat pocket with the other. He took a long step inside, swung the bucket toward the ash can and the flashlight toward the stairs.

No one could hear the gasp he gave—he hoped. The stairway, as far as the torch beam reached, had been swept.

CHAPTER FIVE

The marshal's private office was already crowded when Gus brought in Mrs. Blaine. But wasn't this, F. Millard asked himself, supposed to be just an examination of the people who lived near the scene of the crime? A matter of checking alibis for those who had the opportunity, regardless of motive?

In the absence of Jeff Peters the office deputy sat in the marshal's chair. Gus went by him into a small inner office. Mrs. Blaine sat down beside Beulah. F. Millard looked from her to Klondike who had lost her mother the night before and now sat two chairs away looking smaller and more appealing than ever with puffy eyes and her charming little nose pink and unpowdered. Natalie Blaine, whose husband had just been murdered, was as carefully made up, as smartly dressed, and as exquisitely aloof as if she had gone downtown to shop.

In the chair between her and Klondike, Beulah Raymond returned the appraising glance of her old friend's widow, that flitted on to the girl beyond. Natalie Blaine and Beulah, thought F. Millard, had two things in common, different as they might be in other ways: He couldn't imagine a circumstance in which either would lose her self-control, and they were both of the type known as ageless. The widow's slim, dark, imperious elegance and Beulah's yearly changed hair, bright blue eyes, and lush figure could have fitted any birthday from thirty to forty-five.

F. Millard's gaze traveled on to the man who had been Tom Blaine's partner. Long Ed Griswold, the others called him. Beulah said the partnership had broken up in 1936, but he lived down Second Avenue a few blocks below Bonanza, so Gus had picked him up. She had started to say more, but Gus had told them all to stop talking. Griswold sat with one hand in his lap on a shaggy fur hat that looked like part of a mangy wolf's pelt, the other stroking the back of his nearly bald head. Above a little fringe of brown hair that stopped at his ears the back of his head was flat, as if he'd rubbed out the usual bulge. It rose to a hairless peak polished by generations of hats. His small dark eyes caught F. Millard's, whose glance fled guiltily on to Mae Trent at the moment when her voice, too long restrained, bubbled into the room's silence.

"But, Frank"— she laid a hand like a miniature cream puff on the arm of the man beside her—"do they have a right to make you stop work because there's been a murder on our street?"

"Shut up, Mae," said the office deputy amiably. "You're not supposed to talk."

"It's not about where I was last night! When you take a construction worker off the job in wartime—"

"You know what Gus said," the deputy reminded her. "The murderer might get an alibi from people talking."

Mae Trent flounced. Beside her Frank Ord looked embarrassed. His face dark red to the edge of golden-brown, tousled hair, he slid his big body farther down in the chair and stared at the toes of his mukluks. Whit Hawley's long, uniformed length lounged against the window sill where, without being too obvious, he could look at Klondike Malone. Now, except for Mae's husband, still out of town, and Valentine Voss at the newspaper office, the roll of Bonanza Road neighbors was complete.

F. Millard shivered. Was the killer in the chair beside him? Or across the room? Or—his eyes caught Klondike's above another damp handkerchief— already past the need of an alibi, her body waiting now for honored burial?

Across the room Long Ed Griswold stroked the back of his head, opaque eyes resting first on one, then another of his neighbors.

Funny how much easier it was to tell a man's age than a woman's. Griswold must be sixty-five, Frank Ord around forty, Whit and Valentine Voss in their middle twenties. In spite of tinted hair and girlish clothes, Mae Trent could be fifty. And Klondike, of course, was eighteen.

Only Beulah and Natalie Blaine eluded cataloguing. His eyes came back to the smartly dressed widow, and his hands closed on the arms of his chair. She had lost her air of elegant aloofness. Eyes hidden by lowered lashes, gloved hands clutching each other more tightly in her lap than F. Millard's gripped his chair arms, her creamy cheeks were the color of skimmed milk. This morning in the warehouse when her husband's body was identified, she had hardly changed expression. What had happened after she came into this room to disturb her?

The telephone rang. As the deputy at Jeff Peters's desk reached for the marshal's phone, Gus Ingersoll shot out of the inner room. "I'll get it outside!" he said sharply.

The silence in the marshal's private office became a listening silence.

"Gus," came Ingersoll's voice through the closed door. "Got it? When? O.K., Doc. Thanks."

The autopsy report, said F. Millard's mind. That's what Gus had been waiting for.

When the big deputy returned he was closing a notebook. He nodded at the murdered man's widow. "O.K., Mrs. Blaine. Come in here."

He was halfway through the door of the little side room before he remembered to step back and let her precede him.

Whit growled, "He could have taken Klondike first." The office deputy looked reproving, and the roomful waited in silence.

Natalie Blaine was not away long, and F. Millard could see when she came out that her tenseness hadn't lessened. Her eyes were fastened on the floor as she crossed the room, with the fixity of a tightrope walker who didn't dare look up.

Gus said, "You're next, Klondike," and the others relapsed into waiting.

Klondike was gone much longer. Whit stood away from the window sill and turned to drum on the pane. In the gathering dusk his big restless hands made F. Millard think of birds beating against the glass. A bad-luck omen, his mother used to say. Frank Ord lighted one cigarette after another, breaking up the matches. The floor around his chair was littered.

The dusk deepened, and the motion of Long Ed Griswold's elbow, as again and again he returned to stroking the back of his head, was like the slow flap of vultures' wings or the angle of a bat's.

The deputy flipped on the light, and Beulah reached for a cigarette. She wasn't given to fidgeting or foot and finger tapping, but even Beulah, F. Millard noted, didn't sit relaxed as she ordinarily did, and was smoking more than usual.

In her chair across the room Mae Trent wriggled. She cried suddenly, "Oh, stop that drumming, Whit!" and glared at the office deputy.

At last Klondike came out. She didn't walk Mrs. Blaine's tightrope, but looked almost as tense and forgot to be disdainful of Whit Hawley's help with her coat. The little hand that pulled a red scarf from her pocket and tied it over brown curls trembled, and in spite of the tears she kept blinking back, her eyes were wide and strained. Klondike Malone looked frightened.

The door to the outer office shut behind her, and F. Millard saw Gus Ingersoll standing in the other door looking over his prospects. He pointed at Frank. "You next, Ord."

The others settled into gloomy silence. They didn't have long to wait. In less than ten minutes Frank burst in, snatched the coat off his chair, and slammed out.

Once more Gus stood in the doorway, selecting. He beckoned to Beulah. Mae and F. Millard wriggled into fresh positions. Whit gave up his post at the window and sprawled his long frame in a chair. The office deputy rustled through some papers at the desk, and Long Ed Griswold began again to stroke the back of his flat, peaked head.

Beulah was still gone when Valentine Voss, his cheeks below the rimless glasses red with cold, rushed in with a handful of newspapers. As he passed them out pride as bright as his fiery ears exuded from fedora to galoshes.

Whit reached up from his sprawl for the first copy before F. Millard got one.

Two faces stared out side by side from the printed sheet. One was Tom Blaine's in the full vigor of middle age. The other was one F. Millard could never forget— that of the girl Silver Star.

Here, in sharp black and white, was the face that had been no more than suggested in the dim cone flames of two candles. The same light pompadour, the slightly curved dark brows, the doll-round face. It couldn't vanish now, no matter how long he looked. For a moment he recaptured the same prickle down his spine. But a ghost, he reminded himself, wouldn't use a material broom. A ghost wouldn't need to sweep out footprints.

He settled his spectacles, glancing from one column to another. Here— "Strange Coincidence in Two Deaths"— was the one he wanted to read.

Silver Star, born Dorothy Matilda Starr, had come to Nome at eighteen in 1904. She met Blaine, then a young fellow of twenty-one, on the northbound boat. Youth and a common love of mischief had drawn them quickly together, soon growing into something more. Here young Voss took a flier in early-day reconstruction. He described a typical Nome dance hall with the boy Tom Blaine in the ground floor throng. And then—F. Millard felt his scalp tingle—the reporter described a girl with silver-white hair coming out on the balcony, trying to attract Blaine's attention. The signal that never failed, unless her marksmanship failed, was the throwing of an artificial rose.

The paper slipped through his fingers while F. Millard stared into space. That thing the girl had thrown last night —as it passed his shoulder, he had caught the scent of roses.

He swallowed and picked up the paper. Silver Star used to go through a special routine to indicate to young Tom Blaine there was mischief afoot, a routine made up of a Spanish dance step and giggles and a fluttering of hands.

F. Millard shivered and read on. The girl and boy had kept up their fun through the winter of 1904 and '05, and the date had been set for their wedding. Then one night in the early spring two weeks before the prospective marriage, they saw the preacher's dog tied in front of his schoolma'am girl friend's boardinghouse. One of the tougher dance halls had living quarters upstairs for the girls. What could be more fun, in the estimation of young Tom and Silver Star, than to lead the preacher's well-known dog up the outside stairs and let him come wandering alone, apparently forgotten by his master, down the inside stairway in front of half the town? They unsnapped the dog's chain and set out down the icy street for the dance hall. This outside staircase had no roof like the one on the old Bonanza. Tom had gone first up the snow and ice covered stairs with the dog on the chain while Silver Star tiptoed behind. Then it happened. The dog darted back, and the girl had been jerked off her feet.

For six months after that fall Silver Star had been unable to dance, and after the birth of her only child in 1925 the partial paralysis returned worse than ever until she gradually became a bedridden invalid.

On the date that was to have been their wedding day, Tom Blaine had left town. And that, the paper concluded, was the beginning of the enmity that lasted down through the years, from Nome to Fairbanks and to houses across the street from each other, that lasted till the night they both died.

The columns under "Local Woman Dies" and "Fairbanks Visitor Slain" were continued on the next page. It was amazing how much Valentine Voss had put in. He must have written at top speed, and had most of his facts ready ever since Blaine's disappearance.

Gus Ingersoll's voice broke through F. Millard's preoccupation. "Come in here, Voss. You live on Bonanza Road too."

The grocer looked around, blinking. Mae Trent was just going through the door to the outer office and Beulah was nowhere in sight.

F. Millard returned to the paper, eyes drawn again to the picture of the girl. He shivered and dragged them away. Dorothy Matilda Starr—born in 1886. . . . He read on: of her months at the Bonanza Dance Hall in Fairbanks; of her first marriage, in 1912, to a man named Anderson now living in the States; of her second, in 1923, to Eliot Malone who died in 1930.

F. Millard turned to the column about Tom Blaine. Sixty-one years old. His thirty-year association with Ed Griswold filled a paragraph—a mining partnership at first, that came to include a warehouse and freighting business (the very warehouse, F. Millard noticed with a shudder, where Blaine had met death), a hotel, and even a restaurant. The grocery was mentioned, its sale to F. Millard, Blaine's departure for California and marriage, only a few months ago, to Natalie Archer of San Francisco.

The little man sat reading, now and then lowering the paper, but still insulated in thought. His eyes kept stealing back to the girl's face on the front page. The slam of a door finally roused him.

Whit Hawley was striding away from the side office, his face beneath the tan a furious red. His hair bristled like chunks of pulled taffy. Scowling at F. Millard he snatched up his coat and slammed two more doors behind him.

The grocer blinked. He was all alone. No Whit now, no Mae, no Beulah, no Valentine Voss. Long Ed Griswold no longer sat stroking the back of his head. Even the office deputy had left the marshal's desk.

"Well," said a heavy voice, "got lead in your pants?"

F. Millard jumped. He wasn't alone. Gus Ingersoll had quietly opened the door.

Slowly F. Millard stood up. Gus jerked his head and he followed the big deputy into the room where each of the others had preceded him. Gus nodded toward a chair facing the light and took his place across the desk. The little grocer clamped his teeth together hard. He mustn't let them chatter.

"What time'd you say it was," Gus demanded, "when Blaine come in last night?"

"J-just about eight." F. Millard's voice steadied. "I was getting ready for lodge."

"When'd he leave?"

"I don't know. I just sat there thinking, and when I looked at my watch it was twenty after eight."

"What'd he want to see you about?"

"B-business. I bought his store, you know."

"Yeah, I know." The big man across the desk leaned forward. "And I know you're behind in your payments."

F. Millard's breath gave an audible lurch.

"You didn't go to lodge last night, did you, Smyth?"

"N-no, it was too late after Blaine left."

"Stay home the rest of the evening?"

"Well, no, I took a turn up to Second Avenue and back to try out my new parky and mukluks. And—and I went down to the store later on."

"What'd you do between times?"

F. Millard swallowed. "I—well, I was going to fix the warehouse fire, and I—well, I—"

Gus leaned closer. His eyes were as hard as blue glass. "Did you go in that building last night?"

The little man's tongue touched his lips. His mind raced over stories from *Flatfoot*. A lying suspect usually tripped himself up; F. Millard would be sure to. He wet his lips again. "I—I was in there for just a few minutes between half-past eight and nine. To—to bank the fire."

"Then why didn't you bank it? Why ask Whit Hawley to?"

So Whit had also been playing it honest. Or was he just testing F. Millard?

"Well?" said Gus. "I'm waiting."

F. Millard swallowed. *Stick to the truth*, he told himself, *all the way*. Even if he looked like a fool. Gus sat scowling while the grocer talked. At last he faltered to a stop, and the room was still.

"What about that phone call you told Whit you got," Gus demanded, "the one that took you down to the store?"

"That—that was just made up. I was—I was scared to go back in the warehouse after seeing—what I saw. And Klondike had just told me her mother was dead. But now —look, Gus: Ghosts don't go around sweeping floors. Whoever was there was real—whether she died afterward or not. Even if she didn't kill Blaine from the balcony or come down the stairs inside, she could have run down the outside stairs and caught him at the light. She could have—"

"And you could have made up the whole damn story," the big man interrupted, "to try to ball everything up."

"But—but I can show you where those stairs have been swept!"

"You can handle a broom, can't you, Smyth?"

For an instant F. Millard shut his eyes. When he opened them the first thing he saw was Gus's right hand spreadeagled on the desk, with two joints gone from the second finger. Back in the carefree days before the murder when his troubles had been only financial he had once had lunch next to Gus at the drugstore fountain where Klondike worked. Someone got to kidding the deputy about third degrees. Klondike had laughed and said she asked him how he'd lost those joints when she was ten and Gus had just been made a new deputy, and he told her a prisoner bit them off. Now F. Millard felt that story might be true; he knew how a prisoner could have felt.

He looked up at the cold blue eyes and the gleam of gold teeth. "Will you let me show you, Gus?" he pleaded. "Will you come with me and look at those stairs? Unlock the door so we can see if there are tracks on the balcony floor, or if it's been swept too?"

The phone rang in the outer office. "For you, Gus," the other deputy called.

F. Millard watched the bulky shoulders swing across the marshal's private office, listened to Ingersoll's heavy voice. "Yes. Yes, sure, Mrs. Blaine. You what? O.K., I'll be right over." The receiver clicked. "Damn these women," F. Millard heard Gus grumble, "why can't they make up their minds?"

The big deputy came back to the room where the grocer waited. "I was up on the balcony myself, Smyth. I padlocked the upper door inside, and I didn't see any tracks on the floor, or marks of sweeping, either."

"Did you look?" asked F. Millard simply.

"Well—the killing couldn't of been done from up there, and no tracks on the stairs. … I just flashed the light around the walls to find the door. By the way, that bolt was off and hanging on the jamb by one screw."

"Then don't you see?" the grocer cried. "That proves it's true! Someone could have gone up and down the covered stairs and slipped in the front door and killed him! Someone could—"

"Someone *could*, all right, Smyth," the deputy broke in, "and that someone could still have been you. I'll go down with you soon's *I* do another errand. I'm not giving you a chance to raise a howl afterwards that you didn't get a square deal."

"A-afterwards?" the little man repeated faintly.

"When you go to the pen."

CHAPTER SIX

Flatfoot fan, F. Millard kept reminding himself, ought to enjoy his first inquest. But being chief suspect made a difference. Tom Blaine had almost spoiled F. Millard's pleasure in his first parka and mukluks, now he had spoiled his first inquest.

The Commissioner's Court was jammed Thursday morning, but a seat had been saved for F. Millard. Seats saved too for Mae and Beulah and Natalie Blaine, for a rebellious looking Klondike, with her piquant nose still pink; for Long Ed Griswold, Frank Ord, Whit Hawley, and Valentine Voss. Whether the reporter was present to represent the newspapers, or in the capacity of a suspect, F. Millard didn't know, but all nine sat on the two front benches watched over by Gus Ingersoll.

F. Millard knew he ought to take an interest in the jury, but aside from wondering whether one of them was sober, from remembering that another had an unpaid account at his store, and that he had once sold a pound of garlic to a third who admitted eating it like onions, the grocer let his thoughts return to the day before.

Gus had been true to his word. He'd done his errand— F. Millard asked himself again what Mrs. Blaine could have wanted him for—and picked up F. Millard at the store. Together, after the deputy unfastened the padlock of the law, they went over the warehouse. No other prints but Ingersoll's, going and returning, showed in the dust of the inner stairs. On the floor above they led on till the balcony turned left. Then the tracks were gone—the dust was gone. … All the left-hand balcony, from the outside stairway door, had been swept. There was no grease on the table where the candles had stood, no marks but those of a dustcloth. Gus unlocked the padlock on the door to the outer stairs and cast his light down swept treads that creaked and popped as the two men descended. At the bottom they proved that anyone going up or down could easily have substituted the ash can for the missing lower steps.

Inside again, downstairs, F. Millard had stammered, "D-did you find a f-flower on the floor this morning?"

Gus frowned. "You mean one of the flour sacks leaking?"

"No, I mean f-l-o-w-e-r. Like a—a rose or something."

Even by the light of the single bulb F. Millard had seen the other tense. "I get a fellow-feeling sometimes for cops that use rubber hoses," the deputy muttered, without even a gleam of gold crowns. "Think I didn't read that newspaper story too? Every one of those details was in it about Silver Star meeting Blaine. Too bad you couldn't give me credit for normal brains and thought up something better."

Then Gus had fairly pushed F. Millard out of the warehouse and padlocked both doors again.

The grocer sighed, remembering, and brought his mind back to the courtroom. The commissioner, ex officio coroner, had finished swearing in the jury, and Gus Ingersoll was on the stand telling of his examination of the warehouse. F. Millard heard his own name mentioned as discoverer of the body. All this was old stuff.

He let his eyes stray around the room, wondering if the good-looking man he'd seen at Beulah's last night was among the crowd of onlookers. He was a stranger to F. Millard, but Beulah knew a lot of men he didn't. The grocer smothered another sigh. It was only natural for a woman so jolly and attractive to have plenty of men friends.

He was on his way home from the store last night when he'd stopped in front of her place. After that sickening interview with Gus and fruitless search of the warehouse, he'd gone back to the store, had dinner downtown, and finally, with no more work to linger over, reluctantly started home. The day that had been so dazzling at noon was ending in cloudiness and murk.

No stars put the street lights to shame the night after the murder. The curtain of clouds, sensed rather than seen in the darkness, felt almost suffocating. As he turned down Bonanza Road snow had begun to fall. He saw, with relief, that the street lights were burning again. Nearing Beulah Raymond's bright windows, F. Millard had paused, then started up her shoveled walk.

At one unshaded window was a man's head and shoulders. She already had company. Not Frank. F. Millard had never seen this man before—dark, with a small mustache and an air of well-groomed sophistication. As the grocer hesitated Frank Ord came out of his cabin. He still had on the open-necked flannel shirt, breeches, and mukluks that he wore to work, and hurried, coatless, through the snow.

He caught the smaller man's shoulder. "What's stopping you, Smitty? Come in out of the snow."

In silence F. Millard gestured toward Beulah's lighted windows.

Hunching his neck farther down in his collar Frank paused too, and F. Millard felt a sudden tension in the air. The big man's hand dropped from the grocer's shoulder.

"Oh—I see. I'll make it another time." Frank's voice sounded smothered. He turned back toward his cabin, slowly in spite of the falling flakes, and F. Millard went on to his.

Now he took another survey of the courtroom. But the man who had disconcerted both Frank and himself wasn't here. Through the windows he could see snow still coming down.

Gus Ingersoll was telling something new: the hatchet that had killed Tom Blaine had particles of scarlet fuzz stuck to the wooden handle. F. Millard owned a pair of red mittens bought in a moment of exuberance on attaining sourdough standing. All the women on the block had red mittens, Frank a pair of red wool gloves. Scarlet would hardly be G.I. for a bombardier, but Whit had spent a good many years in Fairbanks before the war, and young Voss, who had never worn anything brighter than brown in F. Millard's sight, would have access to anything in the Hawley house. The grocer's eyes turned to two other pairs of hands: Natalie Blaine's, in fur-lined gray kid, clutched tightly together in her lap; and Ed Griswold's, bare, gnarled and grimy, the wide leather gauntlets of a pair of "Siwash mitts" protruding under the bench below him.

Gus stepped off the stand and the doctor took it— youngish, dapper, with a black mustache and black hair shot with white. A little like the man at Beulah's last night, but not enough for the grocer to confuse them. ". . . between eight and nine Tuesday night," the doctor was saying. "A blow on the back of the head . . ."

Between eight and nine. . . . Blaine had been killed between eight and nine. A cramp of nausea caught F. Millard. He had been next door; taken that brief walk up and down the block on which the warehouse stood; he had been in the warehouse itself. Huddled on the front bench, he pressed folded arms against a quivering stomach.

"Call F. Millard Smyth," a loud voice said, and the little grocer got shakily to his feet.

He went through the business of being sworn in and heard himself answering questions: telling where he had found the body, when, what he had done about it. He kept bracing himself to tell about the woman on the balcony, but no question came that concerned Tuesday night. It seemed to him that his reason for going home for lunch Wednesday morning was unnecessarily dwelt on; so was his business connection with the murdered man, and Blaine's call the night he was killed. Then, before he'd even been able to steady his voice, Klondike Malone was called to the stand, and F. Millard went back to the front bench where the goats had been herded off from the sheep.

Klondike, looking smaller and daintier than ever in the witness chair at the end of the commissioner's big desk, kept making angry little dabs at her nose with a wet balled-up handkerchief as if she couldn't bear to let the public in on her grief. She admitted knowing that the warehouse key was missing, but said Tom Blaine hadn't been at her house Tuesday night, and she hadn't seen him since he came back to Fairbanks on Monday. Reluctantly, very briefly, she repeated the story of washing her hair between eight and nine and calling the doctor for her mother—at nine-fifteen, according to him. She said she hadn't looked at the time.

The United States Attorney's young assistant asking the questions seemed embarrassed. "Klondike," he began, and stopped.

The girl turned from him to her audience of fellow townsmen. Her drowning gray eyes looked beseeching.

"Klon—er—Miss Malone," the young attorney corrected himself. He stuck out his chin and took the plunge. "Did you know that Tom Blaine's will left your mother five thousand dollars?"

A gasp ran through the courtroom, followed by a general buzz. The commissioner rapped for silence. When Klondike could be heard, she stuttered furiously, "Of c-course I didn't know it. He certainly owed it to her though, a whole lot more than that. Oh, why couldn't it have come while she was alive?" She dropped her head into both bent arms and began to sob.

Mae Trent was next on the stand, repeating what she'd already told Gus in the others' presence, that she'd spent Tuesday night from before seven-thirty to twenty after nine getting her hair done at Beulah's, from twelve minutes of eight to nine o'clock under the drier.

Beulah corroborated Mae's testimony, adding that a few minutes after putting her customer under the drier she had gone next door to Frank Ord's and stayed till it was time to take Mae out—at nine o'clock. Both women said they looked at their watches.

Valentine Voss, pink-cheeked and neat as always, said he had spent the whole evening at the newspaper office. He'd been working alone, but several people had been in and out and seen him.

Long Ed, formally referred to as Edward Griswold, sat rubbing his head in the witness chair and denied having seen his former partner since he'd left Fairbanks over a year ago. He'd wanted to see Blaine, too, Griswold said, even called him at the hotel. There was still a business matter between them to be settled. His opaque brown eyes picked out F. Millard. He said he hadn't left home after six o'clock Tuesday night. There was no one, reflected F. Millard, to substantiate that statement.

Whit Hawley, looking awkward and too tall for his uniform, told about F. Millard's asking him to bank the warehouse fire. He said he was in the building only long enough to shake down a bucket of ashes, throw a scuttle of coal in the stove, and refill the scuttle. Not more than ten minutes, probably less—and after his uncle had been killed, according to the doctor's testimony. Between eight and nine, Whit said, he was home alone. Another unsubstantiated statement, the little grocer noted, and immediately felt compunction: What sort of furlough was this for a soldier who'd been fighting two years—coming home to find death next door, murder across the street, and the eyes of suspicion turned on him? Asked whether or not he'd been remembered in his uncle's will, the bombardier said stiffly that he didn't know and didn't care.

The dead man's widow was called to the stand, still pale for all her careful make-up. She was questioned about her marriage to Blaine and his purpose in returning to Alaska.

"My husband seldom talked about business affairs." Natalie Archer Blaine's voice was mannered and expensive-sounding. She looked as if the little courtroom and everyone in it were only things to be endured for the moment. "I understood he still owned gold mines in Alaska, but couldn't operate them for the duration. He was going to look into other minerals."

Any particular kind?"

She shrugged. "He didn't say. Just something that he could get priorities for now."

"How did he act after he came back to Fairbanks? Glad to see his old friends? Or moody—secretive?"

The perfect arch of Natalie Blaine's black brows rose higher. "Traditionally small-town, Mr.—er—I'm afraid I didn't get the name. Much hearty laughter and loud talk and backslapping."

Gus Ingersoll gave an audible snort. "Just too damn vulgar for words," he stage-whispered to Beulah Raymond.

She smiled without taking her eyes from the woman on the witness stand. Beulah looked more relaxed than she had yesterday in the marshal's office. So did the seven other sharers of the two front benches, F. Millard decided, except Klondike, whose hands, when not busy with her handkerchief, were twisted in her lap, and whose big gray eyes in her pointed, responsive little face reminded him of a trapped fox's.

He barely caught the next question. "Did your husband see any more of one person than another, Mrs. Blaine?"

"Not while I was around. He treated everyone with the same familiarity, regardless of position."

"Did he have many callers at the hotel?"

She sighed. "I couldn't do my nails all day on Tuesday for people dropping in. And phone calls!" Slim hands and dark eyes took part in her shrug.

"Any of these folks"—the young attorney indicated the eight on the two front benches—"come to the hotel to see him?"

Her eyes touched each face like a passer-by looking in a show case. "If they did, I didn't see them."

"You heard all but one speak this morning. Did you recognize any of their voices on the phone?"

"No."

"Did your husband look upset after any of his visitors left?"

She shook her head.

"After any of his phone calls?"

She hesitated. "There was one Tuesday morning. He banged up the receiver, and—I don't know how to describe it—he looked half angry and half—nervous is the only word I can think of."

"Did he answer the phone that time, Mrs. Blaine, or did you?"

"I did. He was busy with a caller at the moment, and I handed him the receiver."

"Was the voice a man's or woman's?"

"I really don't know, Mr.—er … It was an odd-sounding voice, almost as if it was disguised. I know that sounds melodramatic, but that's how it impressed me at the time."

"What did you do Tuesday evening yourself, Mrs. Blaine?"

The slim gray-suited figure sat straighter above the carelessly tossed-back mink coat.

"Just a routine question, of course," the attorney said smoothly.

A routine question, reflected F. Millard, that everyone had been asked but himself.

"I went down to the lobby after my husband left," Natalie Blaine said coldly, "picked up a few magazines, and returned to my room."

"Did you notice anything—unusual about him when he left Tuesday night? Any of this nervousness you mentioned after that phone call?"

"Just before he put on the parka he'd had in storage I saw him slip a pistol in his pocket—one of those flat ones I believe they call an automatic."

The roomful waited, eyes bright with interest.

Gus Ingersoll said loudly in the silence without being put on the stand, "There was no gun on the body or in the warehouse."

The young lawyer turned from the deputy marshal to the witness. "Didn't your husband say anything about it? Did you ask him what it was for?"

"Certainly I asked him. He tried to pass it off as an old Alaskan custom. But I saw his face when he was putting the pistol in his pocket. He looked—he looked grim."

Gus Ingersoll conferred in whispers with the assistant United States Attorney. Then the deputy returned to his seat and the young lawyer cleared his throat. "Is there anyone in this room, Mrs. Blaine, that you knew before you came to Fairbanks?"

Natalie looked at her gray-gloved hands. Her voice, when it came, was pitched lower. "Yes—there is."

"Who?"

Another "Who?" F. Millard told himself wildly, and he'd think he was in a haunted house with an owl in the attic and a witch taking off on a broomstick. In the pause while the courtroom waited for Natalie's answer, he saw that snow was still falling.

At last she raised her eyes and looked at F. Millard's bench. Her voice was barely audible as she murmured, "Frank Ord."

"In—er—what capacity did you know Frank Ord, Mrs. Blaine?"

"He used to be my husband."

CHAPTER SEVEN

While the courtroom buzzed F. Millard asked himself if it was to tell of this earlier marriage that Mrs. Blaine had called Gus yesterday. Had the sight of Frank in the marshal's office been responsible for her sudden pallor, the clutch of one hand on the other?

The commissioner's gavel rapped again, Natalie Blaine returned to the bench across the aisle from the grocer, and Frank took the witness chair. The man was gray-pale as he passed his former wife. The woman stared at the floor. "

Where were you Tuesday night, Mr. Ord?" the attorney asked.

Frank had to try twice before his voice came out, and then it was a croak. "Home."

"All evening?"

"All evening."

"Alone?"

"Alo—" He jerked up his head. "Beulah Raymond was there between eight and nine."

"And you didn't go out?" Frank shook himself like a badgered bear. "What difference does it make, when I've got that special hour accounted for? No, I didn't go out. But who'd care if I did? Listen, brother . . ."

An epidemic of gasps hit the courtroom. Even F. Millard's thoughts stuttered as he told himself that he'd always heard inquests were in-f-formal.

". . . as long as we're exposing family secrets—did you know Natalie Archer Blaine's half-brother was in Fairbanks?"

Mouth slightly open, the young lawyer shook his head.

"Well, he is." Frank's loosened hair bobbed. "San Francisco slicker Dwight Archer himself. I saw him last night down at Beulah Raymond's."

"Dwight?" gasped Natalie from the front-row bench. "What's he doing here?"

Gus hurried up to whisper again to the questioning attorney while the general buzzing rose.

Frank was motioned back to his seat and the matter turned over to the jury. Now the front benches, too, took part in the whispering, all but F. Millard and Klondike. The girl stared straight ahead, fishing at intervals for her handkerchief. Once she sneezed and F. Millard jumped. He sat watching the door the jurors had gone through. Accident—suicide—or murder. By person or persons unknown. Or by someone named—F. Millard Smyth? Why hadn't he been asked where he was between eight and nine, like everyone else? Was Gus saving something to spring later? Was he afraid to air that ghost story? Or what? It seemed to F. Millard that the people near by looked at him oddly. Had they, too, noticed that significant omission?

Accident—suicide—or murder. It couldn't be accident. It couldn't be suicide. If they just didn't name the killer.

Outdoors snow still fell, the windowpanes all a gray blur.

It may have seemed forever to F. Millard, but it didn't take the jury long to reach a decision. "Murder, by a person or persons unknown."

The little grocer wondered if people in the back of the room could hear his sigh of relief.

The courtroom began to empty.

"Come home and have lunch with us, Smitty." In spite of high-heeled galoshes, Mae's round eyes were still below the level of his. "Beulah's coming, and I'm trying to catch Frank. Then we can all go to Silver Star's funeral together."

His gaze ahead on Beulah's red curls beneath a black hat that was just as becoming, if not so smart, as Natalie Blaine's, he absentmindedly accepted. He had a question or two to ask Beulah.

Unwilling to miss the rare chance of an elevator ride they lost Frank who plunged through the crowd and clattered downstairs among the first.

A foot of fresh snow furrowed with tracks covered the sidewalks. As F. Millard turned down Second Avenue with Mae and Beulah he flung a glance of pride at the four-storied concrete bulk of the Federal Building they had left, rising in chrome-trimmed modernity above one- and two-story wooden neighbors. He stumbled and returned his gaze to the ground. A block away Long Ed Griswold hunched along through the falling flakes, and almost out of sight Klondike hurried on by herself.

"Honestly, Beulah," gasped Mae, taking two steps to the others' one, "can you imagine Frank Ord married to that woman? That—that frozen-faced—"

"Careful, Mae, don't shock Smitty." But Beulah's chuckle sounded mechanical and lacked its usual richness. "I don't suppose Natalie Archer Blaine would consider mukluks the thing for funerals, but if this keeps up, I'm breaking out mine. There's a pound of melting snow in each of my galoshes."

"Beulah . . F. Millard stopped.

Her bright blue eyes turned sideways.

But he'd rather ask about last night's visitor without Mae listening in, and probably chiming in, without the added distraction of fumbling along through loose snow. "I—I—weren't you astonished at Tom Blaine's will—that five thousand dollars for Mrs. Malone?"

"Astonished that he finally kicked through," Beulah said dryly.

"Why didn't he give it to her years ago?" panted Mae. "When Eliot bumped himself off, and she was left with a five-year-old kid, and a crippled back—and no money!"

"Eliot—was that Klondike's father?" F. Millard asked. "The paper said he died."

"He died, all right," Mae grunted. "At the wrong end of a thirty-eight revolver. Shot himself one day Klondike and Silver Star were out. That was while she was still able to get out a little."

"But he—her husband—"

"You really can't blame Eliot, Smitty," Mae sighed. "He was a trapper. He'd lost his whole catch from the season before—I heard he gambled it away;

and that winter, right at the beginning of the season, he broke his leg out on the trap line alone, and by the time he finally dragged himself to where he could get help both legs were so badly frozen they had to be amputated."

"You have to be pretty hardy to take a thing like that," added Beulah. "And Eliot Malone wasn't. I knew him before he came to Fairbanks. (The winter I worked in that Godforsaken roadhouse, Mae, up on the Chandalar.) I'd been out prospecting that summer and hadn't made enough to get back to town. He was up there trapping, and believe me, all of us who spent the winter in that roadhouse got to know each other too well. Eliot Malone was fun, Smitty, and good-looking in a sort of girlish way—Klondike looks a lot like him—but he wasn't long on guts. I wasn't surprised when I heard he shot himself."

Mae sighed again. "Tough spot to be in, poor devil. And tough on his wife and kid. Silver Star's back kept getting worse, and by the time Klondike was old enough to earn a little money out of school hours, they were up to their eyebrows in debt. That's one of the things that made her trying to borrow more to take her mother Outside so pathetic."

"Klondike's been trying to borrow money recently?" F. Millard asked.

Mae nodded. "Poor kid kept hoping the Outside doctors might be able to fix up her mother, even though the doctors here said nothing could be done."

"I wonder," said Beulah suddenly, "if Tom had helped out Silver Star when the accident first happened, if he'd scraped up the money to send her Out then—I wonder if she'd have been cured?"

"God knows," said Mae, "but at least he'd have avoided nearly forty years of hate. Funny thing—Silver Star told me herself—right after Tom skipped out of Nome so he wouldn't have to marry a cripple or pay her expenses, the miners were going to take up a collection to send her Outside. But she began to get better. I think it was determination to catch up with Tom and get even."

"And think of the way he treated the Hawleys," added Beulah. "After getting them up here to put one over on Long Ed."

"Ed Griswold?" asked F. Millard.

"They were partners in so many things when Tom bought the grocery," Mae explained, "that he was afraid Ed might try to get a cut in it too. When he gave up the creeks Tom had the store transferred to himself and threw out Whit's dad."

"Long as Tom and I've been friends," said Beulah, "we all know he was pretty much of a stinker in some ways."

The three turned down Bonanza Road through the falling snow while Long Ed kept on down Second. Klondike was already out of sight.

In the Trents' well-dusted living room, crowded with an overstaffed chesterfield set, down cushions, and potted plants, Beulah dropped her coat and started to follow her hostess to the kitchen.

The little grocer caught her arm. This close, her perfume was heady, the bare arm soft and firm, satiny under his fingers. "B-B-Beulah," he stammered. He made his voice steady. "What was Blaine's brother-in-law doing at your house last night?"

For a moment, so close he could distinguish each minute piece of mosaic that made up the blue of her eyes, she gave him back look for look. Then the off-center smile he always found so fascinating began to curve her lips. "I won't try to make you jealous, Smitty. Dwight Archer came to see me on business."

His hand dropped, but she stayed beside him. "You may have to explain it to Gus," he said quietly. "It's quite a coincidence when a man turns up this far from home, and his half-sister doesn't know he's here, and his brother-in-law gets murdered."

"I never saw him till he looked me up two or three days before Tom came back. He said he was here after cinnabar, and someone—I think someone he was talking to in a bar—said I had a claim, and he took down my name and address."

"Wonder if that'll satisfy Gus," said F. Millard slowly. "He's a hard man to explain things to—I found out."

"It'd better satisfy him," Beulah retorted. "That's all there is to tell."

"Cinnabar's what mercury comes from, isn't it, Buelah?"

Her off-center smile flashed on full. "Yes, Mr. Grocery man. Worth a damn sight more than it used to be, and you can get priorities to work it. Now can I go and help Mae?"

* * *

Mae and Beulah weren't the only ones in mukluks at Silver Star Malone's funeral. In the church, fur-clad leg after fur-clad leg passed F. Millard's pew. He assured himself that he wouldn't look into the casket. But in the same way that his eyes had kept returning to Silver Star's picture in the paper, he found himself going down the aisle.

The face beneath the artificial flowers on the coffin lid was so startlingly like the one that had bent over the balcony railing that F. Millard almost exclaimed. The pain and bitterness so evident in life were now gone. Given the right make-up and sufficient strength and motive, could the woman who lay before him have put on that little act? Dealt the hatchet blow herself? The little grocer shivered.

Snow laid a blanket of white on the casket as it was lowered into the grave, and half an hour later, when F. Millard hung his coat in the back room of the store, snow was still falling outside.

The afternoon dragged on, growing darker. The swarm of flakes began to thin in the light that streamed out from the windows.

Closing time, dinner, a little more work, and F. Millard started home. Snow was no longer coming down, but the clouds were low and heavy. He wondered, now that the inquest was over, if the official padlocks would be taken off the warehouse and if Gus had remembered to keep up the fire.

Tomorrow Tom Blaine would be buried. . . . What was that? F. Millard stopped. A faint moan, a puff on his cheeks . . . Good gracious, was the wind coming up? He thought of the miles of forest and tundra hedging the town, the tons of fresh snow—and wind screaming over it all. . . .

One funeral today, another tomorrow. ... He bent his head and hurried on, trying to keep in the tire furrows. Tonight he'd stop at Beulah's no matter who was there.

If they all put their heads together . . . Still, that might not be such a good idea. You couldn't tell who . . .

He shivered. A puff of snow blew down his neck, and he shivered again. He'd stop at Beulah's anyway. She always raised his morale.

He could see a light down Bonanza before he turned off Second. Too near the river to be at Mae's or Frank's. At the corner he saw it wasn't at Beulah's. He pushed on faster through the soft snow that had no car furrows on Bonanza, and stopped abruptly. The light was in his own cabin.

He began to run through the hobbling white—down the street and up his own path where another set of prints had been before him. Pushing open the door he found Gus Ingersoll sitting in F. Millard's favorite chair behind F. Millard's table. And on the table—pointing his way— was an automatic.

"O.K., Smyth," said Gus harshly, "I've got the goods on you now."

"G-goods? What are you talking about?"

"Come off it, Smyth. That innocent stuff won't get you anywhere now. I've got the note. The fire didn't do the job you expected."

"Wh-what note, Gus? What fire? I *swear* I don't know what you're talking about!"

"You're going to do the talking now, brother. You're coming down with me and I'll sweat it out of you. I suppose you never saw this before?"

The deputy held out a once-crumpled, half-charred sheet of paper with the name of a local hotel at the top. F. Mil lard could barely make out the hasty scrawl, but he recognized the handwriting:

"Smyth,

"See you Tuesday night at your place—9:30. I've got to have those back payments by the 19th.

"Tom Blaine."

* * *

His sick eyes met the deputy's hard one. The hand with half of one finger gone reached for the automatic.

"I—I'll come quietly," said F. Millard.

CHAPTER EIGHT

Outside, the wind had risen. It hit F. Millard and his captor in ice-cold huffs and puffs. The moaning and siren sounds were louder—and prophetic.

"Wh—where did you find that note?" F. Millard asked between gusts.

"Corner of it sticking out of the ash can at the foot of the warehouse stairs."

"Anyone could put it there, Gus. There's not even a door, let alone a lock, to prevent them."

"I knew you'd say that. But the note's all I need, and I've got it. Oh, you tried to destroy it, all right. Funny things can happen when you throw wadded-up paper in the stove with a scuttle of coal. May get caught in the grate or shook down with the ashes."

"But that only happens once in a lifetime, Gus! It's too much to expect it would now. Why, if I tried to get rid of anything like that I'd wait till I saw it burn up."

Under a street light F. Millard caught a flash of the other's gold crowns. "Hard luck for you, all right. But seeing's believing."

They plodded on through soft snow that now seemed heavy to F. Millard, while the wind did all the talking. He was glad it was dark, that the growing storm cut down their chances of meeting people—people who would see F. Millard Smyth in the custody of the law.

Gus said presently, "Jeff Peters'll sure be surprised when he gets back and finds the Blaine case already solved."

"Under the circumstances," said F. Millard stiffly, "you can't expect congratulations from me."

"Train's stuck at Broad Pass," Gus volunteered. "God knows when Jeff'll get back from Nenana."

"I wish he was here!" burst out the little grocer.

"Wouldn't do you no good, brother. You might think it would if you watched Jeff tip back his chair and chew the fat. Might think an old guy like that'd be softhearted, but there's no one as hell bent on catching murderers as Jeff Peters."

"Murderers ought to be caught," F. Millard muttered, "but not innocent men. . . . What were you doing in my house tonight, anyway? You said you found the note at the warehouse."

"Just hunting around. Don't worry, Smyth; I had a search warrant. Everything was legal."

"What'd you find—Blaine's gun? I don't suppose who ever planted that note would overlook planting the gun on me too."

Gus patted his pocket. "Found a pair of red mittens."

"But those are mine!" F. Millard yelped. "I've worn them a hundred times when I used my hatchet. But not— I didn't have them on—I never used the hatchet on Blaine!"

Gus Ingersoll stalked on through the snow.

"Besides," the little man panted, "I'll bet you'd find a pair just like them—or red gloves—in any house on Bonanza. If you *didn't,* it'd look more suspicious. Do you suppose I'd have left mine around if—"

"Oh, shut up," the deputy growled.

The wind bit in as they turned up Cushman Street to the Federal Building. Climbing the steps, F. Millard glanced furtively right and left. The only man in sight was coming down the bridge approach on Front Street; surely too far away to recognize F. Millard. The door bumped his heels as it shut.

He panted up the shallow inner steps to the lobby and up two long flights beside Gus. No elevator ride tonight. Only *clump, clump* up the stairs and gloomy surmise as to what was in store for him on the third floor. Third floor—third degree—Gus. An all-night session without food? Perhaps even without water. Rubber hoses? Glaring lights? Their steps were loud in the stairwell.

Tobacco wouldn't matter—after more than fifty years without it. Lately Beulah had introduced him to cigars. Would there be any more cozy evenings at Beulah's, with her hair shining under the lamp, and that off-center smile teasing?

The third floor came too soon. They turned in at the door marked "U.S. Marshal."

In the room beyond the outer office a shaded desk lamp burned. Peering over it was a man with lined cheeks like loose leather and thin white hair flattened down like a little boy's.

"Jeff!" cried Gus.

"Mr. Peters!" gasped F. Millard.

He grinned, and the cheek leather cracked. "Hello, boys. Got a gas car in from Nenana. . . . Helping out the marshal's office, Smyth? Or are you a suspect?"

Gus spoke first. "Guess we got our man, Jeff." He jerked his head at F. Millard. "Looked like him all along, but I got more evidence tonight."

"S-someone's trying to frame me, Mr. Peters!" cried F. Millard. "She—or he—killed Tom Blaine in my warehouse with my hatchet, and planted a note—"

Gus broke in and both men talked at once.

Jeff Peters held up a gnarled hand. "Hold your horses, boys. Drag up a couple of chairs and talk one at a time. Why'd you say 'she or he' just now, Smyth, instead of 'he or she?'"

Again F. Millard told the story of Tuesday night and the ghost that couldn't have been a ghost. Again Gus made blistering comment, but now Gus was just a hired man.

At a fast gabble the little grocer covered Tuesday night, Wednesday morning up to finding the body, where Gus determinedly took over; Wednesday afternoon in this very room and the little one opening off it. This morning's inquest they reported in duet.

"I knew," exclaimed F. Millard at the end of the joint recital, "there was something queer about Blaine's visit that night! When he left he said he wouldn't keep me away from lodge. How'd he know I had lodge meeting that night? He just came to town the day before. And he said, 'Now I won't have to see you later.' Was he planning to see me later? Do you think he really wrote that note, and someone else got hold of it?"

"Hell, of course he wrote it," scowled Gus. "No forger that good would be wasting his time in Fairbanks."

"But look," F. Millard cried eagerly, "how would Blaine know all those things about me if someone hadn't told him? If he and whoever it was put their heads together—"

All Gus's gold crowns showed at once. "Yeah, Blaine and his murderer got together and planned how to kill him so they could throw the blame on you! Hell, Jeff, that's the kind of thing Smyth's been handing out ever since Blaine was killed. What do you say I take him along and work him over like I was going to?"

Jeff's faded blue eyes examined both men while F. Millard forgot to breathe. Slowly the old marshal shook his head. "He won't get away, Gus, and neither will any of the others. We'll take our time—and get the right one."

The little grocer exhaled. "Then it w-won't be me."

Gus snorted.

"You boys might as well go home." Jeff Peters pulled out a drawer and bent his big, gaunt frame above it "Guess we can all use a good night's sleep."

"This don't mean you're cleared, Smyth," Gus reminded F. Millard, scowling, as the little man turned the door knob.

The old marshal looked up from his desk. "No one's cleared—till the murderer's caught."

But F. Millard's feet hardly touched the stairs. He was going down a free man. In the street even the moaning of the wind, soaring now and then to a shriek, only made him duck his head and hurry faster for home.

By morning the wind was all shrieks and howls, the new snow on the ground driven fury. Involuntarily dodging as a scoop of snow hit the windowpane, F. Millard looked out on white madness.

And today Tom Blaine would be buried. As soon as the grave was thawed and dug the wind would fill it with snow. If he didn't go to the funeral, would the town think him callous? Not if it saw eye to eye with Gus. The little man squared his shoulders. He was innocent, and he wasn't going to act guilty. His eyes strayed to the copies of *Flatfoot* stacked on a shelf. He'd like to see who came to that funeral—who came, and who stayed away.

Outside, the wind cut like a new bread slicer. He held fur-mittened hands against his face and shrank farther into the parka that, customary or not, he intended to wear to the funeral. If Gus forgot the warehouse fire on a day like this and the canned goods froze—for a moment in spite of the wind the little man straightened—by gracious, F. Millard would sue him!

Gus himself appeared at the store soon after it was open. He held out two keys, with the kind of look that said he hoped they'd burn the little grocer. "Jeff says to keep these till you get new locks on the warehouse. I'm good and sick of walking down there twice a day to throw in coal, and we're through with the joint now, anyway. But don't forget"—he leaned heavily on the counter—"that don't mean we're through with you."

By will alone F. Millard kept himself from cowering before two hundred pounds of Ingersoll topped with vibrant mink tails.

Gus drummed on the counter with his fingers, all but the finger whose drumming joint was missing. The grocer found himself watching it and thinking of Klondike's story.

"I suppose," the deputy said darkly, "I'll be seeing you at the funeral."

* * *

Tom Blaine wasn't buried from a church. When the wind caught the door of the funeral parlor and slammed it behind F. Millard, he found the room dotted with other parka-clad figures. The furry hoods, the skirted furry bodies, and fur mukluks that made no sound when their wearers moved but a slither on the floor gave the whole thing an eerily ritualistic flavor smacking of Black Magic.

At this funeral the casket remained closed, and among the handful of onlookers there were no sounds of weeping.

F. Millard stood unobtrusively by the door as the others filed out to the waiting cars. In conventional (and fashion able) attire the widow passed. Was it the wind that made her shiver at the door? Behind her came the handsome man the grocer had seen at Beulah's, Natalie Blaine's half-brother. Then, each with leather Siwash mitts and reindeer mukluks like a uniform, the parkas began to file out: Mae in gray-tan caribou, Beulah in brown muskrat, Valentine Voss in spotted hair seal, Long Ed Griswold in lank tan canvas furred only around the face, a few other old- timers in canvas. Three or four coonskin coats went by beneath the faces of local businessmen. Whit Hawley passed in uniform.

Except for Frank Ord and Klondike Malone all those who had waited Wednesday afternoon in the marshal's office were present at the murdered man's funeral.

The room was now empty except for a man in a coonskin coat on the other side of the doorway. F. Millard looked up as the other looked down—and met Gus Ingersoll's glare. They walked out together; but not handcuffed together, the little grocer reminded himself.

In the bleak white cemetery they endured for the necessary time the slicing of the wind that whistled past the few tombstones. Then hurried back to the cars, away from the rattle on the coffin of clods already freezing.

At lunch, F. Millard saw with surprise that Klondike was back at work—lipsticked, brown curls fluffed up, and apron as perky as ever. But her big eyes were still swimmy and handkerchiefs still in play. As he gave his order she sneezed, and he remembered she'd sneezed at the inquest. So all those handkerchiefs weren't being wet by grief alone; Klondike had a cold.

Dwight Archer, Blaine's half-brother-in-law, was at the counter too. F. Millard observed with even greater surprise that Natalie Blaine's half-brother was making himself pleasant to the girl who served him lunch. Birdlike little Klondike Malone with those luminous gray eyes was the sort of girl to whom men are instinctively pleasant. But anyone related to Natalie Blaine seemed more the type to snoot a waitress.

All day in the store the little grocer listened to complaints about the weather. The few customers the wind blew in panted, "This reminds me of Nome," or of Juneau, or Valdez. By late afternoon the wind died down, and the whole town sighed with relief.

F. Millard echoed the civic sigh as he went home that night. Fifty below was better than another day like this. Even sixty below. The still, deep cold of the usual Fairbanks winter—Good gracious, he was talking like the Chamber of Commerce. But thank goodness, it seldom blew like this in Fairbanks. Thank goodness, too, he was still a free man, not behind bars. Remembering Gus's eyes this morning at the funeral, he stumbled against a snow drift. And the usually mild old eyes of the marshal when he said last night, "No one's cleared—till the murderer's caught." They hadn't been mild then.

Jeff Peters was right. Until the murderer was caught, all those who had a motive or opportunity, or both—F. Millard shuddered—would be under suspicion. Even—he controlled another shiver—in danger themselves. The first murder was the hardest, and the first, according to *Flatfoot,* often led to a second. And after the second . . .

By the time he reached his cabin and turned on the light, he found he had been shying at every shadow on the street. After the light went on, the telephone rang, and his hand shook so he could hardly take down the receiver.

But the voice that came warmly over the wire stopped the receiver's gyrations. "Come on over, Smitty," urged Beulah. "The gang's gathering for a post-mortem."

A poor choice of words, thought F. Millard, holding back another shiver. Post-mortem—and Blaine on the warehouse floor in that twisted parka. . . .

He cleared his throat. "Thanks, Beulah. Right away? Fine."

Not quite so fine, he admitted, hanging up, as if he and Beulah were going to spend the evening by themselves, but a lot better than waiting alone, wondering how soon Gus would close in again, this time with Jeff behind him.

Next door he found Beulah's living room buzzing. Hers was a replica of Mae's, except for the beehive-shaped hair drier, with a chesterfield set and only a few less house plants. It was already full of people. Frank Ord was sprawled in the middle of the davenport, his hair more mussed than ever, both arms outstretched along the back. Mae sat in the half circle of one brawny arm, her feet not quite touching the floor, and F. Millard felt uncomfortably sure that the vacant place beneath the other arm had been Beulah's. Whit Hawley's long legs hung over the arm of one chair, while pink-cheeked Valentine Voss sat compactly in another.

Whit gave the little grocer a face-slashing grin. "Wait till you hear the latest! Now that dear old Uncle Tom can't contradict, Long Ed Griswold's pulling a fast one. He claims Uncle Tom paid for your store with partnership money, and the Blaine estate owes him half the profits up to the time you bought it, and half the sale price after."

"Why," gasped F. Millard, "nothing showed in the papers the bank's got in escrow that anyone owned it but Blaine!"

"That's what everyone always understood. Supposed to be the reason Uncle Tom sent for Mom and Dad." The soldier's grin was gone now. "He took the store out in Dad's name, so Long Ed wouldn't get a look-in."

"Well, then—"

"It was bought before Blaine and Griswold broke up, so it'll be hard to prove either way." The hard grin slashed Whit's face again. "But, hell, that's the fair Natalie's worry."

F. Millard blinked. "Wouldn't it show in the papers when the partnership was dissolved?"

"What papers?" the younger man snorted. "They wouldn't want a lawyer to know their business."

Beulah laughed. "You'd have to know them to understand, Smitty. They were the closest-mouthed as well as closest-fisted men I ever knew."

"It's not uncommon, Smitty," added Mae. "I'll bet most mining partners don't have papers, and that's what Tom and Long Ed were at first. In the early days plenty of other partnerships were verbal too."

"But when they broke up," F. Millard protested, "they'd have to have some sort of accounting."

"On the backs of envelopes," chuckled Beulah. "I've known too many like them. 'You take this, and I'll take that. This is yours, that's mine, and we'll call it square.' "

"And then they lose the envelopes," finished Valentine Voss.

"My gracious," said F. Millard weakly.

Frank Ord came out of his private engrossment long enough to ask halfheartedly, "No kidding, can't they produce any papers?"

"Not Long Ed," said Whit. "Claims he lost what papers he had when one of his cabins burned on the creeks. Don't know about Uncle Tom. Jeff Peters said he hadn't any with him. Suppose the fair Natalie can have someone go through his things in San Francisco."

"I'll bet they don't find anything about the Blaine- Griswold partnership," said Beulah. "Long Ed's too smart to start something if he doesn't think he has a good chance to make it stick."

"He wasn't called Long Ed for nothing," Mae observed.

"How did he get that name?" F. Millard asked. "He's tallish, but nothing like Sergeant Hawley or Jeff Peters."

Mae laughed. "Not for his height. It was the shape of his head, and the way he used it. A Cockney gave it to him."

"You mean—Long *Head?*"

Mae nodded, her round face rounder with laughter. "You know how his head goes up to a peak, and what with the way he was always coming out on top in a deal and his name being Ed, it was just too much. He couldn't get rid of that name now if he tried."

F. Millard thought of the sharply crooked elbow and stroking arm, of opaque dark eyes on the dead man's widow. Wednesday afternoon in the marshal's office, Long Ed Griswold might have been estimating his chances of making this very scheme stick.

"You damn near have to've been on the creeks yourself to understand those guys," remarked Whit.

"It's a funny life," said Beulah. "You may go a year without seeing anyone but your partner. I never had one myself, but I know what it's like."

"You either get to love him like a brother," said Mae. "or you—"

"—set a stick of dynamite under his bunk and light the fuse and run like hell," put in Whit. "I'll never forget Long Ed and Uncle Tom the summer I spent with them. Sometimes they wouldn't speak for days, and then they'd spend a week arguing over every pan of gravel and mouthful of beans."

The dark eyes behind Valentine Voss's rimless glasses were bright. "Argument's always been Griswold's long suit, hasn't it? I even heard some story about him robbing a clean-up to prove he was right."

Mae, Beulah, and Whit all laughed.

"Don't wonder you thought that," bubbled Mae. "Wasn't it the year you went Outside, Beulah, in 'twenty- nine? Seems Long Ed had been arguing with an old man on the next creek who was working all alone about taking care of his clean-ups. He used to leave them out on the hillside—claimed they were too piddling for anyone to bother—and Long Ed swore Alaska wasn't what it used to be and the old man had better look out. Then, by gosh, he was robbed."

"Do you mean that Griswold—" squeaked F. Millard.

The others laughed again.

Beulah took up the story. "That's what we all thought too, but Tom said Long Ed was digging a ditch with him all day. The deputy marshal only found one set of tracks— made by shoepacks like everyone wore; so Tom's alibi let Long Ed out. And how winning that argument tickled him!"

Good gracious, thought F. Millard, no telling what this kind of talk might lead to. People who'd known Blaine so long might be able to throw light on past events and relationships that could very well tie in with murder.

"Look," the grocer said eagerly, "will you hold every thing till I get back? Since Gus has been fixing the warehouse fire I'm liable to get so interested I'll forget I have it to tend to. It'll only take a minute to throw in coal, and—why there's no telling what we may dig up, getting together like this!"

An odd little silence fell in the room.

Mae broke it. "Oh, have they given the warehouse back to you now?"

"Padlocks and all," said F. Millard. "Gus gave me the keys to theirs till I can get some new ones."

"Oh," said Mae.

And the odd little silence deepened.

"Let's make it a party," said Beulah. "Klondike went back to work today. Let's get her over here, too, so she won't have time to mope."

"Swell idea," applauded Whit.

"I'll get her," said Valentine Voss.

Whit jumped up, but the reporter was closing the door. The tall bombardier kicked a chair leg. "And to think I introduced that 4-F Charley to her! If Val Voss thinks he's going to—"

"Count ten, Whit," soothed Beulah. "She probably wouldn't come if *you* asked her."

Whit gave his hostess a sheepish fraction of a grin. "Guess you're right, Beulah. I'll go out and cool off."

He and F. Millard both started for the door, and Mae turned brightly to Frank, "I know just the right girl for you, Frank, the cutest little—"

For the first time that evening Frank Ord came alive. He sprang up, scattering broken matches. "Oh, God, I'm going out and get drunk as a skunk!"

He flung through the door ahead of the other two men and slammed it in their faces. The little grocer blinked, opened it for himself and Whit, and watched Frank dash up the Ord walk.

"Seems kind of put out," he murmured.

"Poor devil," said Whit unexpectedly. "I know how he feels." He, too, started up the street.

F. Millard turned toward the river. After the wind the paths all had to be shoveled again. No dents marred the smooth whiteness between street and warehouse. This would be his first time alone in it since Blaine's body had been removed. If there was any ghostly presence there now it ought to be a prone figure in a parka with a hatchet embedded in the skull. But after crunching his way to the door, when he unfastened the marshal's padlock his eyes turned instantly upward. Inside the building no faintest light appeared where the edge of the balcony must be. Only blackness.

But no figure that needed to sweep away footprints would be able to pass the marshal's padlocks. Clicking on the flashlight, F. Millard stepped in with more confidence and shut the door behind him.

The boxes that had covered the bloodstain were still scattered, the dark spot on the floor significantly evident in the torch beam. He turned it quickly up toward the light bulb and pulled the cord. Then, trying not to look at the red-brown blot, he piled the three cases of tomatoes back on top of it. Now everything, outwardly at least, was as it had been before last Tuesday night.

When he opened the stove door that faced the door of the building the last of the unburned coal on a glowing bed burst into flame. So Gus hadn't forgotten the fire. It flickered a moment as air from the room filled the stove, then, with no more motion to fan it, rose straight and lemon colored above its bed of orange coals.

F. Millard stood watching the fire—one friendly presence in a room where another presence, with spangled dress and Lorelei ways, had beckoned—had it been to destruction? In a room where a man had been murdered.

He pushed the iron door wider, clattered coal into the scuttle, and returned to the stove, his eyes on the friendly flames.

As he watched they shrank away, farther and farther from the door. His trip for coal wouldn't cause that draft. One mitten tightened on the bail of the scuttle, the other made a fist.

As slowly as a rusted screw turns, his head turned toward the door.

It was closed, just as he'd left it. Then, down the aisle of boxes, he saw a puff of vapor—like the last of a cloud let into a heated room when a door is opened on the cold. As he looked the vapor vanished. His head swung back, and he saw the flames straighten.

Had someone just looked in and gone again? Then the scuttle almost slipped from his fingers. Had whoever looked in *gone?*

F. Millard gave a convulsive swallow that seemed to echo through the room. This was no place to stay in. He'd fill the stove and get out.

But he had barely started for the door, the rattle of coal and clang of iron still in his ears, when the foot stretched out for another step faltered. He pushed back his hood to hear better.

It wasn't repeated—whatever noise had stopped him. The stealthy sounds he heard now were too faint to penetrate a fur hood—the slither of mukluks on boards.

"Who's there?" F. Millard croaked.

Instantly the slithering stopped. The grocer waited. The room waited, pulsing with his heartbeats.

He tried again. "Wh-who's there?"

The silence made no answer.

Before him lay the unobstructed aisle to the door, boxes heaped high on each side. Three nights ago behind one of those tiers . . .

He had no way of knowing from which side the sounds had come. No head showed above any box, no hand or arm.

But he had to get to the door—get there first, before the thing that had happened to Blaine happened also to him.

Thank God the light was on. Though he had no weapon. Nothing in his hand but a flashlight to beat off an attack. His mind raced over the nearest heavy objects. Not even a scuttle of coal. He hadn't taken time to refill it when the flames sent a warning.

Beside the empty scuttle lay a quarter sack of coal. He whirled to pick it up, straightened, and coal settled down in the bottom of the sack with a noise that seemed to his sensitive ears louder than airplane motors.

He whirled back. In time to see a leather Siwash mitt reach out from behind the boxes by the light—the boxes that already hid one bloodstain—and pull the cord.

The room went black.

CHAPTER NINE

Blindly F. Millard waited. And so did someone else. No stir of motion in the dark.

Blaine's gun! If the other had the missing automatic …

Seconds that might have been hours passed before F. Millard could swallow. Before he realized that anyone planning to shoot would have left the light on.

With approaching steps to warn him—the weighted sack to swing, and a flashlight in his left hand—the little grocer could retreat up the balcony stairs and beat off his pursuer.

His right arm quivered. Coal clinked again. He shifted his feet—and heard once more the slither of that other pair of mukluks.

The hand in the leather mitten had been by the light. These steps could be anywhere. Anywhere between him and the door.

His grip tightened on the sack. If he started for the door himself while the sound of his own steps was covered . . .

Groping among the boxes on the other side of the aisle from the light and that reaching hand he fought back a sudden urge to turn on his flash—to find and confront the intruder!

But sanity returned, and with it, fear. His fingers dug harder into the sack, and he fumbled on.

Ahead—on the same side of the aisle as himself—a light flashed. Mukluks—the hint of a parka bottom—then it swung in his face and he scrambled backwards. The light clicked off. He ran—stumbling—bumping boxes. . . .

When at last he paused to listen, he could hear the other still moving. Strange that the steps were no nearer. He must be trying to reach the door ahead of F. Millard—to lie in wait. . . . Even if F. Millard crept up to the balcony and down the outside stairs every move would be followed by ear, and when he neared the foot of those creaking, popping stairs, his adversary would be waiting.

If the fellow could somehow be lured from the door . . .

The grocer set his flashlight down on a box, gripped the sack tighter, and stepped to one side. He drew a long breath, stretched for the button, clicked it—and ducked.

Crouching, breath in, he waited.

The steps went faster now, as if the torch beam spurred them on. F. Millard made a groping dash away from it and stopped to listen again.

Still, in that stealthy shuffle, the steps went on, now seeming farther away.

Another dash. Another pause. The steps still seemed no nearer.

F. Millard sighed. Something—the angle of the flash light, the beam's unwavering steadiness—must have made the other guess. He or she, the stalking cat, wasn't going to be lured from the mousehole.

F. Millard gulped. If the other was at the door he wasn't at the light cord! With a light to show what was coming in time to swing the loaded sack . . .

Stealthy footsteps still groped through the dark.

F. Millard fumbled for the center aisle. Left hand sliding along a box wall, he began to run. The light cord— right here. . . . He pawed air.

Just as his fingers closed on the string a cold draft touched his face. He jerked on the light—and saw the door close and a puff of white vapor billow in.

He dropped his sack and sprinted down the aisle. Outdoors he might run the fellow down—at least recognize him. . . .

F. Millard wrenched at the knob—and crashed against a closed door. Beneath furious jerks it only rattled and stood fast.

The keys were in his pocket. He could run upstairs and let himself out the upper door that was padlocked on the inside. But his wild rattling of this one had covered the crunch of the other's steps. He—or she, the grocer re minded himself—might be waiting now at the ash can, out of sight of passers-by, for that very move.

Even with a shot-put to swing—the little man glanced up the aisle at the quarter sack of coal he had dropped— wouldn't it be better to wait here? If the stalker came back, F. Millard would be cat at the mousehole. Meanwhile he could bang and shout till one of Beulah's gathering guests finally heard him.

Beulah's guests—had one of them been his guest in the warehouse? When he left, only Mae and Beulah remained. Frank was going to get drunk, Whit take a walk, Valentine Voss pick up Klondike. Any one of the three could have followed him here. . . .

He yelled and pounded on the door, then held his ear to the crack. No crunch of snow came in.

At least he wasn't waiting in the dark. But he ought to be! His heart slipped a cog. Suppose whoever had shut him in came back?

And he should have his weighted sack, now lolling on the floor. The dark again—this haunted building . . . *My gracious,* he thought weakly.

Then thrusting out his chin, he started down the aisle. He must get his flashlight too, still burning on the box where he'd left it. He reached it at last, walking with his head screwed around like an owl's, eyes on the door—that stayed shut.

Back at the light bulb he picked up his clumsy weapon by its chicken-limp neck and gave it a tentative swing. If he had to use it . . . He swung harder.

Pulling the light cord he switched on the torch and kept its beam fixed on the door as he walked toward it through the dark.

Now he was ready to meet whoever might come. He pounded again and shouted. Still no sound came in from outdoors.

In the dark his breath sounded labored and loud. Merely for the comfort of his flashlight's narrow beam he couldn't risk the battery's going dead.

Going dead—and Bonanza Road was a dead-end street —and Tom Blaine, right here in this building . . .

With jaws and hands clenched he waited. The darkness pressing around him was heavy with food smells: coffee— apples—something else. . . . His nostrils quivered. Some thing strangely contradictory that at first he thought was age. Once it reminded him of roses—his eyes traveled upward in the dark—then it made him think of candle grease—and then of blood.

He whirled, beating on the door, shouting again and again. When he stopped for breath, he gripped sack and flashlight tighter.

At last he heard the crunch of drifted snow.

He gave another shout, and an answering shout came in. "I can't open the door," F. Millard yelled. "The padlock must be on."

He heard fumbling outside, scraping on wood, the clink of metal.

"Is it locked?" the grocer called.

"No—just"—in grunts between fumbles—"hooked over the staple."

The door opened. F. Millard's flashlight glared into a neat-featured dark face with a black mustache.

The man outside fell back a step. "What the hell? Trying to blind me?"

F. Millard slid out, still clutching the weighted sack. "You're Archer, aren't you? Blaine's brother-in-law?" Fur-lined gloves, galoshes, cloth overcoat, he inventoried. But there'd been time to discard mukluks and mittens and a parka.

The other's teeth showed for a moment beneath his mustache. "Half-brother-in-law," he corrected.

"How come you let me out?"

Teeth gleamed again. "Want to go on pounding and yelling?"

"But what were you doing down here?"

"I always thought Alaskans were noted for the questions they didn't ask," Dwight Archer murmured. "Don't overwhelm me with thanks."

"Don't be funny," scowled F. Millard. "Somebody locked me in there. What do you know about it?"

"You weren't locked in. The padlock was only—"

"It was just the same as locked for anyone inside. There was a murder in that warehouse Tuesday night. I've got a right to ask what you're doing here."

"Oh, was this where Natalie was made a widow? You're one of the police?"

"I own the warehouse," said F. Millard stiffly.

"Well, well, I wish *I* had a flashlight. Would you mind taking that one out of my face?"

"What brought you down here?" the little grocer repeated stubbornly, still keeping his torch beam leveled.

The other shrugged. "I was on my way to Mrs. Raymond's when I heard you kicking up a row."

Beulah lived two houses up the street, but in this still air sounds traveled. "Come along, then," the grocer said abruptly, "I'm headed there myself. Wait till I look at these tracks."

He dropped his sack of coal and turned his flash on the drifted-over walk. For a minute it looked as if only one set of tracks led in from the street, then he realized that anyone else would naturally step in the tracks F. Millard's feet had already made. He poked his flash down the first deep indentation. The impression of Archer's galoshes showed plainly on top. In other holes, edging prints of galoshes, he found parts of mukluk tracks. But even complete mukluk tracks would have told him only whether they were large or small, hard-soled or soft. One mukluk sole was too much like another to leave distinguishing marks.

He flashed his light toward the outside stairs. The snow was smooth and unbroken.

"Ready, Hawkshaw?" Dwight Archer sounded amused.

At Beulah's F. Millard forgot to be polite. While his hostess was introducing Archer, the grocer's eyes ran over the occupants of the living room. "All right," he broke in, "everyone Gus had at the courthouse is here but Frank and Mrs. Blaine and Ed Griswold. . . . Which one of you followed me?"

"What do you mean, 'followed you?'" growled Whit who was sulking across the room from Klondike and Valentine Voss. They both, with Mae and Beulah, stared in apparent astonishment.

"Someone sneaked in the warehouse while I was fixing the fire. If I hadn't caught him at it"— F. Millard paused —"guess I'd be where Blaine is now. You all knew where I was going. . . . Who followed?"

"Then why'd you make those cracks at me?" demanded Dwight Archer. "I certainly had no advance information on your plans."

F. Millard swung back to him. "You could have been watching for me."

Archer touched his small mustache with delicate finger tips. "Forty below's a bit chilly for street-corner loitering."

"If you followed me home you didn't have to wait long. I was only in my cabin long enough to answer the phone, and I couldn't have spent more than ten or fifteen minutes here before I went to the warehouse."

"How could I have counted on that? Natalie's first husband may call me a city slicker, but even Frank never called me clairvoyant"

"With a parky and mukluks you wouldn't mind the cold," returned the grocer. "Or you could have waited in someone's dark cabin; Alaskans don't lock their doors."

"I'll bet they do now," Archer murmured, "on Bonanza Road. Besides if I'd fill the bill, so would that old buzzard with the mangy fur hat who used to be Tom's partner; so would my charming half-sister."

"Well, it sure wasn't me," said Whit Hawley. "I didn't go anywhere near the damn warehouse."

"You been alone ever since you left here, sergeant?" F. Millard asked sharply.

"Why, you little—" Whit glanced at Klondike and swallowed the word. "O.K., I don't have any way to prove it, but I still didn't go anywhere near there."

"Frank hasn't come back," said F. Millard. "He knew where I was going."

"Don't hit a man when he's out, Smitty," Beulah said softly, "in more ways than one."

"And you"—the grocer whirled on Valentine Voss —"how do I know you went right over to Klondike's?"

"But he came in ages ago!" the girl exclaimed. "He wouldn't have had time—"

"How do you know, Klondike, what time he left here?"

"I—why, of course I don't, but I changed my clothes after he came and brushed my hair, and took all kinds of time. And we've been here several minutes."

"I assume you went in another room to get ready," F. Millard commented, "and shut the door."

"Why, you . . . !" Again Whit swallowed what he wanted to say, but this time he sprang to his feet.

"Did Mae stay here, Beulah," the grocer asked, "you two together?"

Mae swelled up like a pigeon gone berserk. "I went home to get more cinnamon for Tom and Jerrys, and if you think—"

"Did she come right back with it, Beulah?" F. Millard persisted.

Her hostess hesitated, and Mae snapped, "No, I didn't! I stopped to fix my hair."

"I got most of the sandwiches made before she came back," admitted Beulah.

"You stayed in the house yourself?" asked the grocer slowly.

For a minute Beulah, too, looked indignant. Then she laughed. "I can show you the sandwiches, and I made them while Mae was gone. But of course I could have done it this afternoon."

"Mr. Smyth!" cried Klondike. "I shouldn't think you'd come to a party where you think everyone's trying to kill you!"

"Not everyone, Miss Klondike," said Archer softly.

"Just one of us."

"I'm not staying," F. Millard said firmly. "And I warn you all right now—I'm going straight to Jeff Peters!"

CHAPTER TEN

At the marshal's "Come in," F. Millard opened the door of Jeff Peters's one-room cabin.

The old man looked up from a chair in front of a square-topped combination cooking and heating stove. Both long legs were propped on the open oven door. "Well, young feller?"

It had been thirty years since anyone had called F. Millard "young feller." His story tumbled out with all youth's breathlessness.

"When the flashlight swung," he ended, "I saw the mukluks were that grayish reindeer nearly everybody wears, but I couldn't see the color of the parka. The Siwash mitt was like any plain leather one with a narrow band of fur on the gauntlet."

The old marshal sat silent, staring beneath white, bushy brows past the stovepipe. Finally he said, "Funny how frost makes different patterns on the windows."

F. Millard blinked indignantly at the suit of damp wool underwear hanging on the other side of the fire. "But I tell you the murderer's got me spotted for his second victim!"

"That one there"—the old marshal pointed a long, bony finger—"looks like what I saw under water from one of those glass-bottom boats at Catalina Island. All it needs is fish. And the one over there"—again the gnarled finger pointed—"looks like my mother's Paisley shawl."

The grocer made a strangling sound.

"Your first notion was the murderer framed you," Jeff said slowly. "If he wanted to frame you, he wouldn't kill you, would he? He'd be losing himself a good goat."

F. Millard groaned. Even his adventure in the warehouse could be twisted against him.

"Ever stop to think, young feller, that it might not of been you they was after? Might be something in the building. . .

"But if I hadn't seen the flames blow, and called out and scared him into turning off the light, I'd have locked the door—with him still in there!"

"Well?" said Jeff calmly. "He'd get out next time you unlocked it. The fire was lit, and he might of brought his lunch. A feller wouldn't be missed at night like he would in the daytime. Perhaps he—or she, of course, you know, young feller—needed lots of time to hunt for something."

"But Gus went all over the warehouse for clues," the grocer objected. "All he found was that broken flashlight Blaine must have dropped when he fell. The flash and that swept balcony and stairs."

"Well, if you'd rather have it someone after you . .

F. Millard shivered. "He did slip out instead of waiting to get me at the door. Though he might have thought he'd try again when I wasn't warned. He or she, of course, as you said. . . . . What could there be in the warehouse anyone would want?"

"Hard to tell," mused Jeff. "I went over it this morning myself before Gus gave you the keys. With a place as old as that most anything might of been left there, anywhere from last week to forty years ago."

"But, Mr. Peters—"

"Make it *Jeff*, young feller, like everyone else. ... Of course, it might not of been someone after something; he might of wanted to leave something."

"Then someone's still trying to frame me!" F. Millard exclaimed.

The marshal tipped back his chair and stretched a long arm for a can of tobacco on the iron bed behind him. "Doc still lets me have one pipe a day. You got one, Smyth?" He held out the can.

F. Millard shook his head. Beulah hadn't tried a pipe on him yet. But smoking experiments were minor matters now. "A parky'd go on over either pants or skirt, and mukluks hide the rest of the leg. There wasn't enough left of the tracks in the holes we all stepped in to tell if they were large or small. Mrs. Blaine and her brother and Long Ed Griswold wouldn't have been expected to show up at Beulah's and Frank Ord said he was leaving . . ."

Jeff filled in the other's pause. "Whit could of said next day he decided not to come back, Voss could of said Klondike wouldn't come, so he wouldn't either; and if Klondike did refuse there'd of been no check on her."

"Only Mae and Beulah . . F. Millard hesitated.

"If Mae hadn't brought back the cinnamon it would of been hard to explain," the marshal agreed, "or if the hostess stayed away from her party. But don't forget we don't know for sure that the guy that followed you was the killer."

"If it was someone wanting to stay till the next time the door was unlocked, it wasn't Beulah or Mae. If not"— the grocer paused—"no one's let out."

In the quiet of the cabin he heard a stick of wood pop in the stove. He turned to the marshal again. "What about this Archer fellow? He told Beulah he's looking for quicksilver property. Why'd he keep it so dark his own sister didn't know it? Or his half-sister, as he's careful to say."

"I been talking to both him and Frank Ord. Archer admits he and his sister aren't pally, but Frank says they hate each other's guts. Says it's always been Natalie that got the breaks, even if Archer was the boy and older. Natalie's mother had the money (old Archer married twice), and all the son by the first wife had was what he could scrounge out of someone else. He's got a home in his half-sister's house—her mother's will saw to that. But I think, instead of helping matters, that keeps them for ever trying to get the best of each other."

"Wonder if his coming up here had something to do with it."

"Might of been trying to get ahead of his sister through Tom," the marshal assented. "Archer told me the same story he told Beulah. He might of thought he could beat Tom to something. Got in just the plane ahead."

"If he was trying to put something over he wouldn't advertise his presence to the Blaine's," agreed F. Millard. "Then after Tom was murdered he'd just about have to lie low. Probably be lying low yet if Frank hadn't given him away."

Got a few highlights from him"—Jeff's leather cheeks crinkled in a grin—

"on Frank and Mrs. Blaine. Archer says when she married Frank he had a big future, or would of, if he'd followed her advice. But Frank didn't want to be a power in the construction business, or shine in society, or even be rich. Guess he's the kind that'd rather use his muscles than his head and have a boss than be one, and Natalie couldn't take it."

F. Millard remembered Frank's gray-white face at the inquest, his moody announcement tonight that he was going to get drunk. "Was their divorce pretty recent, Mr. Pe—uh—Jeff?"

"Four or five years ago, I think. Archer said Frank took it hard. Funny how that chilly type gets hold of a man. Myself, I'd say Natalie Blaine was about as warm and soft as a keg of nails at forty below. Archer says Frank went to Los Angeles after he and his wife busted up, and dropped out of sight. . . . Funny thing about Frank: I checked with some of the Second Avenue neighbors. Old lady that lives nearest says his cabin was dark for a few minutes Tuesday evening. Her daughter'd promised to send her some Red Cross yarn. She used up all she had and was standing at the window watching for her son-in- law's car, with one eye on the clock and one on the street, when she saw Frank's light go out. The clock said seven minutes to eight, and there was no headlights in sight. Then in just five minutes, at two minutes to eight, Frank's light went on again. Her son-in-law didn't come till near ten, and Frank's light stayed on all that time."

"Funny it went off at all," F. Millard mused, "when he said he was home all evening."

"I mentioned that to him," drawled Jeff. "He says he started to go uptown, but he'd only gone about half a block when he remembered Beulah was coming over, and he turned around and went back."

Jeff stretched long arms over his head and glanced side ways at his caller. "Are he and Beulah pretty friendly?"

F. Millard stiffened. "No more friendly than she and I. We're neighbors, you know."

A pause fell between the two men.

"I appreciate what she's done very much," the grocer added primly. "And I'm sure Frank does, too."

"Oh, Beulah's always had the knack of making a fellow comfortable." Jeff's easy drawl speeded up. "I just wondered if Frank was still too much wrapped up in that first wife of his to take an interest in other women."

"Beulah acts no different with him than me. And Frank treats Mae Trent the same as Beulah. He slips an arm around them both, and—well, he's a little too free with his hands to suit me. I gather he's that way with all the women. The chummy type that doesn't get around to matrimony."

"Ever been married yourself, young feller?"

F. Millard shook his head, a flush creeping up under his collar. He'd always thought of himself, except for a brief few months of dreaming about a girl who wasn't for him, as not a marrying man, but lately he'd taken to imagining a light on when he came home from work, the smell of dinner cooking, and perhaps the satin of softly firm arms. . . .

"I don't care what anyone says," he exploded, "I never have believed that talk about Beulah and Blaine!"

"Perhaps you got no call to," the old marshal soothed. "This is a great country for gossip, and a good half of it's guesswork. Beulah never was the conventional type, and when you don't behave the way folks think you ought to, tongues are bound to wag. But she'd never be jealous about Tom's marriage. He kept after her to marry him after she divorced Raymond. If Beulah was a scalp collector guess she could trim a whole belt. Even Long Ed—"

"Not Long Ed Griswold!"

"Sure. He was young once, and crazy about her as Tom was. I always kind of wondered if that wasn't partly why Tom and Beulah got to staking claims for each other. She wouldn't marry either one of them, but anyone could see Tom had the edge, and he took a delight in rubbing it into Long Ed every way he could, even by putting her location notices just as close as he could to theirs, with her name in big letters, by Tom Blaine, her attorney in fact."

F. Millard looked puzzled. "Could he stake for someone else?"

"The law only lets you stake two placer claims per month in one recording district," explained Jeff. "If a feller strikes good ground he wants more. It's an old dodge to get a friend's power of attorney and stake two extra claims for him and count on his deeding you half."

F. Millard blinked.

"Tom and Beulah did it for years, young feller, clear back to the first World War."

"My gracious, she wouldn't be old enough—"

Creases fanned around the other man's eyes. "I wouldn't give away a lady's age, but Beulah Raymond's as old as Mae, if not more so."

Then the hints about her and Blaine weren't so implausible; there hadn't been too much difference in their ages. Still, it worked both ways, reflected F. Millard; there wasn't so much difference between his own age and Beulah's, either.

Jeff took his pipe out of his pocket and knocked clinker tobacco from the bowl. "Tom didn't have it all his own way on the creeks. Long Ed had innings too. He used to get Tom's goat by staking for Silver Star. ... By the way"—the old marshal's eyes held F. Millard's—"someone saw Beulah come out of the Blaines' hotel Monday night."

"It was Tuesday night Blaine was killed!"

Jeff nodded. "She said she went in to see another friend and didn't even look up Tom. I just wondered if she told you different."

F. Millard shook his head.

"Beulah's friend says she was there, all right. I was only thinking out loud." The marshal cupped his pipe bowl in one veiny hand, his eyes on the well-worn stem. "Don't get the idea that Beulah was the only woman in Tom Blaine's life between Silver Star and Natalie. He sure gave the gals in the business a time when he used to come in off the creeks. And not only the gals in the business. Even Mae—"

"Mae Trent?"

"Hell, boy, don't show so plain now under layers of fat, but thirty years ago Mae was an almighty cute little trick. Quite a bit of talk oozed back to Fairbanks the winter she and Tom took the same boat Outside. Now, I don't know a bit more about him and Mae than I do about him and Beulah, except Beulah was the only one I ever heard him say he wanted to marry—so remember it's just gossip."

"It must be wonderful to know so much about folks' backgrounds, Jeff, when you're working on a case. I could listen all night, but I've got to find some way to fix the warehouse fire without getting killed. Do I have to put a bolt on the door so no one can follow me in?"

"Not a bad idea—under the circumstances."

"When an innocent man can't go in his own warehouse . . ." F. Millard stopped. "Look, Jeff, suppose I don't put a bolt on the door. Whoever came in tonight wasn't able to do what he wanted to. Suppose he comes again, and I have a gun—and get him."

Jeff lowered his eyes to the pipe in his hand.

"If Gus goes in with me, whoever's watching'll see him," the little man urged.

Still the gaunt old marshal was silent.

"Wouldn't you—wouldn't you—trust me with a gun?"

Jeff raised faded blue eyes, and F. Millard thought they twinkled. "Gus's chief suspect? Well, hardly."

The grocer gave a baffled sigh, then leaned forward in his chair. "I'm not *your* chief suspect, am I, Jeff? You never would have told me all the things you have if you thought I killed Blaine, would you?"

"Just charge it off to an old man's gabbiness, Smyth."

Gabbiness. ... Was he being treated to a sample of the marshal's famous methods? What Gus referred to as chewing the fat instead of leg work? F. Millard burst out:

"Why wasn't I asked at the inquest where I was between eight and nine? Was Gus afraid to let me tell about the ghost?"

"Guess you hit the nail on the head, young feller, but not for the reason you think. If there's any truth in that story of yours and someone acted the part of Silver Star to get hold of Tom, it might not be so good to let her know it wasn't Tom she got hold of."

"But, my gracious, if she was the one that killed him she certainly knew who was who!"

"I'm not saying yet who killed him. Ever think of Tom seeing that Silver Star act, too? That he might of been in the building—alive—at the very same time you were?"

F. Millard shuddered.

"Looks to me, Smyth, like the best thing you can do for yourself is to find that ghost."

CHAPTER ELEVEN

Before going to work next morning, F. Millard hunted up an old bolt and screwed it inside the warehouse door.

Business put off his ghost hunt till night. All day at the store he kept considering Beulah, Klondike, and Mae, deciding each time that it couldn't have been one of them he had seen on the balcony. But if they stood where that woman had stood and went through the same motions they could give him an idea of size. Size, and maybe more: If Jeff Peters was right and the woman in red still had no idea that the figure she'd seen wasn't Blaine, F. Millard's story might surprise one of them into giving herself away.

The three extra hours the store was open Saturday nights dragged on like another day. F. Millard telephoned Mae and Beulah, extracting mystified promises—in Mae's case, rather short-tempered—to see him before they left for a dance at ten.

Klondike finished her shift early Saturday nights and had no phone at home. He'd have to leave catching her to chance. With her mother only just buried, she'd hardly be taking in the dance, but would she stay home from the movies?

When he turned down Bonanza and saw her windows were lighted, he hurried by the other cabins.

Klondike let him in. Her expressive little face—showing surprise when she opened the door—was freshly made up. The coral-colored sweater and plaid skirt were her newest clothes. Inside he found Whit Hawley belligerently occupying a shabby Morris chair. The bombardier must have had his foot in the door before Klondike saw who it was.

F. Millard backed and filled while Whit glared and the girl's gray eyes flew from one to the other and on to the clock.

"O.K., O.K., Klondike," the soldier said impatiently, "you so bored you think the clock's stopped? Or've you got a date?"

Her pointed chin went up. "None of your business, Whit Hawley."

"I—I . . ." F. Millard stammered.

The others didn't even look his way.

"Well?" said Whit. *"Valentine* Voss still chiseling in?"

"Just because a man has the misfortune to be born on Valentine's Day—"

"Nice timing," the big towhead grinned.

"And isn't a six-foot-two moose, and his eyes keep him out of the service, and he's too sensitive to—"

"Too damn sensitive to live."

"And—"

"Don't tell me it's this Archer guy!"

Klondike sat straighter, a slim, vibrant figure on the edge of a chair. "I tell you it's none of your business. And if Dwight Archer was coming to see me, I'd certainly be proud!"

"Don't kid yourself, Big Eyes. Any day that city slicker bothers with a small-town babe scarcely hatched, there's only two things he's after—her money or her virtue."

Klondike gave a strangled hoot marred by a sneeze.

"Don't forget you've got five thousand dollars now," the bombardier reminded her.

"Five thousand dollars! Chicken feed for a man like Dwight Archer!"

"Ten to one it's chicken feed he offers to invest for you."

F. Millard temporarily gave up his own conversational ambitions. He looked thoughtfully around. Here was none of the overstaffed comfort of Beulah's and Mae's living rooms: scarred wooden chairs unpadded except for the one Whit sat in, a disguised cot for a couch. Through the open kitchen door he could see the water bucket with the handle of a dipper sticking out. A door on the river side showed the grillework of an iron bed.

Klondike's room, he supposed. The door of the other, that had always been her mother's, was closed. If Klondike had been in the kitchen, or even in her bedroom, Silver Star, if she was able to walk, could have slipped out of the house unobserved.

The spatting still went on. "What in hell," grumbled Whit, "you can see in a forty-year-old—"

"Dwight Archer's thirty-nine," the girl corrected haughtily, and sneezed again.

Whit suddenly turned on F. Millard. "What are you doing here, anyway? Trying to give me some more competition?"

Her money or her virtue. . . . The little grocer felt himself blushing. "I just—just wanted to ask Klondike if she'd so something for me."

"What?" barked the soldier.

"Why, it—it's kind of a private matter."

Whit planted himself more firmly in the Morris chair. "I'll listen to whatever you've got to say to Klondike."

"Indeed!" Her chin came up again.

"Neither one of you can put me out."

F. Millard and his birdlike hostess exchanged helpless glances, then both pairs of eyes sought the clock. He still had Beulah and Mae to see, and all three to argue into coming to the warehouse before their evening's dates.

"Look," he began desperately, "I need a few women in —in different shapes and sizes—"

Whit whooped. "Something new in packaged groceries —or a harem?"

F. Millard flushed. "Would you—would you mind, Klondike, coming over with me to the warehouse—"

"Warehouse!" interrupted the other man. "Where Uncle Tom was killed? Last night you said you were followed—"

F. Millard did some interrupting of his own. "I'm talking to Klondike, Sergeant Hawley. I wouldn't ask you to go alone, Klondike, or even just with me. If Beulah and Mae come too … All I want you to do is go up on the balcony . .

Did her small face look paler, or was it only in contrast to her lipstick? In his annoyance over his own awkwardness and flusteration over Whit, the grocer had almost for gotten to watch for her reaction. Was there a flicker of fear in her eyes, a flicker suggesting the terror he had seen at the inquest?

"I saw someone like"—F. Millard hesitated—"like a ghost on the balcony the night Blaine was killed."

"You saw . . ." Klondike stopped, her bright mouth as wide as her eyes. Surely genuine astonishment.

"You saw a ghost?" she finished feebly.

"For God's sake," growled Whit, "come off it."

"Who—who was it?" Once more he saw fear in her eyes. Had she, too, remembered that Silver Star died the night Blaine was killed?

"I—I'm sorry, Klondike," F. Millard said gently. "It looked like your mother."

"My m-mother?" Her voice broke.

"Of course we know there aren't any ghosts," the little man hurried on, "and we've got to find out who'd be—unkind enough to do such a thing. Someone who'd try to put the blame for murder on a woman who couldn't fight back."

"Oh, but no one—"

"Someone was there, Klondike; I saw her. Will you help me find out who it was?"

"What—what do you want me to do, Mr. Smyth?"

"Look here," broke in Whit, "she can't—"

"I wouldn't ask her to do anything dangerous, sergeant. I just want her and Mae and Beulah to go up on the balcony while I watch from below where I was the other night, and get some idea of height and build and what to look for. . . . Will you do it, Klondike?"

"I—I—if the others do, I guess I'll ha— If you think it'll help, of c-course I'll do it."

"Good girl." F. Millard rose. "I'll get them and pick you up."

At least, he corrected himself, knocking on Mae's door a few minutes later, he would try to get them.

Mae, with a blue dressing gown wrapped around her, wasn't as friendly as she'd been before last night. Her eyes got rounder and rounder while he told about the ghost, but when he asked her to take the part of the figure he had seen in the warehouse, her plump little body recaptured its huffy pigeon look.

"If you think you're going to involve me, F. Millard Smyth, your head's only fit for squirrel food. It wasn't me you saw on the balcony, and I'm not giving you the chance to say it was."

"But, Mae, Klondike's coming, and Beulah—I think. If you're the only one who won't, it'll look suspicious."

She bit her thumb and stood blinking. For the first time F. Millard noticed that in spite of the childishness of her gesture and rolypoliness of her figure, Mae Trent didn't look childish. He began to blink too. Actually her round eyes, sometimes more round and sometimes less, only changed expression when she laughed.

Mae wasn't laughing now. Slowly she nodded her head. "Guess you're right. I'll go, then, if the others do."

F. Millard exhaled and reached for the door knob, then abruptly turned back. "Listen, Mae, when you get your head under that drier thing, can you hear what's going on in the house?"

"Gosh, no! It'd have to wake the dead, or you might feel a jar and know something'd banged."

"Then Beulah could go in and out by the back door or be talking to someone in the kitchen and you not even know it?"

Mae nodded. "She said she went over to Frank's the night of the murder. Don't you remember? I wondered later if that wasn't why she hurried me so. My appointment was for seven-fifteen, and I was a few minutes late, but not enough for her to scamp the shampoo and rush me through the pin-curls like she did."

"Listen, Mae: I know it was five days ago, and anything so little—you're pretty warm, aren't you, under the drier?"

She nodded, bewildered. "Sizzling."

"Then you'd notice anything cold. Did Beulah feel cold when she touched you? Her hands or anything?"

"Not her hands. I know because she took hold of my chin while she felt my hair to see if it was dry. But seems to me I did notice—I know! Her skirt! It was cold on my knee, the way it'd be if she ran outdoors to Frank's."

"But how would her hands . . .? She wouldn't put on gloves to go next door!"

"Of course not. She'd wash in hot water after she came in. That beauty school of hers was hipped on sanitation."

With Mae's reluctant promise to join him after she was dressed, F. Millard angled across the street.

Beulah came to the door as friendly as ever. It was like her, he thought, to let bygones be bygones. The radio was playing swing that was more free from static than usual, and the living-room rug was rolled back.

Beulah, in a short black evening dress with a lacy top, held out rounded arms. "Drop your overcoat, Smitty, and give me a whirl. I'm practising up for tonight."

He found himself out on the floor taking awkward steps, with one arm around her waist, and perfume sweet in his nostrils. Not rose, he involuntarily noted. Her body, close to his, was both yielding and firm. How could a bald-headed buzzard like Long Ed Griswold, no matter at what age, ever have the gall to aspire to Beulah?

"I wish I was taller than you," the little man said wistfully.

She leaned back, smiling. Then she withdrew from the curve of his arm and bent over. He heard two sharp thuds, and she was beside him again, close, no taller than himself.

"Just heels, Smitty. See?" She swayed a finger's breadth closer. "I'm no taller than you are now."

Then all at once he found both arms around her instead of one—closing tighter. Clumsily he grazed her cheek with his, and the fragrance of her hair made him breathless. Springtime, violets—whatever it was . . . Good gracious, Mae would be coming over any minute!

Heart still thumping, he drew away. "Mae—Mae—"

Was it bewilderment that followed the softness in her eyes? Now, the look that had been there was gone, and her eyes were a glossy bright blue, almost as hard as Gus's. "Beulah's the name," she said crisply, "not Mae."

"My—my gracious, you surely didn't think I thought you were Mae?"

"When a man looks right at you, muttering 'Mae— Mae,' and you're the only woman in the room—"

"I'd never get you mixed up with any other woman. You're the only—" He'd better stop before he forgot Mae again. "Mae's coming over, and I was scared. . . . You—you're not mad, are you?" he asked softly.

Beulah's off-center smile was more than usually lop-sided, her voice as soft as his. "Of course not, Smitty. It was only—" she laughed apologetically, her old rich chuckle—"a gal doesn't like to think she's slipping."

"Look, Beulah," F. Millard said abruptly, "could Mae have heard you tell Frank you'd go over to his house the night she had her shampoo?"

"Why, I don't know. I don't remember all the circumstances now. Seems to me Mae was here when Frank and I were talking—guess that was Sunday night. Whit Hawley was too, and maybe Val Voss. Any of them could have heard us."

"You always wash your customers' hair in the kitchen and bring them in here to dry?"

She nodded. "And I pin-curl them here—at the mirror behind you."

"When you have someone under the drier, do you usually leave the house?"

"Well, it's not a regular habit, but of course I can't talk to them under the drier. I usually give them some magazines and go on about my business— maybe run over to a neighbor's, or bake a cake, or do my ironing, or even put out a wash. It was different when I had a shop. While one customer's under the drier you're getting the next one ready. But with just one woman to work on, you can't sit around and twiddle your thumbs waiting for her to dry."

"Do the neighbors know that, Beulah?"

"Why, I guess so. I never tried to keep it secret."

"Whatever made you take up beauty operating? It's so different from what your life must have been, prospecting."

"That's the reason, Smitty. I figured I couldn't stay on the creeks forever, and I'd have to work if I stayed in town. Unless I was willing to marry again—or be kept. I told you about Ray, didn't I? My husband? He certainly was good-looking. But it wasn't a wife he wanted. Just a mirror to hang in a flattering light. Guess I never was a mirror for anybody, and Ray— Damn it, Smitty, Ray was tight—tight with money, I mean. I couldn't stand it more than a year. God, it was good to get out prospecting again —and not have to ask a man for money, not have to wheedle it out of him."

The radio played on. Finally Beulah looked at F. Millard and smiled. "But it was beauty operating you asked me about, not why I never married again. The only way I could earn a living in town was by cooking or cleaning or something like that, and I wasn't having any. So when I gave up prospecting I went out to Seattle and took up beauty culture. There was money in it, too; women always want to be good-looking. I hadn't been back here working long before I set up my own shop. And now—guess you could call me a retired capitalist if you wanted to be funny. But I still take a customer or two just to keep my hand in. Never can tell when I may have to go back!"

The radio went on playing, and F. Millard wondered if Beulah would mind if he patted her hand. But the business of the evening was still before them and a few more questions to be asked.

"Look, Beulah: Coming back to Tuesday night, suppose you hadn't gone out while Mae was under the drier —or even if you had, and came back just into the kitchen —if you heard the drier going in the other room, would it have occurred to you to look in and see if she was there?"

"Good Lord, Smitty, you aren't hinting that Mae …?"

"No, no. I—I was just checking up."

"If Mae Trent slipped out from under that drier with her wet head and went down to the warehouse at thirty below, hung around long enough to kill Tom, and then came back and stuck her head under the drier again—she'd be lucky not to have pneumonia. And she doesn't even have a cold."

Whereas Klondike, F. Millard reflected, who had wrapped a towel around her head and just run across the street and back, had come down with a nasty cold. He blinked perplexedly, staring at the drier pushed back of the rolled-up rug.

"Beulah," he said hesitantly, "would you turn that thing on and let me sit under it a while?"

The rug was soon unrolled and the drier trundled over to a chair. F. Millard sat down, and Beulah lowered the beehive arrangement over his head and turned on the switch. Air blew in his face. Now the hive was filled with angry bees dive-bombing around his ears.

If Beulah spoke he didn't know it. She stood beside him, the generous curves of the short black dress visible from the lace yoke down, her head and neck out of sight above the grocer's clamorous bonnet. The black skirt flared as she turned, bent to put on her pumps, and walked to the front door.

Mae Trent came in, with a long green dress and mukluks below her coat. Her round eyes, pouncing on F. Millard and the drier, went rounder, then flew back to Beulah, while her lips moved faster and faster.

Beulah's own lips moved, and both women's hands, but through the racket in his ears no sound penetrated to the grocer. He couldn't even hear the radio. Anyone under the drier could no more have heard voices in the kitchen than a whisper from Mt. McKinley—not voices or the shutting of doors, or the trampling through the back of the house of all the neighbors on Bonanza.

Both women looked grave, one not waiting for the other to stop before her own lips started to move. Their faces kept turning his way.

How loud, F. Millard asked himself, would the beehive sound to someone whose head wasn't in it? Beulah had lowered the thing over him, but he wasn't, he found, fastened to it. He wiggled out from under.

"You don't have to have help," he observed, and in the comparative quiet where now the beehive only buzzed instead of roared, he knew he'd observed it aloud.

He turned swiftly to the women by the door. Both were watching him intently. Mae bit her thumb, her expressionless gray-blue eyes almost narrowed out of their roundness. Beulah's bright irises looked as hard as blue marbles.

CHAPTER TWELVE

F. Millard herded a sulky quartet into the warehouse.

He shot home the inside bolt and Whit snapped, "What do you think you're doing?"

In the beam of his flash F. Millard saw Mae whirl back toward the door. "I'm not going to be locked in this building !" she cried.

"Well, I'm not leaving it unlocked," said F. Millard firmly. "Nothing'll happen to you while we're all here together."

"Then what are you scared of?" scoffed the bombardier.

The little man's lips pressed together. "Someone sneaked in once."

From the dark searchlighted by three torch beams came Beulah's chuckle with almost its normal warmth. "Nice to know he doesn't think it was any of us, or he wouldn't bother to lock the door." She pointed her flash down the center aisle. "How about some more light, Smitty?"

Whit's flash, too, picked out the aisle, and F. Millard walked down the double beam, his own light nosing like a minnow into the shadows at the sides. He pulled the light cord, and the boxes and sacks heaped about him took on sharp-angled substance.

Whit and the three women left the door and started forward.

"What are we supposed to do?" asked Klondike doubtfully.

The grocer pulled two candles out of his overcoat pocket and started for the stairs, gesturing with the clean wick ends toward the balcony on the left. "The only light in the building that night came from two candles on that table. . . . You girls better come up now, so you won't break your necks in the dark."

"Smitty," Mae shrilled after him, "do you think you're going to get us up on that old balcony, and then put out the light—in *this* building?"

F. Millard turned around. "I can't make any comparisons if we don't have the same kind of light. If you girls'll all go up there and come out one at a time where I saw— that other woman, while I stand where I was that night and—"

"See if you can recognize her," Mae finished bitterly. "I tell you it wasn't me."

"I—I'm not very nuts about going up there either, Mr. Smyth," stammered Klondike.

"You don't have to—" began Whit.

"What is this," broke in Beulah, "an old ladies' sewing circle? I'm not scared to go up on the balcony with or without candles." She marched after F. Millard, setting down each mukluked foot firmly.

Slowly, Klondike who hadn't bothered with mukluks or galoshes, clicked on spike heels after Beulah. More slowly, grimacing over her shoulder at Whit, Mae followed.

F. Millard climbed the stairs and followed the left-hand railing to the table. As he lit the candles and stuck them upright in melted paraffin, the three women came up, one by one. On the floor below, Whit stood where F. Millard had stood Tuesday night.

"Sergeant," the little grocer called, "will you turn off the light and come back toward the stove, and let me see if I can—let me see how you look from here?"

"Want to see what the other half saw?" murmured Beulah.

Beyond her, both Klondike's face and Mae's turned toward him.

"I know what she saw, all right," he said quickly, "but we ought to get the whole picture."

As he spoke the electricity went off. The three women, half hidden by the table, seemed to be suspended beyond two stars in a cavern of black. Gradually, as his pupils enlarged, nearer objects took shape in the dimness. The stove was a shadowy blur in the center of the room. On the right, a narrow beam of light crept out from below the front balcony.

"Turn off your flash, sergeant," F. Millard called over the railing. "The candles give enough light."

The beam disappeared. Presently a shadow emerged from the balcony's edge.

"Wait there!" the grocer cried. "That's just about where I was."

If Whit had worn a white parka he would have stood out from the dimness. But in his drab clothing only motion and the pale blur of face and paler hair made him any more conspicuous than the stove. No distinguishable features marked the head's blob.

The woman on the balcony couldn't have recognized him, F. Millard told himself, or known she wasn't playing to Tom Blaine.

He turned, and the candle flames wavered like the flames in the stove last night. Thank goodness, he'd bolted the door tonight in spite of the others' objections.

"When I say Spanish dance step, girls," he directed, "go like this, with a nice big whirl."

Even Mae laughed at his pirouette in overcoat and spectacles and heavy, ear-flapped cap. A hoot of derision came up from the shadows below.

But by the time F. Millard reached the bottom of the stairs, all three women, as tense as ever, stood in a stiff little row at the railing.

He looked up at the candles and figures, and the hair on the back of his neck reminded him of last Tuesday. Now there were three women instead of one, and all swathed in coats.

"I can't compare you with her," objected the grocer, "if you wear your wraps."

"Think this is a beauty contest?" Whit grumbled in his ear.

"It's too shivery in here," Klondike called. "I'm just getting over a cold."

"You hardly keep this place above freezing," complained Mae. "Want to give us all pneumonia?"

"It won't hurt just for a minute," F. Millard coaxed, "just the one of you that's—acting. The woman the other night had a low-cut dress and no coat, and goodness knows how long she was there."

"Maybe she *was* a ghost," observed Beulah.

"You do it first, Beulah," F. Millard urged. "You other girls step back by the booths. She'll show you nothing's going to happen and you won't get too cold, either."

The three on the balcony exchanged glances. Finally Beulah shrugged and took off her coat. The others joined the shadows beyond the candlelight.

"Step farther back from the railing," F. Millard directed.

But even farther back Beulah looked too tall; and, lovely as her bare arms were and the white shoulders beneath the lace yoke, they were rather too plump for the ghost, her waistline more than rather. She stepped forward or back as the grocer directed, and even went through the pirouette while he heard the slide of her mukluks. Then he told her to put on her coat, and called Mae out of the shadows.

If Beulah was too plump, Mae was that much more so. But she seemed the right height. Without comment, F. Millard put her through the same paces. As she whirled in the Spanish dance, he caught himself swallowing hard —Mae's feet made no sound on the floor.

He dampened his lips before asking, "What are you wearing for shoes, Mae?"

"Mukluks." She edged one foot through the railing, and he saw the gray-tan fur that her long dress and the ceiling had hidden.

"Soft soles?"

She nodded, kicking a spindle without sound.

"What are yours, Beulah?" he called.

"Hard soles," came Beulah's voice from the shadows.

Mae put on her coat and, merging with the gloom, remarked, "You'll get a real performance now. Klondike was the star of the high school stage."

Taking off her coat, the girl stepped reluctantly forward. She had changed her sweater and skirt for a more elaborate, though older, dress with long sleeves. The material was dark. On the dimly lit balcony he could barely distinguish the outline of her figure—almost childishly immature compared with that of the woman in red. Her face, as he had known it would be, was far too slender for the round one he had seen.

She whirled in the Spanish dance, and the candle flames bent as they had bent several times, not alone for the pirouette, while the grocer had been watching. Again he thought of last night's flames and was glad he had locked the door.

The girl on the balcony moved stiffly. Strangely, Klondike, who was almost tiny, surely no taller than Mae, now seemed almost as tall as Beulah. Then the click of heels penetrated his abstraction.

"Take off your shoes," he called.

Hugging slim shoulders, she shook her head. "It's too cold."

"Just for a minute," F. Millard coaxed. "It can't hurt you for two or three steps. There's a broom down here if you think the floor's too dusty."

Sulkily she kicked off her slippers. Now Klondike, as well as Mae, was the proper height, and the steps she took were soundless.

"Come over to the railing," prompted the grocer. "Lean forward and beckon."

She moved hesitantly nearer, and beckoned with one slow-motion finger at the end of a stiff, sleeved arm. Her usually responsive face was wooden.

"Smile," F. Millard urged. "Look like you were trying to have fun or—get your man, or something."

Beside him, Whit gave an inarticulate growl.

A grimace briefly stretched the mouth of the girl above them before it drooped again. If Klondike was the star of the high school stage, F. Millard shuddered for it.

"Lean over," he directed, "and call 'Tom' like you were trying to get hold of someone. Call two or three times."

Clutching the railing Klondike frowned, her slim little body defiant. Then abruptly she bent forward and screamed, "Tom — Tom — Tom—Tom!" through the hushed, dark house.

"St-stop! My gracious, stop!" The grocer's head rang like the echoing building while he tried not to let his teeth chatter.

"Ought to wake the dead," came a woman's dry voice from the upper shadows. Mae, thought F. Millard. In the gloom beside him, Whit snorted.

But the test had served its purpose. Klondike's mouth hadn't looked like that of the ghost-silent figure sending out her ghost-hushed call. Klondike's mouth had made a standing-up oval, and the other's an oval lying down.

But it didn't have to be Klondike who had played the ghost. If she knew her mother had, Klondike would have done the sweeping. No wonder she'd looked frightened in the marshal's office and the courtroom, that she acted stiff and self-conscious tonight.

Then another idea, like an incendiary bomb, hit F. Millard and exploded. It didn't have to be Klondike or Silver Star—or even a woman. Right beside him in the shadows—Whit Hawley's towhead was almost platinum, Whit Hawley's waist was slim! Dressed in women's clothes, his lean body padded—if he stood well back from the railing, even when leaning on it, he wouldn't look tall. At no time the other night had F. Millard seen the feet of the woman in red.

Height was only relative. There'd been no one on the balcony to compare that woman with. The booths were too shadowy for guides, and she'd moved around. If it had been Whit . . .

F. Millard must have been staring. The bombardier shifted his feet. "Hell, there's nothing to this," he mum bled. "I'm going home."

"Wait—wait a minute," the grocer stammered. "I— there's one more test."

Whit began to move toward the door, and F. Millard stepped deliberately away, toward the girls. That ought to rid the bombardier of any notions. He heard Whit muttering in the center aisle. "Hold everything, sergeant," F. Millard called back. "I'll unlock the door when we make one more test."

He raised his face to the candles' pale shine. "When I came in Tuesday night, the woman was already here, but she left first—at least she disappeared when the candles went out. I'd like to see if she could have run down the outside steps while I was still in the building."

Mae and Beulah came out of the shadows. Once more the three faced him at the railing.

"And I suppose"—Mae gave a sigh of exaggerated patience—"you want one of us—or *each* of us—to run down those damn stairs and find out."

"The only way to test it, Mae, is to do what I did that night. One of you blow out the candles, and I'll run for the door as fast as I can in the dark."

Mae's voice shot up an octave. "You think one of us is going to run down those outside stairs while you scramble around down here, and the other two of us wait in the dark?"

"But two of you'll be waiting together, and whoever goes down the stairs will have a flashlight. The woman must have had one the other night. It'll only take a few minutes."

"We'll draw straws, I suppose," remarked Beulah.

"It won't be bad," F. Millard cajoled. "Look, Whit, if Klondike takes the stairs, you could meet her at the foot—"

But the voice that came out of the gloom wasn't Whit's. "Darn right I'll meet her at the foot. This is no business for Klondike!" The voice belonged to Valentine Voss.

"What—what are you doing here?" gasped F. Millard.

Candlelight glinted on the reporter's rimless glasses. "Klondike's note said she'd be here. That's enough for me."

"N-note?"

"We had a date. She thumb-tacked a note on her door so I wouldn't think she'd stood me up."

"How—how did you get in here?" F. Millard stammered. "Did Whit just take off the bolt?"

The other shrugged broad shoulders. "Don't know. Whit was inside when I saw him. The door was unlocked. All I had to do was open it."

Voss had only had to open the door. . . . How many times had the candle flames wavered tonight?

CHAPTER THIRTEEN

Time to bank the warehouse fire again, F. Millard told himself grimly next morning. Fires went out and canned goods froze on Sundays just like weekdays.

Maybe it was silly to keep feeling there was someone in the warehouse. The others had laughed at his suggestion that, in a place so large and dimly lighted, with only one man to search a side, anyone in moccasins or soft-soled mukluks could play ring-around-a-rosy with a searcher he would always hear coming.

The three women had waited at the door while F. Millard and Voss went through the building. Naturally they would think the search conclusive; *they* didn't have to go back next morning to bank the fire. He had thrown in last night's coal while Valentine Voss stood watching.

Reason said there was no one in the warehouse; instinct said to take along a weapon. That big monkey wrench— not so heavy it was clumsy, but heavy enough to mean business.

F. Millard put on his overcoat and cap, tucking the ear flap inside—*The better to hear you with, my dear,* came an echo out of childhood.—If there should be anyone to hear in the warehouse.

He hurried down his walk to the street.

Whit hadn't appeared again last night. He might be in the warehouse now— he, Frank, Archer, Long Ed Griswold—or even Natalie Blaine. Though probably the only alien presence was the product of his own imagination.

Slowly the little grocer unfastened the padlock and pushed the door wide.

This time of year eight in the morning, wartime, was as dark as eight at night. The smell of apples and coffee and that indefinable something called age came to greet him out of the dark.

Standing in the doorway, he thrust his flashlight here and there among the boxes.

But this wasn't getting him any nearer the light cord and stove. Tucking the torch under one arm, while his right hand gripped the wrench, he fumbled to bolt the door without turning his back on the room.

He clamped his teeth together and, with the flash held at arm's length before him, began a springing, zigzag progress toward the light. At least he'd be hard to hit— with either a hatchet or a bullet. . . . When were they ever going to find that missing automatic?

He reached the cord and jerked it. The warehouse looked the same as ever— boxes and sacks bright beneath the bulb, shading off to dim and dimmer. Drat meddling Mae Trent for slipping back the bolt last night while he went on ahead! Drat Whit and Klondike and Beulah for letting her! But maybe they were right about the warehouse being empty. There had been no ambush—yet.

F. Millard hurried to the end of the aisle, bent to pick up the coal scuttle he'd filled the night before—and some thing like a cloudburst broke loose.

A rain of gigantic hailstones pelted him, thumped and beat around him. He sprang away, stepped on something that rolled, and crashed to the floor.

The thumping stopped. Finally the sounds of rolling stopped. Quiet closed over the warehouse.

F. Millard sat up. Then jumped up. But nothing stirred except his own pounding heart.

Mystified, he looked down at the little bright things on the floor. Canned baby food! Tiny cans scattered for yards —the cardboard case upended beside the scuttle.

His eyes leaped to the balcony. But nothing showed in the shadows beyond the spindles. He took a tentative step toward the stairs, and roller-skated on another can.

Catching himself, he hesitated. If this was an attempt at murder it was peculiarly bungling. No adult would be killed by that shower of pygmy cans, not even seriously hurt. So why in the name of goodness, pelt a man with baby food? It sounded like a bad joke.

He turned back toward the overturned carton. A string was tied to one corner, lying in loops at his feet. Knot by knot he drew it through his mitten. The string caught. Metal clanked, and the coal scuttle moved.

Again he raised his face. If a box had been balanced on the railing above attached by a string to the bail of the scuttle, when the scuttle was picked up . . .

The racket of dropping cans would cover other sounds —small sounds, like a bolt being drawn. . . .

F. Millard began to run toward the door. And found he was right. The bolt was off. The door unlocked. Some one had just gone out.

CHAPTER FOURTEEN

For the second time F. Millard found himself knocking on the door of Jeff Peters's cabin. Again the old marshal called out, and F. Millard let himself in.

Jeff sat before the stove, both long legs crossed on the oven door just as he'd sat Friday night, only now the smell of boiled coffee and fried bacon filled the room, and light was growing at the windows.

"Had breakfast, young feller?" the old man asked.

F. Millard nodded.

"Then what's on your mind?"

Once more the grocer burst into breathless speech. But this time Jeff didn't change the subject. He stretched a long arm for the telephone beyond his empty plate on the oilcloth-covered table. "I'll send Gus back with you to look the place over. Remember to snap the padlock?"

The little man nodded. "Don't know whether this visitor swept up or not. That front balcony wasn't swept when the other was. But I keep a broom in the warehouse."

"You didn't go up there, yourself?"

F. Millard shook his head.

The marshal set down the phone without taking off the receiver. "Don't look now like he was trying to kill you, does it, young feller?"

"But what does he want, Jeff? He's had plenty of time to plant Blaine's gun or anything else. Of course, if he's trying to'find something . . . Didn't someone say he and Griswold used the old bar for an office? Long Ed or

Mrs. Blaine or her brother might think Tom left something there."

"Could be," agreed the marshal. "Better count Whit Hawley in, too."

"You think . . .?"

"Tom had his office in the warehouse while Whit's dad was in the store. Then, too, anything that might tie in with Klondike Malone interests Whit."

"You think Klondike . . .?"

"Her mother used to dance there. We don't know yet who wants what. I'll try and find out if Whit knew about his uncle's will before Tom was killed."

"Whit didn't show up after he said he was going home last night. He could have stayed in the warehouse, Jeff, instead of someone else coming in."

"No one saw him around town either. We been kind of keeping an eye on you folks, young feller. No one saw Long Ed after he left the pool hall about eight o'clock, or that Archer feller after the first show let out at nine-thirty. I don't guess anyone checked on Mrs. Blaine after she went back to the hotel from supper. That was around half past seven, and the hotel clerk's in and out a good deal. Frank was hoisting a few at different bars all evening, and I saw Beulah and Mae at the dance. One of the neighbor women saw Klondike at the second show with Val Voss."

F. Millard sighed. "I put those four out of the warehouse when I locked the door. What sort of connection do you think these Californians have with things up here, Jeff? Frank Ord, of course, has his job. Mrs. Blaine's connection would be through her husband. And Archer's—well, it might be Blaine, too, or there's this cinnabar claim of Beulah's. Think he and Blaine might have tangled over it?"

"Could be."

"Wonder if that was one of the claims Blaine staked for her, or if Beulah staked it herself?"

Jeff shrugged loose-jointed shoulders. "Location notices are on file in the commissioner's office. Probably tell there, though often as not an attorney in fact's not mentioned; a prospector's apt to think it's not important. But there's another way we can check. When Blaine and Griswold were in that part of the country Beulah was here in town straightening up her mining interests before she went Outside. So if Tom did the staking, it would have to be before she revoked her power of attorney, but late in the summer, because he and Long Ed spent the early part in Porcupine country."

"Location notices give date of staking?"

Jeff nodded. "Beulah was up that way the early part of the summer. She could of staked it then. . . . Say, the commissioner phoned a while ago. Said he was at the office. He could look it up and settle that point right off."

Again the old man's knuckly hand closed on the telephone. This time he lifted the receiver.

While the marshal's slow voice drawled into the mouthpiece and he leaned back with the receiver in his hand to wait for the commissioner's report, F. Millard's attention wandered to the shelf of books over the table. He blinked at volumes of Shakespeare, Plato, and Walt Whitman among a jumble of westerns and textbooks on geology and astronomy. Blinked at the wool socks hanging back of the stove and the leather-cheeked old marshal. Jeff had said to find the ghost.

The little grocer's thoughts returned to last night's experiment in the warehouse. Since the woman in red couldn't have recognized him. . . .

Suddenly he gripped the edge of his chair. The night he saw her—Tuesday night—he hadn't stayed all the time where he told Whit to stand. When she beckoned and sent that soundless call over the railing, he had started around the stove toward the stairs. For a minute—that last minute just before she extinguished the candles—he must have been several feet nearer.

"J-J-Jeff!"

Nursing the receiver, the marshal looked up beneath shaggy white brows.

"She—the ghost—might have recognized me. Just before she put out the candles—" The little grocer hurried to tell what he'd just remembered.

The old marshal nodded. "When Gus goes over to the warehouse, try it on him. . . . What? Oh, yes," he said into the telephone, "not filed till then? Thanks, young feller. I'll do something for you some day."

He hung up the receiver. "Beulah's cinnabar claim was staked June seventh, nineteen twenty-nine; so she must of staked it, not Tom. She filed the location notice the first of September just before she went Outside. Commissioner says she revoked her power of attorney to Tom the twenty-ninth of July."

But F. Millard's thoughts were still in the warehouse. "I never thought I'd want to see Gus again, but if the woman in red could have recognized me . . . You—I don't suppose you'd care to come over to the warehouse instead of Gus?"

Jeff grinned and tipped back his chair. "I've got some head work to do, young feller. Let Ingersoll do the leg work." He reached for the phone again to call Gus.

As the big deputy, mink tails jouncing on his lustrous fur hat, walked down Bonanza Road with the grocer, faces appeared or curtains moved in every house but F. Millard's. Except for the squeal of dry snow underfoot, the two men walked in silence, eyeing each other with distrust.

The first argument started just inside the warehouse when F. Millard bolted the door. The light was still burning as he had left it when he tore out for the marshal.

"For God's sake," snorted Gus, "why the bolt? Joint stuffed with diamonds?"

"It may not mean much to you," returned the little man with dignity, "but my life's worth more to me than any diamond."

Gus snorted again, but F. Millard won the first skirmish. The deputy left the door bolted and started down the aisle.

When he came to the scattered cans he looked down without stooping, glanced at the overturned carton, the scuttle, and the string that attached them; looked up at the balcony, then down again at F. Millard. The silence in the warehouse was unbroken.

The little grocer squirmed. "Well, you—you see how he did it, of course."

Gus made a slight correction: "I see how it was done."

Again silence fell in the warehouse.

"Uh—" began F. Millard, "before you look around upstairs, will you wait here a minute while I go up where I saw the gho—that woman that looked like Silver Star? Jeff Peters said you'd help me."

"The boss told me to," Gus grudgingly conceded. "But if you think I'm going to wait for you to go up and fix something you just remembered you forgot, you got another think coming. I'll go up, and you wait here."

The deputy won that skirmish. F. Millard waited by the scuttle while Ingersoll's number twelves pounded up the stairs and thumped along the balcony.

"There're two candles on that table," F. Millard called. "Light them and I'll turn off the electricity."

"What the hell for?"

"*Jeff* Peters said—"

Gus struck a match.

When both flames were shining, inch-long cones F. Millard pulled the light cord and walked, with dim candlelight to guide him, out from under the balcony. Gus Ingersoll looked even less like the Lorelei with moon-colored hair than had the three women in a row last night.

"Can you recognize my face?" the grocer asked.

Gus shook his head.

The man on the lower floor moved nearer the stove. "Can you now?"

"Well . . ."

A few more steps brought F. Millard to the left of the stove.

"I know you now, all right," called Gus.

"Face—clothes—or general outline? Or is it just because you know who you're looking at?"

The deputy hesitated.

"Suppose I wasn't the man you expected to see—could you tell I wasn't?"

"Well, I could tell you're not Jeff Peters or Whit Hawley."

"But they're so very tall. Could you tell I wasn't Tom Blaine?"

"Sure could," Gus said positively.

No wonder the girl had shaken her head and pointed across the room. Even if she hadn't recognized F. Millard, when she saw she didn't have the right man, she would have to get rid of the wrong one, and hide in the dark till he left.

F. Millard turned on the light and mounted the stairs to join Gus. The deputy had moved on to the front balcony and was flashing his torch around. As the grocer came up Gus muttered, "You sure keep your broom hot, brother."

In the light that rose from the center well and the beams of both flashlights, F. Millard saw that the front balcony, too, had been swept. Beside the railing were two cartons, which must have been propping up the box of baby food that the string tied to the scuttle had brought down on his head.

Gus was watching him. "This sweeping job wipes out your tracks as neat as the first."

"You—you still think—"

"Sure I do, Smyth. So does Jeff. He's just kidding you along till he gets more evidence. You swept that other balcony and the outside stairs just so it couldn't be proved there was no tracks on them but yours. And that's why you swept this today."

"For gracious sake," cried F. Millard, "can't you see? Do you think I've been chasing myself around the warehouse, and scaring myself, and setting traps for myself just to make it harder for you?"

Gus gave him a hard-eyed stare. "Criminals have set booby traps for themselves before now. I notice this wasn't anything that'd hurt you."

The little man's jaws clicked helplessly together. "I'm going over this joint again with a fine-tooth comb," the deputy announced. "And I won't be needing your help."

"Then I'll fix the fire and go back to my cabin. I'm not any crazier for your company than you are for mine."

As haughtily as was compatible with seeing in a dim light, F. Millard felt for the stairs and descended. Without detaching the string from the bail, he emptied the scuttle into the stove.

"I'm going now," he called.

"Go to hell," came down from above.

That, unfortunately, seemed to the little grocer, just where he was heading if anything else happened in this warehouse, or the marshal's office went on suspecting him of murder. If he asked Gus to bolt the door . . . But F. Millard shook his head at the thought of the answer he'd get. Besides, whoever had been in the warehouse overnight had either done what he wanted to do or given up.

His mother used to say it calmed her nerves to make pie. F. Millard wondered whether anything short of apprehending the murderer would calm his, but he'd like a pie. Neither Beulah nor Mae had asked him to dinner as they frequently did on Sundays. If he didn't cook his own, he'd have to go uptown.

His hands were plastered with flour and lard when the knock came on his front door. If this little while was Gus's idea of fine-tooth-combing the warehouse . . .

But what if he'd found all he needed? That last bit of planted evidence that would hang F. Millard Smyth.

Dry-mouthed, he hurried through the kitchen and across the cabin's other room, dripping pastry crumbs at each step.

At the door his mother's training reasserted itself. "Turn the knob," he called. "My hands are greasy."

While it turned he braced himself for arrest, for Gus's wide, triumphant presence and the gleam of hard eyes and gold crowns.

The opening door revealed a slim, fashionable figure in a mink coat and smart gray hat and gloves.

"Why, Mrs. Blaine, what—has anything happened?"

For the first time since he had met her Natalie Blaine smiled—a smoothly arranged parting of exquisite lips over perfect teeth. In a few seconds it was gone. "Aren't you going to ask me in?"

Blinking, F. Millard moved back, and a flake of pastry as big as a quarter fell off one hand to the floor.

Natalie Blaine stepped daintily around it as she entered. Her eyes ran over the room, from the stove with its dome shaped nickel top to the neatly made-up bunk with a year and a half's accumulation of *Flatfoot* on the shelf above it. They traveled on to the table where Gus had sat the night he produced the charred note, and returned to her host's doughy hands.

"Is there anyone else here?" she asked abruptly. "Can we talk a while—in private?"

She hadn't quite turned up her nose when she glanced around the room but its owner felt the omission had been conscious. If Tom Blaine's supercilious wife thought F. Millard was going to drop everything for a Sunday morning chat when he'd just poured the water in his pie crust . . .

"I live alone, Mrs. Blaine. If you'll excuse my not getting a chair and bring one to the kitchen for yourself, we can talk in private as long as you like." Or, at least, he added mentally, till Gus came to take him to jail.

She placed her chair on the living-room side of the door. As he plunged both hands in the big yellow bowl he saw her critical eyes examine the kitchen. Her lips parted—lips of that fashionably purplish hue that always made F. Millard think of heart trouble. "Dear me, isn't a wood stove unbearably warm when you're cooking?"

"Not when it's forty below," said F. Millard loyally. Let her go next door to Beulah's or across the street to Mae's if she wanted electric ranges.

"Isn't that a hand pump, Mr. Smyth? Don't you have running water?"

"Lots of folks do, but not me." Surely she hadn't come down here to comment on life without plumbing.

He felt her gaze on the rolled copy of *Flatfoot* rearing out of his hip pocket and the flour sack tied around his middle.

"No wonder you Alaskans are easy on each other—in business," she said slowly, "to make up for your daily hardships. ... I hate to mention it, Mr. Smyth, but my husband told me you are very much behind in your payments on the store."

He blinked at the woman in the doorway, and his spirits found a new low.

"Do you know my husband's former partner? Have you heard of his cowardly attempt to defraud me?"

"You mean claiming the store was a partnership business?"

"Imagine!" For an instant Natalie Blaine's mouth pressed inward. "I must say I have no faith in that crude Mr. Ingersoll or that old skeleton of a marshal. I've been hearing things about you, Mr. Smyth. The hotel clerk— the Commissioner—quite a number of people say you've had experience with detection—in an amateur way, of course—murder and—er—finding things out about people."

Now she was getting down to business, he decided, and his spirits lifted a little because she had come to him.

"I wonder if you'll help me." For a moment she was almost appealing.

"You'd have a personal interest. . . . If you'll find some way to prevent that man from taking half the store, I'll give you five years to make up your back payments."

The yellow bowl almost tipped over. Natalie Blaine wasn't asking him to find her husband's murder, only to save her money.

She misinterpreted his silence. "I'll give you that offer in writing." She'd come prepared, he noted. Opening her handbag she held out a paper—the same hotel letterhead her husband's note had been written on, the note Gus had found in the ash can.

Momentarily F. Millard's sympathies were with Ed Griswold. But an extra five years would be a big help— if he didn't land in the penitentiary; then, he supposed, it wouldn't matter. Anyway, not if they hanged him.

But if Long Ed was really trying to pull a fast one, this woman was in the right, and it was up to F. Millard to help her. He straightened till the sack around his waist made an inward curve.

"I'll do what I can," he told her. The modesty of his words didn't match the liberality with which he floured the pastry board.

She got up to lay the paper on the living-room table. When she came back her eyes were more nearly smiling than when her lips had smiled.

"May I make a suggestion, Mr. Smyth? Don't overlook Dwight Archer. I wouldn't be surprised if that half-brother of mine was behind this Griswold person's scheme. He's made trouble for me ever since I can remember. Why, even the first time I was married, Dwight used to egg Frank on to stand against me. He never could bear to let me get what I wanted."

She reached for the chair behind her, pulling it nearer the kitchen as she sat down. Her eyes were brighter now, her sculptured face more alive. "What's Dwight here for, anyway? He never heard of Fairbanks before I married Tom. We were married in October and Dwight's been living with us—my mother's will gives him the right. In those months, Mr. Smyth, he could have written back and forth to Alaska and learned the reputation of Tom's former partner. Suppose they began their plans by letter. Dwight left San Francisco before we did. I didn't know he was coming here, but the marshal tells me he arrived on the plane before ours. Dwight could have gone to this Griswold person and they could have completed their plans. And then—when Tom came—put them into execution."

She leaned back. A triumphant half-smile curved her dark lips.

F. Millard forgot he mustn't work his crust too much; he was kneading it like bread dough. "Did your brother leave San Francisco much before you folks, Mrs. Blaine?"

"Two or three days. We stopped several days in Seattle."

"Was that stop your husband's idea or yours?"

"Oh, his. I don't know anyone in Seattle."

"He have a lot of friends there?"

"If so, he didn't introduce them to me. I spent three days in our hotel room, and with accommodations what they are in defense areas you may know it wasn't too pleasant. When he started out the fourth day I followed him. You're not the only amateur detective, Mr. Smyth. He went to five different fur places before I gave up and returned to the hotel. Of course I thought he was buying me something, and it was just like him to go to those— cheap-John holes in the wall, if you'll pardon the slang, instead of good stores. But the next day we took the plane, and he didn't say a word about furs."

For a moment the only sounds in the cabin were the crackle of wood in the old-fashioned range and the slap on the board of F. Millard's toughening pastry.

In the silence the telephone rang.

The little grocer dropped the dough and started forward, then looked from his hands to his neatly gloved guest's. "Would you mind—"

Natalie Blaine walked gracefully across the room to the wall telephone. "Yes?" she said into the mouthpiece. As she held the receiver to her ear, her shoulders beneath the mink coat stiffened. She turned around, her face pinched-white.

Staring, the grocer mumbled, "Ought to wash my hands. . . ."

She pushed the received toward him. "T-take it."

He took it. "H-hello," he stammered.

The voice at the other end of the wire was one he didn't recognize, low with a peculiar quality of hoarseness. "F. Millard Smyth?"

Stupidly, the grocer nodded.

"F. Millard Smyth?" the voice repeated.

"Yes. Who's this?"

"Never mind. You have something I want."

"Oh, d-do I?"

"And I have something you want—some information. Would you like to arrange a trade?"

"A t-trade?"

"How much do you want to see the ghost?"

F. Millard gurgled.

"Enough to give me back my property?"

"But I don't know—"

"Oh, yes, you know you have it. Something you didn't I give Gus. You wouldn't have kept it if you didn't believe in me."

"But I—"

"I don't expect it for nothing. If you'll leave the warehouse door unlocked tonight, I guarantee you'll see the ghost."

F. Millard swallowed.

"The upstairs door, so no one but you and I'll know." The voice at the other end waited. Then repeated, "How much do you want to see the ghost?"

"I—I want to, all right. I *need* to. But—"

"Then we'll just exchange." The voice came promptly. "We'll both leave the marshal's office out of this, and keep it between ourselves. You agree?"

Leave the marshal's office out? Had the woman in red killed Tom Blaine? But what if F. Millard was convicted for it? He might have to have her evidence. He had to know who she was.

"Silver Star will come back tonight," the husky voice went on, "if you leave the door unlocked and don't tell the marshal's office."

"What—what time?" gasped F. Millard.

"Nine o'clock. Remember—if you tell, she won't come!" The telephone clicked in his ear.

He turned to the pallid-faced woman shaking inside her mink coat.

"That—that voice," she stammered. "It was the one I told about at the inquest—the one that called Tom the day he was killed!"

CHAPTER FIFTEEN

F. Millard slid into a revolving chair at the drugstore lunch counter. What else was there for a bachelor whose neighbors didn't ask him to Sunday dinner, and whose pie crust was more ceramic than the plate?

Klondike, over her cold at last, was skimming about behind the counter, slim and quick and charmingly flurried with her rumpled brown curls and flying apron strings. Her light soprano repeating orders and half-mechanical pleasantries didn't sound like that low, hoarse voice on the telephone this morning. But if he could eat and watch a suspect at the same time, a disciple of *Flatfoot* would naturally choose a restaurant that served detection with meals.

As he gave his order, the last two chairs at the counter were filled, one on each side of F. Millard. Dwight Archer sat down on his right and Whit Hawley plunked himself on the left.

Archer ignored the little grocer, Whit barely spoke. Both had their eyes on the slim, aproned girl behind the counter.

F. Millard crawled back into reflection. The telephone operator hadn't been able to identify the voice that called him this morning, but said that the call had come from the public booth in the hotel where the Blaines had been staying. It had taken persuasion to prevent Mrs. Blaine's ringing up Jeff Peters. But a nip-and-tuck argument finally convinced her that interference from the marshal's office would only upset a delicate balance, and she finally agreed to wait. If nothing came of the appointment, or F. Millard *failed to return*—goose flesh sprang out all over his body —she would notify the marshal. Then he'd spent the rest of the day stewing over whether or not to tell the marshal, himself.

F. Millard blinked his way back to the clatter of heavy dishes and scrape and clink of forks. He found himself not only eating, but halfway through the food on his plate. Klondike was coming toward him with a laden plate in each hand. She paused and glanced down, then, reaching across the grocer, pushed the plate with the smaller helping at Whit, and shyly, with a luminous smile, set the other in front of Archer.

F. Millard saw the brown, oversize hand on his left clench into a fist. On the right Archer's delicate fingers touched his mustache.

The smaller plateful was consumed long before the large one, but Whit Hawley grimly waited. F. Millard dawdled over dessert.

Finally Archer rose and selected a smartly cut overcoat from among the shaggy coonskins, parkas, and sheep-lined leather jackets on the hooks. As he started for the cash register, Whit was just behind him.

The little grocer fumbled for his own threadbare coat and hurried after both. The nearer Archer came to the end of the counter, the more Whit lagged.

Now Archer, too, showed signs of stalling, while Klondike waited at the cash register with a pucker between her upslanted brows.

Whit turned abruptly to the little man padding behind him. "Where you been all day?" He gave F. Millard an ungentle clap on the shoulder.

The grocer pulled away. "I've been sitting next to you for the last half hour."

The bombardier said nothing. Eyes glazed, he stared through his companion while his ears seemed almost to bend back.

F. Millard, too, tried to listen, but could hear only the murmur of Archer's voice, not what he was saying.

Klondike turned pink and said softly. "I wish I could, but I'm afraid tonight . . ."

The soldier and F. Millard moved closer.

Archer, leaning over the register, managed to put into only two words a hint of intimacy. "Tomorrow night?"

Klondike nodded. Her face still flushed, she gave him another smile, and something stirred in F. Millard. Poor child, she hadn't smiled for almost a week.

Whit cleared his throat and wiggled the check in large brown fingers. Archer moved on to the door.

"I don't suppose . . Whit paused. His back, bent slightly toward Klondike, didn't look very hopeful.

"Right," the girl said crisply, handing him change.

F. Millard laid down his dollar and a half and hurried after the others.

On the sidewalk, Whit stood watching the well-tailored swing of Archer's overcoat passing the next lamp-post. The soldier's lips were moving as the little man came alongside.

". . . coming in here over a week without even saying good morning to her till that five thousand dollars came up. It's made no difference to me in a year and a half. Why, Val Voss'd be better than—"

F. Millard blinked. "Do you mean you've known about the will for a year and a half? Klondike didn't have the five thousand till your uncle—"

"What the hell are you talking about?" Whit's eyes were off the swinging coattails now, boring into F. Millard.

But you—you said—"

"Chr-rist, if you saw a guy like Archer chasing your girl, you'd shoot off your mouth, too. If he doesn't look out . . ." Whit's eyes returned to the overcoat, now half a block away but still distinct in the bright downtown illumination.

"Did your uncle tell you about his will, sergeant?" F. Millard persisted.

The bombardier's attention came back to the man at his side. "Hell, how could he? Wasn't married then. Hadn't even met the gal."

"I mean that he was going to leave Klondike's mother five thousand dollars."

Whit gave the little man a scowl that made his wince. "I never saw my uncle's will. And I didn't know what was in it. See? Now make something of that!"

He flung off up Second. F. Millard blinked after him, then turned downstream to look for Archer. The tailored overcoat was crossing Second Avenue at Cushman.

The grocer broke into a trot. By the time he reached Cushman the coat was out of sight. He hurried down the short block to Front Street. Across the river, beneath a yellow splash of northern lights, the dim shape of a church spire rose beyond an empty bridge. On his left, where the curve of Front paralleled the frozen Chena, the swinging coattails passed a lighted store window.

He caught Archer unlocking his hotel room. The door was half open and the man going in when F. Millard spoke.

Archer jumped, with an involuntary motion to close the door. Then he pushed it wider. "Looking for some one?"

"I've been trying to catch you," F. Millard panted. "I'd like to see you a minute."

The other shrugged. "Wait till I take off my coat and turn the light on."

Why not turn the light on first? Were wall switches too modern for this hotel? While his host was inside in the darkness, the grocer felt along the wall near the door. As he found a switch and flipped it on, Archer tossed his coat to a chair. But not before F. Millard had seen a pair of mukluks standing beside it. The coat now covered them.

The eyes of the two men met.

The grocer spoke first. "Do you wear mukluks in San Francisco, Mr. Archer?"

The other looked the little grocer up and down. "You're the fellow that owns the warehouse, aren't you?" His tone was as disdainful as his sister's. "The one I let out on an unsuspecting world."

"The name's Smyth," said F. Millard stiffly.

"And the world no longer unsuspecting—I gather, after the other night. Do your friends run when they see you coming?"

"At least they don't try to hide things as obviously as you do, Mr. Archer. Why don't you want me to see those mukluks?"

"For God's sake, did you think I threw my coat over them on purpose?"

Once more their eyes met. F. Millard pushed the coat aside and picked up the mukluks—gray-tan reindeer, well worn.

Archer shrugged again. "I bought them to keep out your delightful forty below."

The grocer's eyes were fixed on the ankle of one mukluk where the hair was almost rubbed off.

"Secondhand," the other added.

"Look here," said F. Millard abruptly, "if you killed Blaine, you'll keep quiet, of course, like you're doing. If you didn't, and got mixed up in it without knowing what it was all about, I'd advise you to tell the marshal. You'll get off easier."

"Your sojourn in the warehouse must have affected your brain, Smyth. I'm not given to getting mixed up in murder."

"Then I'd advise you to give up your other game—before it gets too big to handle." The little grocer straightened. *Flatfoot*—and Alaska—had taught him a thing or two about handling suspects, or maybe it was desperation from being chief suspect himself.

Archer touched his black mustache. "I suppose you think you're going to crack this case ahead of the marshal."

F. Millard flushed.

"O.K. You've been giving me advice. Now let me give you some: Better watch your step, Smyth. You're playing with T.N.T."

A door slammed down the hall, and the hotel was quiet. Across the frozen river a dog began to howl.

"Every murder case is T.N.T.," said F. Millard, suppressing a shiver.

"Not for those that mind their own business." Again Archer touched his mustache with delicate fingertips, eyeing his visitor above them. Then he looked pointedly at his wrist watch and turned the door knob. "Much as I enjoy your fascinating conversation, I've got a date tonight." With the door half open, he suddenly closed it. "Speaking of T.N.T.—there's an envelope in the hotel safe with my name on it. The marshal ought to have it—if anything happens to me."

Then F. Millard found himself in the hall with the sound of a key turning behind him.

He pulled out his own watch. The mysterious voice on the telephone had said nine o'clock; he still had two hours in which to keep himself from running to the marshal.

On the street, he turned downriver. The blanketed Chena beside him curved through the town in the starlight like a great white snake. Beyond the man-made streets and blocks of cabins the wilderness pressed close—the wilderness where the white snake crawled.

On the opposite bank a dog howled again, and the Malemute Chorus swelled. F. Millard's steps went faster. Tonight was like that other night, almost a week ago, with stars that shamed the street lights, and the whips of the Aurora, now red and green and yellow, snapping soundlessly over the sky.

He dashed around the banked turn at the end of Front Street and sprinted the short block to Second as if the howling dogs were after him. But the wail rose and fell and rose again in a crescendo of mournful abandon. Just as he reached Bonanza Road the chorus died away, and he walked the last block in numbed silence.

Tonight was so much like that other night that his eyes, when he reached Bonanza, flew to the street lights. Both burning, thank goodness.

Frank's house was dark, as it often was; bright oblongs, speckled with house plants, fell on the snow from Mae's windows; light shone at the edge of drawn blinds at Beulah's and the Hawleys'. Klondike wouldn't be off shift for another half-hour, and F. Millard still had nearly two in which to change his mind.

But he wasn't going to change it. Identifying the woman in red was too important. He wondered, as he jerked the light cord in his cabin and took off his coat, what she thought he had that was hers. Hers, that is, if the ghost was a woman. If Whit had known beforehand about the provision for Silver Star in his uncle's will . . .

Oh, dear, if the ghost was Whit . . . F. Millard thought of Gus now with positive longing. At least the deputy hadn't arrested F. Millard today. Did that mean no fresh evidence? Or was Gus taking it to Jeff?

The little grocer pulled the rolled copy of *Flatfoot* out of his pocket and made himself sit down and read. When he stepped again to the window that faced the warehouse he saw that the street light at the door was still burning, and now a window at Malones' was bright too.

He drew out his father's big watch. Still half an hour before the rendezvous. In fifteen minutes he would unlock the door and come back to watch from his window.

At last those fifteen minutes passed. He picked up his coat, and dropped it. To open the upper door, padlocked on the inside, he would have to go in from below. Suppose the person who phoned was waiting now at the top of the outside stairs, waiting for the padlock to come off, so he could rush in and overwhelm the little grocer. Or perhaps with Blaine's automatic. . . .

Grimly F. Millard picked up the wrench he had taken with him this morning. Almost any kind of death would be preferable to hanging; he had to identify the ghost.

The warehouse, when he opened the door, was silent and black. The beam of his flash showed him the way to the light. He pulled the cord, and, gripping the heavy wrench, passed the stove, climbed the stairs, and stopped at the upper door. On the other side . . . Was this padlock, so smooth and cold through his mitten, all that stood between him and death?

He turned the key and sprang back. But the outer stairs remained as silent as the building.

Running down to the lower floor, he turned off the light and drew back the bolt. The outdoor air was fresh and cold, and the street light near enough to outshine the stars.

Back in his own cabin he waited in the dark.

Another fifteen minutes dragged by with F. Millard's nose bumping the window. It was after nine and no one had gone into the warehouse. Yet she might have stolen in while he was on his way back to his cabin or been waiting on the upper landing in silence. He couldn't risk a slip-up.

He fumbled with his coat sleeves in the dark. Once more he picked up the wrench, opened the door, and slowly approached the warehouse.

Bonanza Road seemed more still than ever, breathlessly still. The northern lights had whipped themselves out, and the stars were cold, bright rhinestones. His steps barely squeaked in the fast-packing snow, and his breath was quick and shallow.

Then the downstairs padlock was in his hands, the key in the lock. He sucked in a last drink of clean, outdoor night, and turned the knob.

CHAPTER SIXTEEN

Tightly gripping wrench and flashlight, he waited at the door till the last possible wisp of steam on his glasses should be dry. But it wasn't steam obscuring the light. There was no light. Only blackness shut him in.

He waited, but no glimmer showed beneath the balcony's edge.

He didn't dare make himself a target by turning on the flash. Perhaps he shouldn't even be near the door. He took a swift step sideways, banged into something that toppled, and leaped away from a thunder of cans.

The light of his flash would have been no more of a give-away. Holding his breath till the last can came to rest, he listened in the dark.

The warehouse was utterly still.

For hour-long minutes he waited, and the black building waited, too.

Finally, holding the torch with his overcoat, he looked at his watch. Nearly half-past nine, twenty minutes since he'd left home.

Then he heard outdoors the hasty crunch of feet and the squeal of cold metal on metal—the lid pushed down on the ash can by the weight of a foot. Then the pop and creak of the outside stairs.

Feeling with his feet for fallen cans, F. Millard groped his way back to the center aisle and hurried to the edge of the balcony. Above, he heard the outer door open and saw the small, downturned beam of a flash. It picked out a booth along the wall, and except for its glow, disappeared where an unseen hand laid it down. Shadows moved grotesquely in the glow, and he heard a rustle like silk.

For an instant the light flared brighter and outlined a woman's head and shoulders. It dimmed, but the outline, though fainter, remained. The figure shifted, and two candles, with flames bent almost horizontal, came in sight as the woman turned.

A woman in spangled red, with white shoulders rising from a low-cut bodice. But the hair—her hair was brown!

Yet there was no mistaking her: the tiny waist, the generous curve of hip and breast, the shapely arms, the doll-round face—all but the moon-colored pompadour. This was the ghost, with dark hair.

A candle in each hand, she walked toward the railing, not near enough, F. Millard noted from below, to show her feet, and he heard no sound of steps. She peered down into the shadows.

He stepped out from under the front balcony, and the woman in red waved a candle, spangles glinting on her dress. She walked, again without sound, to the table, and stuck her candles beside the unlighted ones left there last night.

Then she swung into the Spanish dance step. Her skirt swirled and the graceful body swayed as it had last Tuesday night. Arms upflung in the final pirouette, she whirled to a stop, and smiled.

That sudden, flashing smile of Silver Star's had been rare. Rare, yet somehow—was it the smile or the woman's brown hair that reminded him of someone?

Then something happened to the face beneath the brown pompadour. The girl's hand went up to her mouth. When it came away her cheeks looked oddly collapsed. Thin face —brown hair—a smile like—

"Klondike!" the grocer cried. He laid down the wrench. She smiled again. Now he knew the smile—her only physical inheritance from her mother. With cheeks filled out, hair white, and body padded, with Klondike a budding actress . . .

She began to run along the balcony toward the stairs. "I didn't have time to powder my hair. So many people came in tonight—"

F. Millard hurried to the foot of the stairs. "Powder it! Was that what made it white?"

"And that's why I had to wash it. That's what—" she stopped by the railing, her face only a blur in the shadows —"that's what makes me feel so bad, to think I rushed right out to the kitchen to wash my hair instead of stopping in Mother's room. I might have seen she needed a doctor—in time."

At least F. Millard knew now that Silver Star's heart attack had not been brought on by climbing the stairs. "But, Klondike, why . . .?"

The girl on the balcony straightened. He could see the pale shoulders squaring. Then she started down the stairs.

"I'll tell you all about it—as soon as you give me my rose."

"Rose? What—you don't mean that thing you threw at me?"

She ran down the last few steps, eyes wide with apprehension. "Of course that's what I mean. Just like Mother used to throw at Tom Blaine. A velvet rose. I even put rose perfume on it!"

"It—it missed me. I didn't hear it land and didn't stop to look for it then, and when I asked Gus—"

"Oh," Klondike groaned, "did you have to tell Gus?"

"You don't need to worry." The man's voice was grim. "He didn't believe me."

"Then he didn't find it?"

"I'll say he didn't. Nothing to bear out my story. He swore I made up the whole thing."

Klondike gave a sigh of relief. "Maybe I can find it now."

"Not after Gus pawed through the place as many times as he did. Even *Jeff* went over it once. I don't know, Klondike; it might be worse if—someone else—found it"

The girl caught her breath. In the half-dark he saw her shiver. "Let's—let's go over by the stove. I'm cold."

As they neared the candles' circle of dim light, F. Millard saw tanned moose-hide moccasins come and go at the hem of her dress. He pointed. "Did you wear those Tuesday night? Is that why you didn't make any noise?"

"No. I had on hard-soled mukluks and took them off. That's how I caught cold—dancing in sock feet, and waiting up there without a coat. It wasn't running across the street with my hair wet."

"Why did you—not want to make a noise, Klondike?"

"Whoever heard of a spook pounding around on heels? Or skidding on waterproof soles?"

"A—a spook?"

"Well, reincarnation—whatever you want to call bringing back someone's lost youth."

"Why bring back your mother's, Klondike?"

"To remind Tom Blaine. To make him think of the happy times they used to have before they—hated each other. So he'd—remember—and feel sorry—and want to help."

"You—knew he was leaving your mother money in his will?"

"How could I? Anyway, I wanted money *then.* I wouldn't have wanted to wait till he—Mr. Smyth! You didn't think I killed him?"

F. Millard said nothing, uncomfortably.

"My gosh, I'd expect that from Gus, but not you."

"What did you do after you put out the candles?"

"Waited till you got out, and then wrapped the candles in the paper I'd spread on the table to catch the grease, and beat it down the outside stairs. Then I dashed in the front door just long enough to untie the light cord—and scrammed."

"Untie the light cord?"

"Well, I didn't want Tom Blaine to turn on the light when he came in and spoil my nice ghostly effect. He probably wouldn't even see my two little candles. So I climbed on a pile of boxes and tied knots in the cord till it was too high for him to reach."

"If you were so anxious to see him, Klondike, why didn't you wait till he came?"

"I don't know," she admitted. "I was cold and—well, some way I began to get scared. I didn't feel I was doing anything wrong, and yet . . . Gosh, Mr. Smyth, when you get to fooling around with spooks, pretty soon you feel spooky yourself. I just decided I'd have to find some other way to raise money, and beat it while the going was good."

"What made you think he'd be here in the first place, Klondike—here in my warehouse that night?"

"I phoned him at the hotel, talking the same hoarse way I talked to you, and told him if he didn't come to the old Bonanza at eight-forty-five that night he'd regret it all his life. He sounded kind of funny, but he said, 'Don't worry, you don't have to disguise your voice; I'll be there and hung up. I was flabbergasted to have him agree like that, but glad I didn't have to argue. So I dug out Mother's old dress and began to get ready."

"You chose Tuesday night because you thought I'd be at the lodge?"

"That's why I made the appointment for quarter of nine," she amended. "But of course I took Tuesday when I knew he was coming down to see you."

"When you knew . . . F. Millard gulped. His mitten closed on her firm young arm. "How did you know he was coming to see me?"

"I read the note. I wouldn't have if I'd known it was yours, but there wasn't any name on the outside, or any envelope, and when you see a note under your door you naturally think it's for you. I didn't know till I opened it, and then it was so short I'd read it."

"What—what did it say?"

"Why, don't you remember? When I saw it was for you I ran over and stuck it under your door. Tom Blaine must have sent it down by some kid who got the wrong house. If he said the last cabin on Bonanza—"

"Listen, Klondike, I'm not kidding. I want to know what that note said."

"Why, something about seeing you Tuesday night at your place and—and having to have the money by the nineteenth. I'm awfully sorry, Mr. Smyth; I had no idea—"

"What time was it, Klondike—when you found the note under your door and stuck it under mine?"

"Sometime after midnight Monday. I don't know how long it had been there, because I hadn't been home since I came down to fix Mother's lunch and left her dinner by the bed, and of course she couldn't get up. I went to the show with Val Voss after work and we got something to eat and fooled around, and it was after midnight when I got home. I opened the door, and there was the note. I nearly had kittens when I read it and found it was yours. So I ran right over and stuck it under your door. Val wanted to do it for me, but it was such a private matter I thought I should tend to it myself."

"Did Voss read it too?"

"I don't know. He was standing right beside me."

If there was any reason for Valentine Voss to have wanted that note he could simply have opened the door and removed it after Klondike went back home. F. Millard was asleep and his door never locked—in those days.

"I didn't know till you said you'd seen M-Mother's ghost that the man in the white parky was you," the girl exclaimed. "I thought it was Tom Blaine. And I put on that lousy performance last night so you wouldn't guess the ghost was me. I thought of course you had the rose, and if I could get it from you no one would ever connect me with the murder."

"And that's why you swept the balcony and outside stairs?"

In the dim light from the candles she nodded, and he noticed the lines of make-up—horizontal to widen her face—running across her forehead and out from her chin, the down swoop of the pompadour that made her face shorter. With court plaster across the upslant of her brows and the brown strokes that made them seem level, with cotton in her cheeks, a smile like her mother's, and moon colored hair—no wonder she looked like Silver Star!

"I had to get rid of everything that showed I'd been there, Mr. Smyth. After Val Voss told me . . ." She stopped.

"Told you what?"

"Honestly, when there's been a murder, you get so you're afraid to open your head. If you don't implicate someone else, you get yourself in deeper. But this couldn't implicate Val. He was working the night of the murder when the doctor or the—the undertaker called the news paper about Mother. He got home too late to come over, but when he saw my light next morning he asked me for her picture and—and the main facts and dates and things. It must have been half-past six, but I—I couldn't sleep and I was just making a cup of coffee. You wouldn't think I'd have wanted to talk about her, and yet—maybe it was going through that act of hers in the old dance hall—I just talked and talked, all about her time in Nome and the early years in Fairbanks, and I told him about her first husband and my own dad. I seemed to get comfort out of talking about her, like she wasn't so far away."

He hadn't the heart to ask her what this had to do with erasing the evidence of her presence in the warehouse.

"It was while I was talking about Mother's accident," she went on, "that Val told me Tom Blaine was missing."

"How would Voss know it that early?"

"Gus phoned. Said Mrs. Blaine had just called him, and he'd phoned the hospital and was trying Val next to see if anything had been reported to the paper. So of course I knew I'd have to get rid of everything that could possibly connect me with—" She stopped again, suddenly as if she'd jammed on foot brake and emergency together.

No wonder, thought F. Millard. How would she know it was the warehouse that she must clear of signs of her presence? How could she know—unless she knew what the warehouse contained?

"Of course I didn't know then there'd been a murder," she rushed on. "But I'd seen Blaine's note about coming down here, and I—I'd told him to meet me in the warehouse, and—well, I didn't know where he was going to turn up—or—or in what shape"—she stopped to swallow —"and people might think putting on that act like—like Mother was a funny way to get money out of someone, especially after the way he and Mother felt about each other, and—and—well, I just didn't know what to do— so I thought I'd better get rid of every indication that any Malone had been up to anything. So after Val left I took the broom and went over there—it was still dark, of course —and did the sweeping. But I couldn't find the rose!"

In the pale light the two stared at each other.

Finally Klondike put out a small hand. "You—you do understand, don't you, Mr. Smyth?"

"Well, I—you actually thought Blaine would give you money?"

"I guess it was crazy. The more I think about it now the crazier it sounds, but then it seemed like the best idea! The one method left when so many had failed. Mother needed help so badly. I kept feeling, if we only had money to send her Outside! But it's too late now." In the candle light Klondike's eyes were wet. She looked appealingly at F. Millard. "Do you wonder I've been scared, Mr. Smyth? Everything I did was so innocent, and could look so dreadfully—guilty."

He opened his mouth and shut it again. Everything could be innocent and look guilty, or guilty and made to sound innocent—by a wispy young girl who was an actress.

"Of course, you know," he said slowly, "I'll have to tell Jeff."

She drew away, her eyes growing larger. Then she flung up her chin and straightened defiant shoulders. "Go ahead and tell him, then! You don't have any more proof than you ever did. I'll just deny the whole thing. It's only your word against mine."

Now it was F. Millard's turn to droop.

The girl softened. "Let's work together, Mr. Smyth. We're both in an awful spot."

He gave her a feeble smile. "Did you put out the street lights Tuesday night?"

"Gosh, no. I thought they burned out or something." "What time did you come over here?"

"Tuesday night? About eight-thirty. Our appointment was quarter of nine. But I had to get here in time to tie up the light and get the stage set."

"You didn't see or hear anything then?"

Shaking her head, she shivered in the spangled dress. "You don't think he was already—my gosh, you must be right. I didn't look around when I climbed up to fix the light. I was in a hurry, and didn't think— But I touched the bulb, tying up the cord—and it was warm."

"Warm! My gracious, Klondike, he must have—"

She nodded, shuddering. "The murderer must have just dragged the body away and put the boxes over the blood —maybe the very boxes I climbed on."

"And maybe he was hiding behind some others, waiting for you to leave." F. Millard shuddered too.

"All I thought," Klondike whispered, "was how lucky I was to miss you. I thought you must have stayed home from lodge and just been in to fix the fire."

Both moved closer to the stove, and the warehouse was still.

"Funny you didn't hear the rose land that I threw at you," said Klondike at last. "Though of course your parky hood was up, and that would cut off small sounds."

"There're some empty coal sacks on a box behind where I stood. It could have lit there."

"But if the murderer found it, Mr. Smyth! I've got to get it back!"

"I know just how you feel," F. Millard sighed.

The old dance hall with its two flickering cones of light on the balcony was heavy with frustration.

Klondike turned toward the stairs. "I'd better get my coat and go home. Hope I'll have time to change before anyone sees me. The neighbors have been dropping in a lot since Mother died. Thought I'd never get here tonight, so many of them came. I laid out the dress and tied on padding where it'd do the most good, and even did my hair without powder, and still I kept being interrupted. Finally I had to turn off the lights and lock the door. I made up my face and finished dressing by one shaded candle."

He helped her into her coat, re-padlocked the upper door and bolted the front one behind her. He pulled out his watch. They'd been here nearly an hour. Without Klondike, the old building was more empty than ever, more lonely. Turning off the light he found his way to the door with the flash, and the warehouse seemed even more black.

When he pulled open the door and stepped out, the concerted wail of the Malemute Chorus made him cringe. Then he straightened. What if tonight was clear, like that other night? What if he had seen the ghost? What if the sled dogs were howling again? As long as the street lights were burning. . . .

He swung around and looked up. His mouth went dry, and his mittens damp. Both street lights had gone out.

CHAPTER SEVENTEEN

After reaching his cabin, F. Millard moved from window to window in the dark. The night-tinged snow gave the out-of-doors a faint visibility splotched and crisscrossed with shadows. The biggest and blackest was the old Bonanza Dance Hall. None of the shadows moved.

He groped his way from the river side of the cabin to the front. Across the street the Malone house showed no light; Klondike must be changing in the dark. Lights were on at the Hawleys' and Trents'. The bright squares in the cabins only made the street shadows more dense. At least his own firewood wasn't one of them now; it was sawed, and stacked by the kitchen door. No matter how intently he peered, none of the street shadows moved.

On the south he could see only Beulah's cabin. The slit of starlight between his house and hers showed no one on her path. Her windows were dark on the side next to him, but through the raised kitchen blind he could see a light in the bedroom.

Somewhere in the distance a lone dog howled and from all over town unseen canine throats throbbed in answer.

F. Millard thrust clenched hands into the pockets of the overcoat he hadn't taken off. Then jerked one out and pawed for the light cord. Blaine's body had been in his warehouse. If someone was still trying to frame him . . .

Grabbing up the wrench he poked his head behind the closet curtain and under the bunk and table. Pulled on the kitchen light and jerked up the trapdoor to the vegetable cellar.

The back shed—a cache, to Alaskans—had to be searched with a flashlight.

Bumping into the frozen hind quarter of caribou that hung from the rafters was bad, but there was nothing behind the galvanized iron wash tub, or the now solid barrel of last summer's rain water, or the case of cleaning fluid.

He stepped out on the snow and peered behind the wood pile. Nothing there but more snow.

Keeping one mittened hand on a rounded log, making the hand lie still, he tried to reason with himself. Electric power was a variable matter in Alaska. The street lights had been off the night before the murder as well as the night Blaine was killed. Surely they hadn't been put out both times—had they?

There was one way to tell about tonight. The icicle chunks thrown last Tuesday would be buried by snow and wind. If there were any on the street now . . .

He hurried down his shoveled path.

The lights had been on when he went to the warehouse tonight. Wouldn't he have heard, inside, the pop of a breaking bulb? Perhaps not after Klondike came and they got to talking, or while she was climbing the covered stairs that popped at every tread with age and cold. Unless Klondike herself—in the thumping and rolling of cans when he knocked over the box Gus had left out of place . . .

Flashing his light about F. Millard scuffed up and down in the street before the warehouse. Then he hit it—a broken chunk of icicle that went skimming away from his toe.

He kicked a second, a third—and knew there could be no doubt.

The little man stood shivering in the street. He wasn't going back to his cabin to wait for another body to be dumped in his lap. He'd have a look around first, and then, with or without more than the lights to report, he was going to see Jeff Peters.

Peering at the seven silent houses he decided to start with the boys'. There was no use going to the warehouse, and he knew where Klondike had spent most of the last hour. He wasn't going calling; this was strictly Peeping Tom.

On tiptoe, gripping wrench and flash, he made his way along the Hawleys' back path. Nothing untoward in the yard or in what he could see of the back shed cache. Keeping well out of the light from the living-room windows he peered inside. This was no time for scruples; the stage had been set for death.

A long-legged figure in uniform strode by the window, and the little grocer ducked. It passed again, then again. Whit's face was sizzling red, his pulled-taffy hair every which way. At intervals one arm shot out, always in the same direction. His lips moved furiously, then clamped together hard.

By creeping closer F. Millard could see Valentine Voss returning the soldier's glare, feet wide apart and back to the stove, light mirrored in his glasses like shooting sparks. He made no useless gestures. Both hands were clenched at his sides. His face, instead of reddening, had grown paler. His lips moved, too, close together and less often than Whit's.

The grocer eased a step nearer, but the extra sash to keep out cold kept in all but the loudest sounds—no more intelligible than barking. This was as tantalizing as sitting under the drier. F. Millard wished his own storm windows were that tight, and reluctantly moved on to the Trents'.

The light here was also in the living room. A silk- and bead-draped lamp revealed every careful curl of Mae's determinedly brown hair as she bent over a paper on the table. Her hand moved rapidly across it as he watched. Once she stopped, blinked, licked her pencil, and wrote on. A letter, he supposed, to "the old man"—that husband she adored who spent so much time away from home. No wonder she wouldn't let her hair gray. It was too bad she couldn't take off weight. He moved on to the back of the house without any results for his pains.

Across the street Frank's cabin was dark. As Mae was alone and the only light at Beulah's was in her bedroom, Frank must be making the rounds of the saloons again. He carelessly shoveled paths gave away no sinister secrets.

F. Millard turned slowly toward Beulah's. He was glad that the lighted window, with the shade discreetly lowered, wasn't on the side of the house with the path. This spying business—but it had to be done, with a murderer loose.

Walking softly so his steps wouldn't crunch he went up the dark path. Everything he could see by a sparing use of his flash looked as it always did—neat and comfortable and cared for. As he started to leave, a light came on in the kitchen.

He ducked back from the yellow rectangle flung on the snow. Beulah walked across the kitchen wearing a pink negligee with a tight rubber cap on her head and a bath towel over one arm. Beautiful, he thought, even in that cap. A light sprang on in the bathroom, opening, Alaska fashion, off the kitchen, and Beulah shut the door.

Now, except for Malones', the neighborhood had been covered. Yet perhaps, even though Klondike had been with him, he shouldn't neglect her back yard.

It was there—in the shoveled path near the Malones' kitchen door—that he saw the patch of black. For a moment his feet and heart stopped together, then the heart bounded on, while his mind told the feet to wait, and his right hand tightened on the wrench.

If someone was crouched there only pretending to look—the way that black thing looked . . .

He listened, and the wilderness cupping the town seemed to listen for snow-covered miles.

Then he tried to steady himself. A housekeeper as careless as Klondike might have left a wash tub out, or a sack of coal, or some chunks of wood for splitting. . . .

But it wasn't a tub or wood or coal, F. Millard knew before he turned on his flash. The light picked out first a man's felt hat upside down on the snow, then two feet in men's galoshes, a custom-made cloth overcoat with a scarf high on the back of the neck, and hanging down like a Chinese pigtail—the handle of an ax.

The wrench slid out of F. Millard's hand and the light wavered as it rose to the head of the ax and the head of the man, to black hair matted with blood. The snow by the ax was red.

The light came back to the custom-made coat that F. Millard couldn't help recognizing. This victim, too, had fallen forward and lay in a heap half in and half out of the walk a few feet from Klondike's back door.

The door was on the river side of the house opening directly from the kitchen instead of from a cache. Beyond the hatless head with the ax sticking out were only black trees and brush and the frozen Chena, above it only stars. With no one home at Malones', the victim and his killer would be cut off from the world. Was Klondike in there now taking off her mother's dress by the light of a hooded candle?

F. Millard stepped to the near-by door and knocked, rattled the knob, and called. When the key finally turned he was making so much noise he didn't hear it, and jumped when the door opened and Klondike's soprano came out of the darkness.

"For gosh sake, Mr. Smyth, I've only just taken off that dress and haven't fixed my hair yet. Whatever is the matter?"

"Will you run over to my house, Klondike, and phone the marshal?"

"What for? Why don't you go? I've got to comb out this pompadour."

"I can't leave you with— You run along, Klondike. It doesn't matter about your hair."

"Leave me with what? I guess you think if Jeff saw this hair-do it'd give your story some support. What are you in a stew about?"

"I hate to tell you. Right outside your house, and all— but you'll have to know sometime, and I'll stay here. Tell Jeff that Archer's been—hurt, and—"

"Archer!" she gasped. "Not Dwight Archer?"

"Tell Jeff to come over as quick as he can." Klondike stepped half out of the dark doorway. "You don't mean Dwight Archer's out there in the yard—hurt— and you're leaving him there? We'll bring him in and call the doctor!"

"It's the marshal we want, Klondike."

"You don't—" in the starlight F. Millard saw her hand catch the door jamb— "you don't mean he's—dead?"

"You guessed it, I'm sorry to say. Now will you call Jeff?"

She took a wavering step forward.

"Don't come out." He put an arm in front of her. "You won't—Archer was murdered, Klondike. Go on through the house and call *Jeff*. You know where my phone is. The door isn't locked."

The light was too faint to see her expression but he heard her swallow. This was no time for hysterics. "Hurry up, Klondike," he said sharply. "If we want to catch who ever did it, there's no time to waste."

The girl wheeled. A light came on in the living room, and he heard the front door close.

F. Millard turned slowly back to the dark huddle on the snow. One arm was flung out with fingers spread, the other bent under the body. That ax—would a weapon as hard to conceal as an ax be carried far? His eyes found the wood pile, a mass of shadow in the grayness, and his flashlight found the chopping block. No ax was there.

Suppose Whit or Valentine Voss had found Archer trying to get into Klondike's house—an ax on the chop ping block by the door . . .?

But jealousy over Silver Star's daughter wouldn't tie up with Blaine's killing.

Then F. Millard's flashlight almost followed his wrench to the snow. Why assume the Malone house had been empty when Archer was killed? Klondike had smiled at him, given him the largest plate of dinner—but couldn't all that have been an act? If Archer knew something to connect her with Blaine's murder . . .

F. Millard looked at the pole across the street where the light was no longer burning. The Malone cabin was directly across from his own, the warehouse nearer the river. If the light had been on, it would have shone right into this yard.

He heard steps, and a shadow came around the corner of the house. "A-are you there, Mr. Smyth?" quavered Klondike.

F. Millard hurried to put himself between her and the dark blot on the snow, spilled over the side of the path. Besides, he had a question or two he wanted to ask before the marshal took over.

"Klondike, when you went to the warehouse tonight were the street lights on?"

"The street lights?" The shadow that was Klondike twisted backward. "Why, they're off now, aren't they? I didn't notice."

"How about then? Were they off then, too?"

"Darned if I— They must have been burning; I didn't need my flash till I started up the covered stairs. What difference does a thing like street lights make when—when Dwight Archer . . .?"

"Might make a lot of difference—if whoever killed him put them out."

"Then they must have done it, the—the whole thing must have happened while we were in the warehouse. . . . Oh, why ever did I say I'd meet you tonight? If I'd only been home I might have been able to save him!"

Klondike began to cry with unrestrained sobs like a child's.

F. Millard took her by the shoulder, forcing himself to be stern. "Are you sure you didn't put them out, yourself?"

The sobbing broke off as the girl flung up her head. Beneath her sweater, he could feel her shoulder tighten. "Why, you—you . . she stuttered furiously. "Have you the nerve to stand there and . . .?"

Steps crunched in the snow, and he shook Klondike's shoulder. She stiffened into silence. A long shaggy-looking shadow came around the corner of the house. F. Millard's flashlight showed a flapping bearskin coat and the lined face of Jeff Peters inside a fur hat whose two side flaps had been untied and hung down like a setter's ears. Tonight even Jeff was doing leg work.

The marshal's flash examined F. Millard and Klondike. "Well," he grunted, his easy drawl gone, "what's this about Archer?"

F. Millard moved aside, and Jeff's flash found the dark shape. Klondike gave a choking gasp and began to sob again.

"Go on inside," Jeff told her authoritatively. "Light all the lights on this side of the house and pull the blinds clear up. And don't come out again."

She ran past them. The back door banged. Lights began to come on in the house. Her slim form appeared at each window, snapping up every shade. A yellow oblong from the kitchen fell directly on the body. F. Millard and Jeff turned back to it again.

"Used an ax this time," the marshal mumbled. His flashlight, like F. Millard's earlier, found the empty chopping block. It came back to the hat near the body, then scalloped the window patch on the snow. The torch beam paused.

Jeff looked down at the little grocer. "Did you drop your flash when you found him?"

Blinking, F. Millard shook his head.

"Someone did."

Near the hat, in the heaped-up snow beside the trail, was a cylindrical dent, bulb-shaped at one end, tapered at the other to the print of a wire ring.

"You haven't touched him, have you?" the marshal asked.

Again F. Millard shook his head.

"Not all corpses are so thoughtful where they land," said Jeff, and the grocer was thankful that Klondike had gone in the house. "Falling on his face this way in the snow tossed out of the trail, if anyone moved him it'd show. See where someone picked up the flashlight?" Jeff's flash pointed out small furrows marring the print of the torch that was gone.

With a loud puffing and squeal of brakes, a car stopped

in front of the house. A door slammed, and Jeff raised his voice, "Face her this way, Gus, till the lights hit me."

The car backed and filled until the Malones' yard was lighted from the street as well as the house.

Gus and the doctor hurried up the walk.

"You here again, Smyth?" grunted Gus. Then he bent over the corpse. "Same type of killing, Jeff. Notice how they always repeat themselves?" In the light from the kitchen window his hard blue eyes found F. Millard again. The big deputy straightened and stubbed his toe. "What the hell's this wrench doing here?"

"That—that's mine," F. Millard faltered.

"My God, what you won't do to try to put us off the track!"

"For gracious sake, Gus," the grocer exclaimed, "why would I bring a wrench if I already had an ax?"

"Let's get him over, boys," said the doctor, his dark face and mustache reminding F. Millard uncomfortably of the face they would soon have to see. "Here's the ax, Jeff. Ready to move him?"

"Guess so," drawled the marshal. "Take it easy."

Bending with Gus and the doctor, F. Millard was conscious of a shadow enlarging as Klondike pressed against the window.

Like the first—the body of Tom Blaine—the second body was turned over.

The thick black hair with wings of gray, the neat features and black mustache of Dwight Archer came into view. The hand of the arm bent beneath him was tightly closed.

"What's he holding?" Jeff pointed. "Looks like leaves."

Gus loosened the cramped fingers. "My God, it's a flower! It's a velvet rose!"

CHAPTER EIGHTEEN

The marshal's office again. The middle of the night. And those who had waited there the other time trickling in again—Long Ed Griswold and Natalie Blaine and all the Bonanza Road neighbors.

In silence, enforced this time by Gus, each took a seat. Klondike was a tight little knot in a chair too large, watching F. Millard with big eyes by turns anxious and defiant. Mae sat tapping her foot, Beulah flicking at her cigarette when there was no ash to flick off, lighting too many. A litter of crushed stubs and broken matches had already begun to collect around Frank who sat unsteadily, staring at his former wife. Natalie kept her own eyes on her folded hands, raising them only briefly to the grocer or Ed Griswold.

When Long Ed came in, F. Millard had watched him lay his wolf-skin hat and wide-gauntleted Siwash mitts on the floor beneath his chair—mittens of tanned caribou hide with a band of fur like the one that had pulled the light cord in the warehouse, like those worn by most old-timers and F. Millard's Bonanza Road neighbors. Now Long Ed pushed them back with his feet, and the grocer blinked at his mukluks. Ankle-length, white reindeer with curled-up Laplander toes seemed somehow out of keeping with Griswold's grease-spotted wool breeches and lank canvas parka. He was stroking the back of his head again with that slow, vulture-wing flap of one elbow; his opaque dark eyes—F. Millard started—fixed on the little grocer.

Valentine Voss and Whit seemed for the moment united in worry over Klondike. Both sat anxiously staring at the small girl in the oversize chair. Whit's big hands were working.

Jeff strolled loose-jointedly through from the outer office. He glanced at the litter around Frank's chair, the full ash tray beside Beulah, Mae's tapping foot, and Whit's restless hands.

"Got your hair fixed different, Klondike," the old man drawled.

The girl jumped. "W-why, it's just like I always wear it."

Jeff's eyes stayed on the tumbled brown curls. "Guess it is—now. I was thinking of earlier, when I saw you at the window."

I—combed it before I left home."

"Looked more combed then than now," the marshal said dryly. His glance traveled on to Long Ed.

F. Millard dodged the black-lashed fury of Klondike's glance and watched Griswold's stroking hand slide into the lap of his parka.

"Didn't ever think I'd see you in harem slippers, Ed. He-Lapps may wear them, but they always make me think of a fat Turk and dancing girls." Jeff's cheek leather crinkled disarmingly.

All eyes were now fixed on the turned-up toes of Long Ed's Lapland mukluks. Frank gave a muddled grin.

Long Ed grinned back at Jeff, showing yellow, decaying teeth. "Feel silly, myself. Couldn't find mine and borrowed these off a Cheechawka neighbor. They're not bad though, Jeff, once you get over feeling everyone's looking at your toes."

F. Millard's eyes fled guiltily.

"Guess I'll take you first, Smyth." Jeff held open the door of the little room where Gus had interviewed each of them before.

Inside, the grocer again drew the chair that faced the light, but now the man on the other side of the desk wasn't leaning half across it with eyes and words like whips.

The marshal took out his pipe and sat nursing the bowl. "How come you found the body?" he asked easily. "What were you doing in Klondike's back yard?"

Beginning with the mysterious telephone call F. Millard rushed through his story of meeting the ghost. "Of course," he finished, "Klondike can just deny the whole thing. She swears she's going to. And I've got no way to prove it—as usual. She did leave two candles in the warehouse beside the two we used last night, but you and Gus can claim I put all four of them there."

"Hmmm," said Jeff.

"Can't you see it's all just what a kid like Klondike would do, Jeff? Just the crazy, dramatic sort of stunt she'd think of?"

"Hmmm," said the marshal again.

"But Mrs. Blaine answered the phone, Jeff! This time I have someone to back me up."

"Mrs. Blaine can prove you got the call. She can't swear it was Klondike who made it."

The little room was still.

"What about that rose?" F. Millard demanded. "Klondike had to have it—and it was found in Archer's dead hand."

"You could of put it there."

"His arm was bent clear under him! You said yourself no one could move him without leaving marks."

"You could of handed it to him just before you swung the ax."

It was like a bad dream: the old man with the boyishly plastered-down white hair and the mild eyes under shaggy brows—telling F. Millard how he could have committed murder.

The little man jumped. "My gracious, I didn't tell you about seeing Archer. I followed him after dinner. . . ." He told about the mukluks and Archer's warning and the envelope in the hotel safe.

The marshal's loosely strung old bones seemed to tighten. "No clerk on the desk this time of night. Archer talk like he was about to stick his neck out?"

"I just couldn't figure him out. I had the impression that he knew something—or might even be the killer himself and was giving me warning."

"Looks like your first guess was right," said Jeff dryly.

"And then, his sister—Mrs. Blaine—was so suspicious of him. He said he had a date. Do you think he meant a date with the killer?"

"That was pretty early in the evening, wasn't it, right after supper? Doc's not through with the body yet, but he says Archer was killed between nine and ten. How'd you happen to be trailing him, anyway?"

So F. Millard filled out the rest of his day, beginning with Natalie Blaine's visit in the morning.

Finally Jeff stood up and reached for the door knob. "Wait out here, Smyth. I'll check the other folks' stories with yours."

He let F. Millard through the door and poked out his own lined face. "All right, Klondike, you're next."

She drew a hiccupy breath that was almost a sob and shot a defiant glance at F. Millard as the door shut behind her.

The mess around Frank's chair had grown while the grocer was gone, Beulah's ash tray was overflowing, Mae was tapping the other foot. Whit's gaze was now transferred to the door through which Klondike had vanished, and Voss's to the mastodon ivory paper weight carved like a seal on the marshal's desk. Natalie Blaine had given up the contemplation of her hands to examine with mental lorgnettes the side-show freaks about her. Her gaze crossed Long Ed Griswold's, and the man's opaque eyes held it. F. Millard watched them stare at each other. The woman gave up first, and the man's hand went to the back of his head to begin its endless stroking.

The night dragged into early morning, and the crowd began to dwindle. The office deputy relieved Gus, who scooped up his mink hat and left. Finally Jeff was alone in one room, and F. Millard in the other.

The marshal came in and sat down at his desk. His bony fingers smoothed the dark ivory paperweight.

"I—I don't suppose," F. Millard stammered, "Klondike backed me up."

"I'll say she didn't. Claims she spent the whole evening at home. Wanted to finish going through her mother's things, and so many folks kept dropping in she finally turned out the lights and locked the door and worked by a candle. Silver Star's room's on the other side of the house from where the body was, and Klondike claims that's why she heard no noise."

"Little liar," the grocer muttered.

Jeff grinned. "Of course she wasn't under oath—if that'd make any difference. The others bore out your story, though. Mae said she was writing her husband, and Beulah said she was giving herself a beauty treatment. Whit and Val Voss said they had something to talk over and agreed to be home before ten."

"Talk over!" F. Millard snorted. "If you'd seen them . . . Did they say how much before ten?"

"They both said they got there on the dot but didn't have any alibis from nine to ten."

"What about Griswold and Natalie Blaine? Did they have alibis?"

The marshal's faded eyes held F. Millard's. "Don't guess it'll hurt to tell you they both claimed they was home, but they've got no one to prove it by. Frank was in half the bars in town before ten, but no one timed how long he stayed or how long it took him to get from one to another."

The hall door banged, steps pounded across the outer office, and Gus burst in.

"You still got him, I see," he said to Jeff, with a blistering side glance at F. Millard. "Listen, Jeff, why let him go? He said he didn't drop his flashlight by the body. If it slipped out of his hand in honest shock when he found the stiff, he wouldn't deny it. Only if he dropped it *when he killed Archer—*"

"If I had a chance," F. Millard broke in, "to say I dropped it innocently, and didn't take advantage of it—"

"All killers get rattled sometimes," said Gus. "Listen, Jeff—his flashlight fits that hole."

CHAPTER NINETEEN

ll the next day—at work in the store, even at the inquest—F. Millard kept telling himself that dozens of people had flashlights like his, sold by a popular mail-order house. But it was the flashlights of the suspects that counted. And every time he sought reassurance, a picture came of Mae's, smart and flat like a woman's compact; Beulah's ladylike pencil that she complained she couldn't get batteries for; and the old-fashioned torch that belonged to Klondike, very long in the shank and wide-flaring at the bulb. He couldn't remember ever seeing Frank or the boys across the street carry flashlights, but they might have them at home.

The inquest this morning had been only routine, disappointingly unexciting for the spectators that crowded the little courtroom. No disclosures like those in the Blaine case were made at all, and, aside from Jeff and Gus and the doctor, the only witnesses called were Mrs. Blaine, F. Millard, and Klondike.

Natalie Blaine merely identified her brother's body.

Asked for an explanation of his finding Archer, the grocer said that, since there'd been one murder on the block, the street lights' going out had alarmed him and he'd walked about the neighborhood to check up.

Neither he nor Klondike was questioned about their other activities of the night before. The girl confirmed his coming to her back door with the report about Archer and sending her to telephone. Her answer to the next question gave the spectators their only thrill. She said, when she cut her morning's kindling, that she found her ax had been sharpened. The audience sucked in its breath.

Asked why she hadn't reported the sharpening of the ax, Klondike looked astonished. People, she explained without looking at Whit or Valentine Voss standing in the crowd near the door, were always doing things for her and her invalid mother, and she supposed that someone had discovered how very dull her ax was.

That had been all of the inquest.

At least, F. Millard thought with relief, he wouldn't have to go to Archer's funeral. The body was to be shipped to California.

He hung his grocer's apron on a nail in the back room of the store and again tried to reassure himself about the flashlight. He ate a restaurant dinner, avoiding Klondike's place of business, and started home.

The stars were out again tonight—myriads that made him feel like an indistinguishable speck in a powdering of specks called a town, spilled on the snow and forgotten. Stars like a million flashlights. . . . Good gracious, he should have bought a new flashlight! No telling how long the authorities would keep his old one. What kind, he asked himself abruptly, did Ed Griswold have?

Then a nebulous nagging became all at once thought. Those worn mukluks in Archer's room—Long Ed Griswold "couldn't find" his. . . .

F. Millard passed Bonanza Road and hurried on down Second. This ought to be the cabin: the little one with a sagging front corner and extra-wide eaves, wedged in between taller neighbors. He knocked on the flimsy outer door that served, with canvas tacked over the screen, as a storm door in winter.

Both doors opened and Long Ed Griswold's peaked bald head was outlined against the light.

The two men exchanged stares, then Long Ed moved back and motioned the other inside.

The cabin had only one room, larger than it looked from the street, its walls lined up to the low ceiling with the hoardings of years.

Long Ed nodded toward a chair by the stove, clattered a pair of snowshoes with broken webbing off another, and drew it up for himself.

F. Millard cleared his throat. "Uh—you said something last night that made me wonder—did you know Dwight Archer, Mr. Griswold?"

"Fella that got killed? I didn't what you'd call know him. We chinned a few times after it come out at Tom's inquest who he was. I used to be Tom's partner, you know, and he was his brother-in-law."

"Did he ever come to your cabin?"

"Why . . ." Griswold paused; his hand went to the back of his head and the stroking motion began. "Seems like he did a time or two. Why?"

"Archer had a pair of mukluks in his hotel room—old ones—just like you wore at Blaine's inquest."

"They're the commonest kind."

F. Millard surveyed his host's feet clad in softly tanned moose-hide moccasins trimmed with red beads. "I wondered if he could have gotten yours," the grocer murmured.

"You mean swiped them? Couldn't pick them up by mistake."

A little silence fell over the cluttered room while the two men stared at each other. Then F. Millard suggested, "You could have lent them to him."

"Well, I didn't," said Long Ed shortly. "Hardly knew him to speak to. If that bastard swiped my mukluks . .

His voice died away and they sat in silence.

Griswold broke it with a question of his own. "Get to know Tom pretty well, Smyth, before he went Outside?"

"Why—I thought so; but the way things turned out, I guess I didn't."

"Suppose he was pretty careful when he sold you the store not to mention he had a partner back in 'thirty-one when he bought it?"

"He said the grocery was separate. And had a deed in his name."

Long Ed cocked his jaw and wagged his bald head. "He bought it with partnership funds. Guess that'll make it half mine in any court of law."

F. Millard thought of Natalie Blaine's agreement in the bureau drawer under his socks. If he was ever going to get anywhere . . . He swallowed and tried to sound aggressive. "Looks kind of funny, Griswold, for you not to claim it till Blaine's dead."

"What do I care for looks?" Long Ed showed brownish teeth. "He owed it to me. Why shouldn't I go after what's mine just because he's dead?"

"But his widow—"

"Hell, his widow's got plenty and to spare. And if she didn't she'd scrounge it out of an orphan. Tom was always a swindler, Smyth. I never did let him get away with it, and I'm not going to now."

F. Millard sighed. Anyway, his neck was more important than his pocket. "Got a flashlight?" he asked abruptly. "I pulled out a handkerchief just outside your door, and I think some coins came too. It was too dark to see without a light."

Long Ed got up quickly. "Whyn't you say so instead of sitting here gassing? I've got a flash, somewheres in this mess."

While his host pawed among empty lard buckets and old dog muzzles and into boxes with unidentified contents that jingled, F. Millard looked around the cluttered room. Looked—then stared—and felt the palms of his hands go damp.

In one corner, half hidden by a portable oven, was a grindstone. And Klondike's ax had been sharpened.

He was shaking so he hardly looked at what he had come to see when it was held out to him—Long Ed Griswold's flashlight. Finally the fact registered that it had a long shank and a flaring lens, and he found himself picking up the nickels and dimes with which he had salted Griswold's path.

He was walking down Bonanza, already past Frank's and almost past Beulah's when he heard a call.

"Smitty! Isn't that you, Smitty? Come in a minute."

Beulah's eye-filling proportions were outlined against her open door. She beckoned with a sweep of her arm.

Inside, the living room was cozy with pink-shaped lamps and warm air coming up the registers. F. Millard took off his coat with a sigh.

"What's it going to be tonight, Smitty? Cigars for you, I hope. They smell so mannish and expensive."

He chose one from the box she held out and went through what he hoped were the proper motions of biting one end and lighting the other.

"I've been listening for you all evening," she said, "even kept a plate of dinner warm till I decided you must have eaten."

Puffing madly, F. Millard set down his cigar to pant. "Don't make me sorry for myself. When I think of one of your meals—and the one I ate! What did you want me for? Anything happen?"

"Anything happen! With another murder last night?"

"But that was last night."

"What about tonight? And tomorrow night? And the next? Tom's gun's still missing. I—" her three-cornered smile was disconcerted—"I'm getting nervous, Smitty. Think I'll take to locking my door."

"A woman's got a right to feel nervous." F. Millard tried not to think of the number of times in the past week that he'd locked his own door. "It may not be an Alaskan custom, but locking up's only sensible now. I wish I had the right . . ." He paused.

Beulah waited a few seconds, too. Then she laughed, the sound a little strained. "When I think of the gal I used to be! Living alone on the creeks, sometimes without even a gun. Maybe that's the difference between being very young and—not so young. Even your tastes change; have you noticed, Smitty? I used to be so restless, always up one creek and down another. ... Now I want a pretty home and guests for dinner and someone to talk to. I was never lonesome when I was a kid, never cared who or what . . ."

She stopped, and her words seemed to hang in the air. This wasn't like Beulah. She'd never even suggested before that she wasn't as young as Klondike.

"When you're a kid you go your own way regardless, but later— Why, Smitty, now I actually care what the neighbors think!" Her off-center smile flashed ruefully. Then she shook herself and jumped up. Her smile became laughter, a little too loud. "Who are we to talk like old folks? What the hell do we know about age? Turn up the radio and I'll light the center light. Who's afraid of the big bad wolf?"

The little grocer blinked up at her from the davenport.

Her laughter climbed a note higher. "Guess that dates me. Old slang always does." Then the derision vanished. She sat down beside F. Millard and laid a fuchsia-nailed hand on his arm. "I'm not goofy, Smitty, just upset. Alaska never used to be like this. I love it like you do—only more so. When I went to that beauty school in Seattle I thought I could kid myself into staying. God, when I think about that winter! If Mae hadn't come out in the spring I'd have just about gone nuts. And Long Ed Griswold came a boat later on a business trip. I swear I've never been so glad to see him before or since. I got so I went down to the pier to meet every boat from Alaska. Every time anyone I knew got off, I'd hang onto him like a leech. I don't know whether it was funny or pathetic. And then, when I ran short of money—" She broke off.

The room, cozy with warmth and light, was still for nearly a minute before Beulah gave F. Millard the smile he found so captivating, this time a little downturned. "Hell, Smitty, I sound just like Eliot Malone—as spineless as a jellyfish. However Klondike may feel about growing up without a father and having an invalid mother to support, she and Silver Star were better *off* without him. Poor Eliot, he was so attractive, and so weak."

"Did you say he lost a whole season's furs gambling one year?"

Beulah nodded. "The season before his accident. He used to gamble half the night when I knew him on the Chandalar. But that was before he was married. When he had a kid and an ailing wife . . ." she shook her head.

"Did it happen up here or Outside?"

"Seattle. The spring of the winter I was there. I met the boat he came on. We left the pier together, and I had dinner with him. I just wish I'd kept him with me—and to hell with what would have been said—till he got those furs safely sold."

"He gambled with the furs themselves instead of the money?"

"That's what I heard."

"Oh, well, Beulah, he'd probably have lost the money going back on the boat."

She shook her head. "Too many Alaskans on board. They'd have made sure he got back with his stake. I can't help blaming myself some, too."

"Beulah, d-darling"—F. Millard leaned closer—"you'd take care of all the world—"

A quick knock came on the door, and it started to open. The grocer bit his lip and sat straighter.

Mae Trent poked her round face through the door, and her round body sidled in. "You all right, Beulah? But I see you got a protector. Lord, with the killing going on around here … ! You know, I lock the door every time I step out! What's Alaska coming to?"

"You take the words right out of my mouth," said Beulah dryly. "Hang up your coat, Mae. Cigarettes on the table."

"Boy, what a night!" Mae plumped herself down on the other side of F. Millard, bouncing the little man higher. "I told Jeff Peters a thing or two while he had me at the courthouse. Honest to God"—she wagged her brightly browned curls—"this is bad. One dead man in Smitty's warehouse, and one in Klondike's back yard. Why the hell would anyone want to kill Archer? We hardly knew him."

The three stared at each other in a silence that grew and pressed.

Mae swallowed. "That—that does sound bad, doesn't it? I didn't mean . . ." She stopped again. "Hell, let's forget about murder. I came over to ask you, Beulah, how you think I'd look with short hair. Those Victory cuts are pretty cute."

"On some people," the other woman returned. "If you were taller, thinner—maybe younger."

Mae pouted. "Perhaps I'll just change the color then. What's yours going to be next year?"

Beulah considered. "Well, I haven't been a blonde for a couple of years."

"Maybe I'm a fool to stick to brown because that's the color my hair used to be. I wouldn't make a bad blonde, myself. Gosh, when I see the way the old man lets himself get fat and bald, without even bothering—guess I'm just a fool. . . ." She stopped.

"Your husband can afford not to bother," Beulah murmured.

Mae shot her a steely glance out of eyes no longer round, and retaliated. "Did you ever think of letting yours go gray—for a change?"

Beulah stiffened. "Any day I . . ." She drew a long breath and F. Millard saw her relax. "What saps we are, Mae. I'm going to keep on as long as I can, and you are too. You know it."

Something bumped against the front door, and the three on the couch leaned forward, hands going suddenly tight. The door knob turned, and slid back. Both women looked at F. Millard.

Slowly, fists ready, he started for the door. As he reached it the bump was repeated. The knob turned again, and the door flew open so fast he had to jump back.

Whit Hawley plunged in. "Got anything to drink, Beulah?" His words were inclined to run together. "Voss hid the bottle."

But not in time, F. Millard decided, watching the bombardier fumble for a chair.

"Coming up, Whit." Beulah was halfway to the kitchen.

Surely she must have noticed. Should F. Millard follow and tell her Whit had had enough? But he began to speak again, and the little grocer waited.

"Val Vosh's got no alibi for last night," the soldier muttered thickly, "but he couldn't of killed Uncle Tom." He shook his light head solemnly, staring up at F. Millard.

The grocer co-operatively shook his, too. "You don't think so, sergeant?"

"And you don' either, shrimp. He couldn' of walked clear down here and back, let alone tomahawked Uncle Tom, with guys passing his desk all the time. It's a mile an' a half from the newspaper offish an' back."

"If he had a car—" mused F. Millard.

"Who'd len' a car to *him?*" Whit's voice turned querulous again. "Jush like a widow. She acts jush like a widow."

"Who?"

Mae winked at F. Millard and patted the place he had left on the couch. From the kitchen came the smell of coffee. He might have known Beulah'd understand. He sat down beside Mae, and they both leaned toward Whit.

"Who acts like a widow?" F. Millard persisted.

"It's only me they think's a murderer, not Val Vosh," Whit muttered. "Maybe ought to let him have her. What she sees in Archer!" He turned seriously to the grocer. "Think she carries on like a widow becaush it was her back yard?"

Of course it would be Klondike Whit was thinking of, drunk or sober.

Beulah came in with a tray of steaming cups.

The bombardier shook his head. "Not coffee, Beulah."

"Val Voss must have found my bottle, too," his hostess said gravely. "We're all having coffee."

They had hardly begun to drink it when another knock came at the door. Beulah answered this one, herself.

"Listen, honey," came a man's voice, "we better have a little talk—"

"Just in time for coffee, Frank," smiled Beulah. "Sit down and I'll get another cup."

Big Frank Ord lounged in, coatless in spite of the cold, plaid wool shirt open at the neck and hair more rumpled than ever. F. Millard couldn't help seeing the other man's masculine attractiveness or remembering that easy "honey." Tonight two things were noticeable about Frank: He was completely sober and looked worried.

He started to follow Beulah. F. Millard laid down his cup and headed for the kitchen too.

Frank's tousled curls were close to Beulah's neat ones above the deep sink where she washed her customers' hair. F. Millard caught the murmur, ". . . no reason to suspect her—"

His foot slid on waxed linoleum, and the others turned.

Frank frowned and Beulah smiled. "Get down a cup and saucer, Frank," she said, "and I'll fill it up."

The big man scowled at the small one. "What the hell do you have to come snooping around for?"

"Now, Frank—" began Beulah.

F. Millard dredged for an excuse he could use aloud. "What—what's Mae sore about?" he stammered. "When she was talking about her hair—both of you letting—"

"Didn't you know about her husband?" Beulah interrupted.

"Hell," said Frank, "you been living here all this time and never knew Mae's trying to keep up with a husband ten years younger than she is?"

"Ten y—!" No wonder she always called him "the old man," thought F. Millard; Mae was whistling in the dark. "Trent's no older than you are,

Frank?"

The curls above the plaid shirt caught light like golden- brown wires as Frank nodded.

"But Mae must be close to fif—"

"Skip it, boys." Beulah's crooked smile was strained. "A gal crazy about her husband has a right to do what she can. Anyway, it's their problem."

With a hand on each man's arm, she pushed them out of the kitchen.

Frank made for F. Millard's vacant place beside Mae in the middle of the couch. But Beulah didn't sit on Frank's other side as she usually did. She drew a chair near Whit.

"Why should she act like a widow?" the bombardier muttered.

"Drink your coffee," said Beulah.

"Is there any reason," said Mae abruptly, leaning forward, "why it has to be one person that killed them both?"

All the faces turned her way. No one needed to ask whom she meant.

"She acksh jush like a widow," repeated Whit.

"I wonder," said Beulah slowly, "how many people knew Tom was going to be down here that night?"

Mae's round eyes turned to F. Millard. "Besides Smitty," she finished.

"I didn't—" the grocer began.

"But the note—" She stopped more abruptly than she'd started.

"What note, Mae?" F. Millard's quiet voice dug in like a power saw.

"Why, didn't—didn't—" she floundered —"didn't some one say you had a note from Tom?"

"Who'd know but him and me?"

"Why—why—I don't know."

"If I'd had a note from Blaine, wouldn't I have destroyed it—under the circumstances?"

"Why, I—I should think so."

"Then how would you know about it, Mae?"

"Damn it, Smitty!" Her plump body quivered. "You're worse than Gus. It wasn't my fault anyway. There it was, sticking under my door. Of course I picked it up and read it!"

Just like Klondike. F. Millard gripped the edge of the couch. "What time did you find the note, Mae?"

"It was there when I got home Monday night about eleven-thirty."

"What'd you do with it?"

"Soon's I read it and saw it was yours, I stuck it under your door."

Where someone else could retrieve it and stick it under Klondike's. . . . The little grocer deliberated. "Where were you Monday night, Mae?"

"None of your business, F. Millard Smyth! You're not the marshal."

"I don't know, Mae," Beulah put in. "We all have to help get this killing stopped. And it doesn't look so good for anyone to hold out."

"What right's she got to act like a widow?" Whit persisted.

Mae sat blinking and biting her thumb. Then she clasped both hands in her lap and straightened. "O.K., you may be right. I went over to see Ora Wells on the other side of town."

"Were you there all evening?"

"N-no. I stopped in to see a couple of other folks, but they weren't home."

"Look here," said F. Millard suddenly. "Did any of the rest of you get that note under your door?"

"Not I." Beulah shook her head.

"Me neither," growled Frank.

"Nothing under my door," said Whit, and stared. The coffee must be taking effect.

"Good grief, Smitty," cried Mae, "a fellow could get the wrong house once, but not five times."

Not unless he had a purpose.

"Besides," she added decisively, "I stuck it under your door."

No use pressing the matter, thought F. Millard. Better not make too much of a point of it.

"What about the rose in his—in Archer's hand?" asked Beulah. "That's what bothers me."

"Don't they lay out corpses with a lily or something?" suggested Frank.

"Sort of a graveyard sense of humor?" countered Mae.

The kind that would pelt a man with— "Canned baby food!" mumbled F.

Millard.

"Hunh?" grunted Frank.

"I don't think it's the lily-in-the-hand idea," the grocer said louder and faster, "or he'd have been on his back, all neatly laid out. He must have had the rose when he was hit." Klondike's face came back too vividly, her tense: "I've got to have that rose." But neither Klondike nor anyone else could have moved the body when it fell in loose snow, without leaving a record. . . .

The little grocer looked up suddenly and found Whit's eyes fixed on him.

"Well, it may be the rose that bothers Beulah and the note that bothers Smitty, but it's having another murder gets me," announced Mae.

Whit grinned foolishly. "Jush like a widow," he murmured.

"That's it!" Mae gave a bounce. "It's that woman—that frozen-faced brunette Tom married. She didn't act any more like a widow when her own husband was killed than if—than if it had been Smitty!"

The room, for an instant, was tense.

"Don't you ever think Natalie—" Frank began truculently.

And Beulah said quickly, "Lots of people are like that She's not the type to show her feelings."

"Not the type to have any," muttered Mae. Then she spoke louder. "It's a funny thing when a man gets killed in a town where he doesn't know a soul—but one woman."

Frank banged down his coffee cup so hard he broke the saucer. "Are you hinting that Natalie . . .?"

Mae's pudgy hand patted his arm. "Now just keep your shirt on, Frankie. You're not married to her any more, and you must know what she's like. You know she wasn't upset when Tom was killed, and you know how she felt about Archer—"

"No one kills her own brother," protested Beulah.

"Half-brother," Mae corrected. "And I've heard, I don't know how many times, that they hated each other like poison. Besides, if Smitty thinks Tom's note's so important —who'd be more likely to know about it than his wife?"

The room was so still that the kitchen matches Frank was breaking made a series of sharp little pops.

"And who'd be more likely to get the wrong house," finished Mae, "than a stranger in town?"

"Surely you're not suggesting that the beautiful, pampered Mrs. Blaine delivered her husband's notes?"

"She might have been going for a walk, or had a special reason, or—"

"Nuts," said Beulah briefly.

"Not nuts at all," returned Mae. "It's still mighty funny that she's the only one in town connected with both corpses."

A knock on the door made everyone jump. Beulah crossed the room and stood for a moment in the doorway while the others heard a murmur outside.

When she turned, her face looked anxious. "Jeff Peters is here to see Smitty."

CHAPTER TWENTY

In the grocer's cabin Jeff occupied the chair in which Gus had once waited for F. Millard with Blaine's charred note and a gun on the table.

"Had to hunt up Long Ed tonight," the marshal said. "Thought I'd check with you again while I was in the neighborhood. Archer didn't say what he had in that envelope, did he?"

F. Millard shook his head, blinking across the table at the old man who still wore his shabby marten hat and bearskin coat. The little grocer hunched nearer. "You didn't— I don't suppose you'd tell me— My gracious, wasn't the envelope there?"

"The envelope was."

"You don't mean—someone beat you to what was in it?"

"I don't know. It's an almighty funny thing. Seems like Archer told the hotel clerk, too, if anything happened to him to turn that envelope over to us. So, bright and early this morning, soon as the news reached him, the clerk pops around with the envelope. Gus and I hadn't got down to the office yet, so the feller gives it to the deputy at the desk. And now here's the funny part: The envelope was sealed, the clerk swore he just took it out of the safe, but all there was in it was a blank sheet of paper!"

"A blank she—"

"Incidentally," drawled the marshal, "Archer's room at the hotel had been searched. It got an almighty quick going over, but someone sure hunted for something."

"You don't suppose . . .?"

"If that envelope hadn't been locked in the safe, I'd of thought someone steamed it open and stuck in a blank sheet, but with it locked up . . ." Jeff's shaggy bearskin coat lifted in a shrug that outdid Natalie Blaine's.

"Where is it now?" asked F. Millard.

"That's the hell of it. Feller laid it on my desk, and when the school kids come in on their paper salvage drive it must of got knocked off and one of them stuck it in with the waste paper—no writing on it or nothing."

The two sat gloomily staring at each other.

Jeff sighed. "I don't go much on invisible ink and that sort of stuff, but if Archer kept that paper locked up . . . I got me a couple of deputies pawing through the paper salvage."

"Think Archer was just bluffing? Pretending he had something on someone that he was going to give you?"

"Then they sure called his bluff."

"Anyone in the hotel see who came out of his room?"

Jeff sighed. "That'd be too much to hope for. Feller next door heard someone moving around, but thought it was Archer. And a woman down the hall come out of her room about the time the sounds stopped and saw someone in a parky going downstairs, but didn't see the face or notice the color of the parky."

F. Millard sat blinking and trying to think.

"Don't know as it's any of your business," said Jeff slowly, "but you'd be surprised what Archer had in his overcoat pocket."

The grocer looked up quickly.

"Bet he wished for a gun a hundred times, but he done the best he could for a substitute. Hotel man's wife keeps a flock of house plants in the lobby, and one of them's got some ornamental rocks stuck around it. They was all there yesterday, she said, when she watered the flowers, but last night we found the biggest rock in the end of one of Archer's socks in his overcoat pocket."

"Then he did have a date with the murderer, Jeff! Or why would he fix up a blackjack?"

"I been trying to find out where he went last night after you saw him at the hotel."

F. Millard drummed on the table. "You said you went down to Ed Griswold's. Did you happen to notice—"

"Yeah, I know he's got a grindstone. ... So you been there, too, have you, Smyth?"

"You know those mukluks in Archer's room . . .?"

Jeff nodded. "One of the reasons I went to Long Ed's."

"He admit they were his?"

"I'll say he did. Swore Archer stole them and acted mad. Said he missed them Friday afternoon."

"Friday afternoon," repeated F. Millard. "It was Friday night that someone followed me into the warehouse, and I saw a pair of mukluks just like those when the fellow turned on his flashlight."

"Yeah," said Jeff.

"I wonder why Griswold borrowed those Lapland mukluks, Jeff? He had on moccasins tonight that could just as well've been worn outdoors; couple of pairs of wool socks under them, too."

"He'd know those turned-up Lapp toes'd catch my eye. There's not so many pairs in Fairbanks. Might of wanted to call attention to his own mukluks being gone without making too much of a point of it; he's not supposed to know about that skirmish in the warehouse."

In the pondering quiet the two men heard heavy steps outdoors. Frank Ord lunged in without knocking, his face a mottled crimson.

"Listen, Peters"—he didn't even look at F. Millard—"if you think—you got no right—I tell you she never—"

Jeff pushed an empty chair toward him. "Sit down, young feller. Take it easy."

But Frank only grabbed the back of the chair as if he might use it for a weapon. "If I'd had any notion before that you thought—that Natalie—I began to sweat about it tonight and came over to talk to Beulah, and Mae said . . ." he drew a rasping breath. "Look here, Peters, I don't know anything about Archer's death, but Natalie had nothing to do with Blaine's—and I can prove it."

Jeff watched under shaggy brows.

"You said he was killed between eight and nine Tuesday night," Frank rushed on. "Well, from ten after eight to nearly half-past nine I was looking right at her every minute."

The marshal drawled, "Mrs. Blaine over at your place too that night, with you and Beulah?"

Frank shook back tumbled hair defiantly. "I wasn't home, and neither was Beulah—at my place, that is. My wi— Natalie was at the hotel."

"But—" F. Millard began.

"I'm telling the truth this time, Peters."

Jeff's tone was unexcited. "Why not before?"

"What would you do if you were in love with your ex-wife, and her second husband was killed three doors away? Even if that didn't make me chief suspect, who wants to be laughed at—or pitied? Well, I don't now, either, and I feel like a heel for what I'm doing to Beulah—but I'm not going to have Natalie up for murder!"

"Get on with the rat killing, young feller," said Jeff. "Let's hear what you got to say."

Frank sighed and sat down in the chair he'd been gripping. He pulled out cigarettes and broke two or three matches before he got a light. "I started uptown, like I said, Tuesday night, but I didn't turn around and go back because I remembered Beulah was coming over. I went back because I met Blaine."

"You knew him?" asked the marshal.

"He didn't know me, but I knew who he was, all right. Think I wouldn't know who Natalie married? Oh, yes, I heard they were coming up here, and I had him spotted." Frank tore up his last paper match and fished a handful of wooden ones out of his plaid shirt pocket.

"So you recognized Blaine," murmured Jeff.

A wooden match snapped loudly. "Sure, I did, and I figured Natalie didn't know anyone here. She'd be at the hotel alone, and I might get to see her."

"Then why'd you go back home?" demanded F. Millard. "Or do you claim now it wasn't you that turned on the light in your cabin?"

"Would you want the whole town to see you spying on your ex-wife? But everyone in parkies and mukluks looks alike if you don't see their faces. I went back to the house for my parky, and left the light on so it'd look like I'd been home in case anyone thought he recognized me uptown. I didn't have to angle for a peek at the hotel register; just as I came alongside the big lobby window, I saw her on the stairs. She glanced around the room and went over to the table with the magazines and stood there looking at them."

Frank paused, and another match snapped. For a minute F. Millard could see Natalie Blaine, slim and lovely and aloofly elegant—perhaps in that chic gray suit—picking up and discarding the hotel magazines—whether Frank had seen her or not. After all, she had told at the inquest about going down to the lobby for something to read.

"Then she went back upstairs, and—well, I just thought I'd take a turn around the building and look at the lighted windows. As I glanced up at one on the second floor, she passed it."

F. Millard gave an audible sniff: Too coincidental for *Flatfoot*. Jeff's faded blue eyes flicked his way and returned to Frank.

"I just caught a glimpse of her head. Then she moved farther back, and I couldn't see her. Listen, Peters, this may sound screwy, but if you knew Natalie, you'd know I couldn't just go ahead and call on her the way a man might his ex-wife. If I'd showed up at Natalie's door, I swear she'd have rung for the clerk, if not the city cop, and said I was annoying her." He paused, and his out-thrust chin defied the marshal. "There's a one-story building next door, with a ladder leaning against it—and there was no one in sight. I climbed the ladder and stood on the roof and watched her. It must have been nearly half-past eight, and I stayed there an hour, till she pulled down the shade."

"She was in the room all the time?" asked Jeff.

Frank nodded. "She glanced at the magazines and did her nails, just the way she used to. I remember how she always—" He broke off and lit his third cigarette. When he looked up his brown eyes were black. "She was there all the time. I watched her."

"What about your first story, Frank?" Jeff's voice was still unexcited. "You said Beulah went to your cabin while Mae was under the drier."

Frank's face turned a deeper red, and two more matches snapped. "Guess I was kind of crying on her shoulder. When I came home from the hotel I went over to Beulah's and—hell, after seeing Natalie again, and all, I just slopped over on Beulah, and she said if anyone ever claimed they saw me, I could say we spent that time together. Then, of course, when Blaine's body was found—and me in the spot I was in—I jumped at the chance of an alibi."

"You say you talked to Beulah Tuesday night," Jeff commented. "Why should she hand you out an alibi before the body was discovered unless—"

The grocer's heart squeezed.

"—she knew she'd need one herself?" Jeff finished.

Frank squirmed and began to splinter a broken match stick. "Well—"

Running steps came again in the snow, made by lighter feet than Frank's. Then a quick rat-tat on the door.

F. Millard opened it for Beulah, whose unrouged cheeks were pale, brightly lipsticked mouth cherry-tight.

She gave him a strained little smile and crossed the room to Jeff. "I suppose he's—told you what he said he was going to?"

The marshal nodded. "If you mean his new version of where he was Tuesday night."

"Guess there's no way to prove he's lying. If I could show you there weren't any tracks on the roof—but with all the snow we've had since Tuesday, how can I?" She sounded as hopeless as Klondike had when she talked about the rose.

F. Millard made a strangled sound and pointed at Frank. All eyes went to the red-faced man breaking matches. "Look at him, Jeff! Look at the mess around his chair! Would it be humanly possible for Frank Ord to wait any place an hour without leaving behind a stack of cigarette butts and broken matches?"

"Oh, Smitty!" Beulah's eyes were bright.

"We had an almighty big wind since," said the marshal slowly.

"But the snow came first," cried Beulah. "If Frank did wait on the roof like that he'd have messed up God knows how many cigarettes and matches!

There'd be nothing to disturb them up there. Wouldn't that much snow have anchored it all down before the wind started?"

"That spot's kind of sheltered"—Jeff's voice was thoughtful—"with the hotel on one side and a two-story building on Third. Guess if there was any mess on the roof, it ought to be there now—under drifted snow."

"If he really did what he claims, there'd be bound to be something to show it. Oh, Jeff"—she laid a hand on the old man's arm—"do you have to wait till morning to look?"

" 'Fraid so." The marshal's bony fingers beat a tattoo on the table. "Look here, Beulah: Suppose we do find a bunch of stubs and matches there—what's your story going to be then?"

"But I don't have an alternate story—like Frank. I can only tell the truth, and I've told it. I don't have—someone I want to protect at all costs—and anyone else's expense."

"God, Beulah," groaned Frank, "I feel like a heel. I hate like hell to do this to you, but when a man's wife—"

"She's no more your wife than—than Mae is."

All they could see of Frank's head was rumpled curls, gold-brown in the light. "Guess you're right," he mumbled.

"What was Mrs. Blaine wearing that night?" F. Millard asked abruptly.

Frank's face came up. "Something dark and close-fitting. She looked love—"

"Never mind how she looked," broke in Beulah. "What color was the dress?"

"God knows," he said blankly. "It was dark. Might have been black, or dark blue, or green or brown."

The woman's voice was acid. "Gives himself plenty of latitude."

"She had something bright on one shoulder," Frank added. "It sparkled like a pin or that fish-scaly stuff."

"Sequins?" suggested Beulah.

Frank nodded.

The clothes could be checked, thought F. Millard. No woman like Natalie Blaine could go into a lobby without someone's noticing what she wore.

"By the way, Frank," Jeff Peters drawled, "when Beulah come in you was just starting to tell us why she'd hand you out an alibi without even being asked. Better make it good, or after what turned up she'll be farther out on the limb than ever."

"Who said I handed Frank an alibi?" demanded Beulah.

"He did," the marshal said dryly.

Frank's face went deeper red. He raised unhappy eyes to hers. "I—I—you know I'd never give you away—if things were different. If it wasn't Natalie they suspected—"

"Skip it," Beulah said bitterly. "Go ahead with your story. I'd like to hear what else you thought up."

"I didn't think it up," he said gruffly. "You know you told me you didn't want anyone to know you had a soldier there." *

"S-soldier!" gasped F. Millard.

Now Beulah's face was crimson. "You mean to sit there and say, Frank Ord, that I told you I was—carrying on with a soldier, while I was giving Mae Trent a shampoo? Why, you—you filthy-minded . . ." She turned helplessly to F. Millard. "That's just the kind of story he would tell; it's the kind Frank understands. You—you don't believe it, do you, Smitty?"

F. Millard felt a rush of warmth. It wasn't her safety Beulah was thinking of now. She had turned to him, not to Jeff. "Of course not," the little man said loyally.

"While you was fixing alibis, folks," drawled Jeff, "you should of cooked up a few for last night."

"I forgot to ask you," exclaimed F. Millard. "Besides the ones that had a right to be there—yours and mine and Klondike's and Gus's and the doctor's—did you find any other tracks in Malones' back yard?"

"Yeah," said the marshal. "A few—made by a pair of mukluks."

CHAPTER TWENTY-ONE

Getting out of bed next morning F. Millard told himself firmly that he'd had enough of stumbling to the warehouse light cord in the dark. Last night and yesterday morning—even though the place had been locked tight and both keys were in his pocket—it had been all he could do to force himself down that black aisle of boxes. He'd buy another flashlight today if the stores weren't out, but the fire still had to be fixed this morning before he went uptown.

By dressing fast he might catch Frank; no use trying to borrow anything from Mae or Beulah till after ten. One trouser leg dragged while F. Millard hopped to the front window. Against the yet night-colored sky two of the chimneys across the street had that smokeless look of coal fires untouched since the night-before's banking. From Klondike's came the fine gray yarn that meant a dying wood fire.

As he watched, the Hawley stovepipe gave a spurt of heavy smoke. One of the boys must be up. In confirmation, a light came on in the front of the house.

F. Millard pulled on the rest of his clothes and hurried across the street.

Whit looked the worse for wear this morning, the little man thought, as the bombardier opened the door in pajamas less brown than his face. His pale hair stood up like shocked hay, and bare toes curled away from the cold.

"For God's sake, come in," he commanded, "or we'll never get the place warm."

The grocer stammered out his request for a flashlight. "There's one here some place," said Whit. "I'll look it up."

As F. Millard's fingers closed around the flashlight Whit brought back from the kitchen, the smaller man gave an involuntary start. He looked down—and blinked. This flash was exactly like his.

Slowly he turned it over—and blinked again. On the unornamented tapered end that held the ring two letters had been cut. If V.V.—or any other initials—had been scratched on the torch dropped Sunday night, no wonder it had been retrieved.

"O.K.," said Whit gruffly, "go ahead and tell me I made a spectacle of myself last night. Tell me I had no business going over to Beulah's place or any place else when I didn't know what I was saying. Tell me I've got myself in deeper—and maybe her too."

"Her?"

"Oh, God, if you'd ever been so crazy about someone that even her mourning for a dead man made you jealous! O.K., I know I'm not good enough for her. Why, Valentine Voss and his yen to be local editor would be better for her than a guy who'll always want to go chasing off to wars and fires—the kind that stays up all night and sleeps all day, and gets ulcers from too much to drink. At least Voss has sense enough to keep out of—murder."

F. Millard's eyes dropped to the V.V. on the flashlight, and returned to Whit's twisted face.

"So I hated Archer," flung out the bombardier. "If he'd wanted to marry her, it would have been different. But it wasn't marriage . . . He stopped and swallowed, jerked up his chin again. "The whole town knows I hated Tom Blaine—dear Uncle Tom who got Mom and Dad up here—to use. Generous Uncle Tom who paid all three Hawleys' passage to Alaska, and kept Dad on starvation wages—when Dad was supposed to own the store! Big- hearted Uncle Tom who kicked the Hawleys out when he came in off the creeks; so Mom and Dad went back to the States more in debt than when they came up. And look at what he did to Klondike's mother!"

"It—it's a shame," F. Millard stammered, "about everything."

"It's a damn sight more than that, brother. So if you ever go Outside again, look me up at McNeil Island."

McNeil Island, F. Millard's mind echoed, the Federal penitentiary in the state of Washington where Alaskan criminals were sent. "McNeil Island?" he echoed aloud.

"Providing I only get life. But I guess—with capital punishment—or would it be a military prison?"

"My g-gracious, sergeant, I have to fix the warehouse fire and get to work. Th-thanks for the flashlight."

For all the work he was getting done he might as well have stayed home, F. Millard decided at the store a few hours later. Dead men in parkas and tailored overcoats floated like mirages in front of the eggs; a dead hand clutching a rose, a Siwash mitt on a hand that moved. Instead of, "How much are potatoes today?" the questions he kept hearing were: Who circulated that note up and down Bonanza? What about that blank sheet of paper in Archer's envelope? Had the deputies found it yet? He could check on the cigarette-stub-searching for himself. The Blaines' hotel was only a few doors away. When F. Millard took off his apron, his clerk gave a sigh of relief.

Next to the hotel, on the roof where Frank said he had stood, three deputies were shoveling and sifting snow. At least it was a change from pawing through waste paper, and they'd be sure of quick results. But they hadn't yet come to results; each dug and sifted doggedly, while a few curious soldiers, old-timers, and housewives stared up from the street.

Examining every shovelful would take hours. Klondike's shift began at eleven. If he caught her now . . . The clerk could handle the store just as well without him this morning.

Back on Bonanza he found Klondike in a skimpy green wash dress with one pocket half ripped off and a flowered scarf tied round her hair. Grudgingly she moved aside and he entered a torn-up room.

"I'm cleaning house," she said stiffly, "and I haven't time . . . Besides, you're not going to make me change my story. I spent Sunday evening going through Mother's things, and I wasn't anywhere near the warehouse—that anyone can prove!"

"You don't have to pretend with me, Klondike. You and I know where you were last night. Seems to me, if you didn't put out the street lights before you came to the warehouse, or leave that—souvenir in your yard—"

"Mr. Smyth! How can you—?"

"—someone," the grocer continued firmly, "must have known you were out. Did you tell anyone you wouldn't be home?"

She shook her head so vigorously that a brown curl escaped from the bandanna. Then the curl bobbed the other way. "Oh, yes, I did—Dwight Archer. In the restaurant Sunday night after dinner when he paid his check."

There at the cash register, F. Millard remembered, when she'd turned pink and said, "I'm afraid tonight. . ." He hadn't caught the rest, but Whit had been closer, his ears undoubtedly strained harder than F. Millard's.

Klondike was still sighing when the grocer exclaimed, "Did you tell him where you were going?"

"My gosh, Mr. Smyth, of course not! How dumb do you think I am? I just said I wouldn't be home."

"You said several people dropped in Sunday night while you were dressing. Remember who they were?"

Klondike sat down on the floor by a stack of books. "I've got to get this cleaning done before I go to work." She opened a book and clapped it together. Dust sprayed out like steam. F. Millard sneezed.

"Whit and Val, of course. Thought I'd never get rid of them. And then blest if"—she clapped another book together—"Mae and Beulah and Long Ed Griswold didn't all come in—separately, of course, which took longer."

Unanimous again—almost. Only Frank Ord and Natalie Blaine— F. Millard blinked. Mrs. Blaine had been no more than a foot from the telephone the morning Klondike called. That hoarse, creepy voice—some tones carried farther than others, some even outside a receiver. . . .

Thoughts played hopscotch in his mind, then jumped back to Sunday night. Whit and Valentine Voss had been at Malones', Beulah and Mae and Long Ed. . . .

"Do you know Ed Griswold well, Klondike? Is he in the habit of coming to see you?"

She giggled. "Not me. He used to come to see Mother. He's dropped in once or twice since—since she died." She slapped shut an oversize book with an oversize spurt of dust. F. Millard sneezed again.

"You weren't dressed, of course, when they came?"

"In that dance-hall red? I should say not. I didn't even do my hair till toward the last. Guess only Long Ed saw it pompadoured."

"Was that red dress with the spangles where anyone might have seen it? On your bed when one of the women went in to powder her nose?"

"It was on the bed, but no one went into my room, and I shut the door—I'm sure I did—when I went to answer each knock."

She popped another book, and some rounded pieces of paper jumped out from the leaves. Spreading it open, she cried, "Oh, look, they're paper dolls! I haven't seen them since— Look at those styles! Short in front and a dip in the back. I couldn't have been more than five or six. . . . Oh, Mr. Smyth"—she raised a suddenly serious face —"Tom Blaine was over here the day I played with those dolls—here in this house. I'll bet it was the only time he ever was. Dad was in bed after he came out of the hospital just before he—shot himself. Mother had to go uptown and I remember she cut out those dolls from a magazine and told me to be a good girl and not bother Daddy, but to play in his room so I could get him anything he asked for. I was nearly six; it was just before he—died."

"That's funny," F. Millard said slowly, "when your mother and Blaine were so bitter, to have him come over here even when she was out. . . . Too bad you weren't older. I don't suppose you can remember anything they said?"

Bright lips parted, she sat staring at the paper figures in her lap. "I remember Mother'd said for me to stay, so I wouldn't go out of the room. Dad said something about he'd like to bury the hatchet. That intrigued me because I thought of our hatchet that Mother wouldn't let me play with, going down in the ground, and I thought it'd have to be summer because the ground was too hard in winter. . . . Why, it was Dad said to bury the hatchet—he must have been the one who wanted the get-together, not Mr. Blaine!"

Her luminous gray eyes came up for confirmation from F. Millard.

He nodded.

"That's just the kind of thing he would do, Mr. Smyth. Dad was so good-natured—and kindly. I remember— But you wouldn't be interested in that. Mae told me after Mother died that Dad always used to be distressed about her quarrel with Blaine. It would have been just like him to want to try to make it up before he—did what he did."

"Can you remember anything else they said, Klondike?"

She shook her head, eyes returning to the dolls in her green cotton lap. One after another she picked up each flatly limp figure cut from fashion plates of the late twenties. Over one she gave a little exclamation. "Dad said something about furs. I remember because this lady wore a fox. I thought it was so lovely, and I wondered if my Daddy'd caught it for her. He said—" she looked up at F. Millard, batting long lashes—"he said they'd been stolen."

"Stolen? What on earth . . .?"

"Lord knows. I remember hunting madly for that paper doll again, but she still had her fur all right. And it seems to me—oh, yes, it was this other doll. Dad said the word 'favor,' and I thought it was such a pretty word and this was such a pretty lady I named her Favor. Aren't kids crazy?"

Stolen furs—bury the hatchet—favor. . . . "Try hard, Klondike. See if you can't remember more."

"Could it really be important, Mr. Smyth?"

"I haven't the faintest idea. But the whole thing was so queer—Blaine's coming here, and their talking of stolen furs. I don't suppose anything that far back could possibly be connected with his murder, and yet, Klondike, you can't tell when some stray bit of information may be the very clue we need. So if you can remember any more . ."

Slowly she shook her head, while the one curl escaped from the flowered scarf quivered. "I just remember that Dad seemed upset. Kind of almost ashamed about some thing. Funny how anything like this"—she touched the paper dolls in her lap—"can bring so much back. I don't think I've seen them since that day. I suppose I left them lying around and Mother put them in this book and we both forgot all about them."

A little silence fell in the room with the chairs pushed into one corner and books scattered over the floor.

"I think," Klondike said softly, "that Dad was eager for people to like him.

Looking back now, and from what I've heard, I think he must have been the kind who'd be easy to take in. I was too little then to know what furs he was talking about. I don't know whether he ever had any stolen or not. All I ever heard that was special about him and furs was the time he gambled away his whole season's catch." She sighed. "Anyway, it isn't Dad you're interested in; it's Tom Blaine."

Finally F. Millard started back uptown. On the roof of the building beside the hotel the three deputy marshals still shoveled and sifted. He ate an impatient lunch and, returning, found the roof empty. But even as his muscles bunched to run for a telephone, Gus started back up the ladder. The deputies, too, had merely gone to lunch.

In the store F. Millard made so many mistakes and intercepted so many furtive glances among the customers that he retired to the back room to keep books. Ostensibly to work, actually to sit and stare at the ledgers and try to find one logical answer to fit all the questions that whirled in his head. Now two more rode the merry-go- round: Why had Eliot Malone been talking to Blaine about stolen furs? What favor had one done the other?

His eyes dropped to his tapping fingers. The ledgers they drummed on had once belonged to Tom Blaine. When F. Millard bought the store, Blaine had given him the books, tearing out the used pages. Good gracious, they'd come from the warehouse! Could it be these ledgers that someone had been looking for? But they wouldn't have done him any good even if he'd known where to find them. F. Millard had checked last year when he made his first entries in the books, and knew the used pages were gone.

His clerk came to ask a question at the hole cut through the partition between the store and back room. The square taken out, hinged and looked back on F. Millard's side, hid one ear and half a cheek. Past the clerk's other ear, down the row of shelves, F. Millard saw the grocery clock.

He gave the man an absent-minded answer and reached for his coat. The clock had said it was time to take another look at the snow-sifting.

Half a block away beside the one-story building next to the hotel the three peaks of snow on the ground were higher than ever. There were no men on the nearly flat roof, its iron corrugations laid bare.

F. Millard sprinted for the store. Inside, bumping into a departing housewife half again his weight, he caromed against the vegetable display along the window. By the time he picked up his customer's packages and the scattered beets and turnips, the telephone was in use.

He jiggled at his clerk's elbow while the man took down a long order. Finally the last item was written and F. Millard snatched the still warm receiver off the hook. It seemed an hour before he got Jeff, but at last the old marshal's drawl came over the wire.

"Uh—listen, Jeff"—now, in front of the customers, F. Millard was suddenly tongue-tied—"did you find—uh— those cigarettes? No matches either? Th-thanks. I'm glad to hear it."

So glad he had to fist both hands in his pockets to keep from waving and clamp his lips together to keep from shouting as he hurried to the back room. Imagine Frank trying to sacrifice Beulah for a woman like Natalie Blaine!

In the little room behind the partition he took off cap and overcoat and flung them at the ceiling, kicked off both galoshes. Then picking up the heavy coat, he whirled it around like a super-limber dancing partner, scattering the books and papers on his desk, making the typewriter rock.

That brought him to. Years of training reasserted themselves, and he bent to pick things up. The tangle of grocery slips would all have to be put in order again; and the old ledgers, already weakened by the pages Tom Blaine had torn out, were so sprawled and upheaved that F. Millard wondered if the bindings had stood the strain. Examining each as he picked up the books, he turned the third sideways and bent closer.

On the end paper at the back a few words had been written in Blaine's characteristic hand: On the first line, "Ed—," on the second, "Lord's office at two."

The book quivered in F. Millard's grasp. It must have lain, spread open like this where Long Ed wouldn't miss it, on the old dance-hall bar that Blaine and Griswold had used for a desk. Weighted down, perhaps, with an inkwell. The first thing that had come to Blaine's impatient hand without his having to stop to find a sheet of paper. Lord's office. . . .

F. Millard must have seen this note when he was given the books. But it had meant nothing to him then, not even enough to remember. Now . . .

Professional men had offices: doctors—lawyers . . .

If Blaine and Griswold had gone to a lawyer . . .

A shadow caught F. Millard's attention, a shadow that moved on the wall. When he rushed in from the telephone he hadn't turned on the light, and the little back room was dim. Light shining through the unglazed window into the store was bright on the opposite wall. It was there that the shadow moved. A shadow like the flap of one large black wing.

Rigidly F. Millard turned.

In front of the shelves of groceries in the square where the clerk's face had been was the shiny, bald peak of Long Ed Griswold's head. His stroking arm was busy again, his eyes on the open ledger.

CHAPTER TWENTY-TWO

F. Millard leaned across Jeff's desk in the marshal's private office. "But if Lord was a lawyer, Jeff, and Blaine and Long Ed both had an appointment with him, that certainly sounds like partnership business."

The marshal sat tapping his pipestem against bony knuckles. "Lord was a lawyer, all right. He went Outside three years ago to open an office in Spokane and was killed in an auto accident right after he arrived."

"Whit seemed to think Blaine and Griswold never had anything in writing, but why would they go to a lawyer unless—"

"I've known plenty of folks that never had a written partnership agreement, young feller, but when it come to breaking up they went to a lawyer to get it done right. Seems like it'd be natural for folks that had their fingers in as many pies as Long Ed and Tom, and were such almighty suspicious fellers anyway."

"Suppose the surviving partner knew something had happened to the dead partner's papers. If they'd been lost or destroyed or something. . . . Just suppose—" The grocer gurgled.

The man across the desk nodded. "Long Ed might of seen a good chance to make a crooked deal stick. Of course he'd have to be sure Tom's widow wouldn't spring any dissolution papers on him."

"That's where Archer might come in, Jeff. He lived in the same house with Blaine. Suppose Archer knew some thing had happened to those papers. Or swiped them, himself! If a man was grasping enough, it might even look worthwhile to—" F. Millard broke off.

"To commit murder?" Jeff asked dryly.

"What did that lawyer do with his papers when he went Outside? If he drew up any for Blaine and Griswold wouldn't there be carbon copies in his files?"

"Ought to be," agreed the marshal. "If we can find the files."

F. Millard was breathing fast. "With the lawyer dead, Long Ed might have counted on getting that ledger before anyone found the note. He must have thought it was still in the warehouse under the old dance-hall bar."

"He see you bring it over here now?" asked Jeff.

F. Millard shivered. "I ran too fast to look around."

"Lord wasn't sure he was going to stay Outside when he left," said the marshal slowly. "Seems like I heard one of the lawyers say he stored his files with an outfit that rents warehouse space. Might be I could get them."

"By gracious, if you could, and it's like I think—Griswold wouldn't have a leg to stand on!"

"Guess you need those extra five years—eh, Smyth?"

"Extra five— You know about that offer of Mrs. Blaine's?"

Lines crinkled the leather skin around the old marshal's eyes. "Under the socks in your bureau. We searched your place again—after Archer was killed. … By the way, Gus found a flashlight like yours thrown into the snow by the river a good ten yards off the road."

F. Millard sat up straighter. "Then that lets me out. Gus took mine out of my cabin."

"After making the mistake of picking it up," Jeff drawled, "the killer'd realize it would of been less incriminating, with so many others like it, to of left the flash by the body than have it found in his house."

"But mine was in my house," F. Millard repeated.

"So he'd take a chance on our not finding it in the snow where he could get it later to drop through the ice."

"But mine was in my—"

"That's how the ordinary suspect would reason, Smyth. You're a steady reader of *Flatfoot* and you've seen a few actual murders. You're not the ordinary suspect. You'd figure you ought to do the way he would, and leaving another flashlight in your house would just baffle the marshal's office."

"Then I'm supposed to have two flashlights?"

"Some folks do," said Jeff simply.

After a silence, strained on F. Millard's side of the desk, the marshal spoke again as casually as ever. "Looks to me like Archer must of been holding the flashlight and his hat in one hand, and they dropped when he fell on the hand with the rose."

"Then why would the murderer pick up the flash, Jeff?"

"It might of been his and he'd given it to Archer. It's instinct to keep something you own from pointing at you."

"Wish you wouldn't keep saying 'you.'"

Jeff grinned.

"Anyway," said F. Millard, "why wouldn't Archer be wearing his hat—at forty below?"

"The flashlight says he was looking at something, and all I can think of he'd have to take his hat off to see would be something along the wall where a hat brim would get in his way."

"Along the wall," repeated F. Millard. "There was a cupboard by the kitchen door to keep frozen food and a wash tub hanging on a nail. . . . You think that tub—"

Jeff nodded. "Seems likely. She could of hid the rose there herself, or someone planted it. When Archer took it out, with his hat off, bending over to look—he'd make a perfect target."

F. Millard thought of the wooden pigtail down Archer's back, and shuddered.

"What'd Long Ed say, Smyth, when you caught him looking at the ledger?"

"Said he came in for groceries and heard a noise in the back room. I forgot about noise when I was throwing things around."

"You were so almighty glad we didn't find any cigarette stubs on that roof?"

"Beulah's worth a hundred Natalie Blaines. You know it, Jeff. By the way, there's something else at Malones' you might be interested in—some paper dolls."

Jeff's shaggy brows drew together, faded eyes peering out from below, while F. Millard told of the memories those paper dolls had evoked.

"That," the grocer ended, "was all Klondike could remember."

"Hmmm," the marshal murmured. "Wonder how hard she's trying."

While F. Millard audibly speculated, Jeff sat in a sort of coma. Even when the grocer returned to the flashlight argument, he drew no more than a grunt from the old man humped across the desk.

Finally F. Millard returned to the store—to his side glancing customers and the spinning roulette wheel of thought.

The wheel spun till eight o'clock. Customers and clerk had been gone two hours before F. Millard realized he was hungry. He had his coat on, one thumb on the latch, and was reaching to switch off the store light, when the latch was jerked from his hand and the door flung open.

Klondike Malone sprang in, brown curls as wild as her eyes, her waitress apron spilling out of her coat. She caught F. Millard's arm frantically. "We've got to do something, Mr. Smyth—right now! They've arrested Whit!"

CHAPTER TWENTY-THREE

"A-arrested Whit!" F. Millard stammered. "Did he get so drunk—"

"Drunk! They arrested him for murder! Tom Blaine and Dwight Archer, both. But he didn't do it! No matter how things look I know he didn't! They haven't tried to find anyone else. I'm going straight up there and tell Jeff everything I ever heard of about anyone connected with Blaine! I'll tell about Long Ed robbing a clean-up, and—"

"Long Ed robbing . . . Hey, Klondike, do you know what you're talking about?"

"That's what he told Mother. I thought he was kidding, but Jeff can make him talk. And I'll tell about Mae's baby and—"

"Mae's baby!" F. Millard snatched his arm away from Klondike to grab hers. "Mae's baby?"

"She'd be grown up now, I guess. Mae told Mother one time they thought I was out playing. And I'll tell Jeff. I don't care if it is a dirty trick. And I'll tell about Long Ed saying one of Beulah's locations was crooked, and the time I saw Frank and Mrs.—"

"Klondike!" He gave her a shake. "Do you know half the things you're saying?"

"I never said I could prove them. Let Jeff do that. I'll tell everything I ever heard or even thought of—to save Whit! I—I'll even tell about the ghost."

F. Millard closed his hand around her elbow and pushed her toward the door. "Come and see him now. I'll take you."

They hurried down Second and across Cushman to the courthouse. The elevator had stopped running, and they climbed the stairs as he and Gus had climbed them Thursday night.

When they entered the marshal's outer office, Jeff looked up from his desk in the other room. Beneath the overhead light his shaggy eyebrows cast peaked shadows on his cheeks.

"K-Klondike," F. Millard stuttered, "has a f-few things she wants to say."

Jeff glanced from one to the other, his gaze resting on the grocer. "Had supper yet, young feller?"

F. Millard shook his head impatiently.

"Skin out and get it then, and come on back when you're through."

The little man clumped downstairs; if he'd been going up he'd have kicked the risers. Fifty years ago his mother had said, "Run out and play now, darling," while the grownups talked.

He wolfed his dinner, but when he returned to the marshal's office Klondike had gone.

Jeff sat stroking the ivory paper weight carved like a seal. He peered out beneath hooding brows. "Got a job for you tonight, young feller."

"Where's Klondike?" F. Millard burst out.

"Home. That's what I want you to tell them."

"Tell them Klondike's home, for gracious sake? Tell who?"

"Mrs. Blaine, and Beulah, and Mae, and Frank, and Long Ed. Better tell Val Voss, too."

"What do they care if Klondike's gone home? Can't the lunch counter get anyone in her place?"

Jeff grinned, and the overhead light cast a network of shadows on his cheeks. "Guess the lunch counter'll have to look after itself; I got me a killer to catch."

"Then Whit's arrest—"

"Did what I wanted it to. Now it's the other feller's move."

The room, for a moment, was silent.

"Don't let on I told you to tell or that Klondike's been to see me. Say she's threatening to dish out the dirt and you're worried about her. Don't forget to mention that she knocked off work for the evening and went home to try and remember something that keeps almost coming to her about her dad when she was little."

"But, *Jeff,* what if the killer …?"

"Go ahead and do what I say," the marshal drawled. "Don't fret, there'll be more deputies around Klondike's place than a porcupine has quills."

F. Millard sighed. "And here I have to work tonight! One of the pilots just brought in a big order from the Colville River country and wants me to get it out to the airfield by three in the morning so he can start at four. I'll have to spend the whole evening at the store getting that order put up."

"Better tell the folks that too, young feller. Someone may be almighty glad to know you won't have your specs trained on him right across the street from Klondike's. If we nab anyone before you get back. I'll let you know at the store."

Six calls, thought F. Millard going down the stairs; six different stories to arrange. While he was uptown he might as well see if Valentine Voss was still at the newspaper office.

He was. When F. Millard opened the door, Voss's neat dark head turned from the typewriter and light glinted on his glasses.

F. Millard cast about wildly for a diplomatic approach. None came, and he blurted out something about having to work tonight and being worried over Klondike. That part was real; even with her cabin surrounded by deputy marshals, Klondike herself was the bait.

Valentine Voss swept all his papers together in one drawer—a reckless gesture for him—and closed up his typewriter with a bang. "I'll go right down there! If she's been talking too much, and the wrong person heard—"

"Oh, I—I wouldn't go to her house," F. Millard stammered. Good gracious, that would spoil everything! "Having someone to talk to would keep her from remembering, and what she remembers may help solve the case. Why not just—just be next door where she could call you?" he finished lamely.

"Don't say anything to anyone else," the reporter cautioned.

F. Millard suppressed an hysterical tendency to giggle. He was only going to tell five others—the five other murder suspects.

From the newspaper office he crossed the street to Natalie Blaine's hotel.

The clerk rang her room and told F. Millard to wait in the writing room off the lobby.

The little room, an afterthought conversion of a bed room, tonight seemed too solitary, almost disturbingly separate from the lobby and the life of the hotel.

It was several minutes before Natalie Blaine came down. When she did, F. Millard blinked. Frank couldn't be blamed for finding her lovely to look at. The curved rouged lips, the delicate nose, the arched black brows above dark, oval eyes were as perfect as a painting's, almost as still. F. Millard thought of some movie he'd seen—or was it a story he read?—of a beautiful woman who had no soul. The black dress clung to exquisite lines, and the little grocer averted his eyes.

He had thought out his approach to Mrs. Blaine. "I dropped in to talk about that matter of Griswold and the store."

A sparkle lit the still eyes. "Have you found out anything, Mr. Smyth? Can you prove it's a fraud?"

"I can't tell yet," he hedged. "I—uh—I'm not through working on it. I just came to ask—uh—if your husband ever mentioned any Fairbanks lawyers."

Natalie Blaine shook her well-groomed head. "I don't think he approved of lawyers."

"You don't know Klondike Malone very well, do you, Mrs. Blaine?"

"Klondike Malone?" The arched brows rose. "What extraordinary names they have up here."

"You know—the pretty girl whose mother and— Well, uh—your brother was found in her yard. She—testified about the ax."

"Oh, the little waitress." Coin-cut face still, the woman waited.

"She—you know it's a funny thing. She went home tonight to try and remember a conversation she heard when she was little. Something about some stolen furs that your husband and her father were talking about. She thinks it may link up with something else she heard recently and help solve the murders."

Had the still face changed, or was it already like marble?

He fumbled for his hat. "I—I've got to work at the store tonight. I'll let you know about that Griswold matter. . .

She laid a white hand on his arm and he caught the hint of a perfume more subtle than Beulah's. "How nice it would be, Mr. Smyth—so well arranged—if this Griswold person should be convicted of the murders."

F. Millard shook off her hand and hurried into the lobby where there were other people, and on out-of-doors to clean air. He passed his store and pounded along down Second.

Under a street lamp halfway to Bonanza, he saw a parka-clad figure approaching. Even while he told himself that dozens of people wore parkas in weather like this, his heart did an extra flip-flop. Then he saw Frank Ord's face in the hood.

"Hey, Frank!" the little man called.

The other stopped.

"Going to be away long, Frank? I'm worried about Klondike."

"What's the matter now?"

"She said she's going to tell the marshal something she knows about one of us and—"

"Well?"

"She seems to think it's pretty damaging, and she's staying home to try to remember something about Tom Blaine and her dad that happened when she was little."

"Well, for God's sake, Smitty—"

"I thought—I have to be down at the store tonight, and I thought you'd see nothing happened to her. If she told the wrong person—"

"Ask another sourdough. The way you all stick together . . . When Natalie needs help— Hell, me for the nearest bar."

Frank strode on up Second and F. Millard continued downstream.

On Bonanza he saw three lighted cabins: Mae's at the corner, Beulah's across the street nearer the river, and Klondike's farthest of all. He knocked on Beulah's door first.

Inside, the pink-shaded lamps, the furnace heat, and the sight of his hostess in a blue dress that matched her eyes almost made him forget his errand. He sighed and rebuttoned the coat he had automatically started to take off.

"I'm worried about Klondike." He plunged right in. "She keeps saying she's going to tell Jeff everything she knows, and I—if the wrong person heard her . . ."

On the davenport Beulah shook her head. "I see what you mean, all right. Let's hope she hasn't said it some place she shouldn't."

"I'd like to stay and look out for her, but I've got a big order to put up at the store. You'll listen for her, won't you, Beulah?"

"Thought she was on the late shift at the restaurant tonight. You don't mean she's home alone!"

F. Millard nodded unhappily. "She'd been thinking about something that happened when she was little—some conversation she overheard between her dad and Tom Blaine about stolen furs, and she's got it firmly fixed in her mind that it had something to do with the murder. She quit work and came home to try and remember what it was."

"Hope she didn't tell anyone that!"

"Goodness knows how many besides me."

"I'll certainly listen for her, Smitty. Think I better go over, or will that interrupt the flow of thought?"

"I'm afraid it would, and what she remembers may be important." He picked up his cap, fingering the ear flap.

"Don't rush off mad," said Beulah softly.

"Wish I didn't have to, but it's going to take me most of the night to get that stuff ready for the plane." He stepped out into the cold and shut the door.

Perhaps, F. Millard decided, hurrying across Bonanza, it was just as well that the street lights were out. It wouldn't look so good if Beulah saw him trot right over to Mae's. Mae and Beulah and Klondike, Whit and Frank and Valentine Voss—if the murderer was one of them— the little grocer shivered. For a moment he was glad that he had work to do tonight that would take him away from Bonanza, away from the closing net. If Natalie Blaine or Long Ed Griswold should be caught he wouldn't care, but if it was one of his neighbors . . .

Mae answered his knock, in an elaborate red hostess gown, high-lighted with costume jewelry. *Mae's baby—* was Mae a scarlet woman—and Tom Blaine . . .?

"What's the matter, Smitty? Cat got your tongue? Come in so I can shut the door."

Her voice released him. Mae was still Mae whatever had happened in the past. He went into his by now familiar routine about being worried over Klondike.

"Little sap," said Mae when he stopped. "She ought to've had the sense to keep still till she talked to the marshal. You didn't think I could do anything about it, did you?"

"Well, no. I don't know what any of us can do—now. Guess I'm just trying to share my worry. You're so big- hearted about other people's troubles."

Mae's round face beamed. "Guess I could go over there . . ."

"Oh, no," he said quickly, reaching for the door knob. "That'd wreck her train of thought. If what she's trying to remember did have something to do with the killings . . ." His voice trailed off as Mae's had.

Deciding he probably looked as scatterbrained as he sounded, he mentioned his errand at the store and stepped out once more into the cold. It seemed even more icy now than when he left the marshal's office. He huddled farther into his coat and wished he'd been born a turtle—with the shell fur-lined.

As he knocked at Long Ed's canvas-covered storm door he found himself hoping it wouldn't open, that one interview could be skipped.

But the door began to ease toward him, and Griswold's peaked head was poked out. "Dropped any more money?" he asked sardonically.

"I—I just wanted to talk a minute. Mind if I come in?"

The aperture widened grudgingly. "If it wasn't so cold —I'm not crazy about letting folks in any more, not in this neighborhood."

The hodgepodge inside looked neither higher nor lower, but the grindstone—F. Millard's eyes flew instantly to the spot where he'd seen it—was now out of sight.

"What do you want?" his unwilling host grunted.

"I wondered if you could give me any idea—Klondike's all excited about some conversation she heard when she was a child, just before her father killed himself. Seems Blaine went to their house—"

"To Silver Star's? You've got things mixed up."

"Klondike swears it's true. She remembers a lot of things they said. Quit work and went home tonight so she could think back and remember the rest. Something about stolen furs."

Griswold shook his polished head. "Don't know nothing about furs."

"She thinks it ties in with the murders. Thought maybe you could give me a lead. Well, I won't take any more of your time. I've got to work most of the night, myself— at the store."

Long Ed's hand found the back of his head and began its up and down strokes. "Cold night to walk back up town."

A colder night, the grocer reflected, to wait in this neighborhood of bloodstains and blade-edged death. To wait and watch the net close. The thermometer must have dropped; in less than a block his nose felt raw. He could stop at his cabin for parka and mukluks— But he hurried past Bonanza with his head turned the other way. Better to take a chance on frostbite than go down that street again—till everything was settled.

All the suspects knew now that Klondike was home alone. One of them would want to make sure she didn't remember too much. Whit alone hadn't been told. Funny that no one had mentioned his arrest.

Overhead the northern lights played wild crack-the-whip. In and out among the stars red, green, and yellow knots tangled and untangled without sound. A dog howled in a near-by yard. Another answered a few blocks away.

F. Millard stepped up his pace, and the full Malemute Chorus broke out.

His fingers curled in his mittens as he thought of Klondike, alone. Feverishly he reminded himself that this wasn't like those other nights when the Aurora had writhed and the sled dogs howled; he wasn't going to the warehouse tonight. He was going in the other direction —faster and faster by the block.

And Klondike, he reminded himself, had protection. He stepped up his pace still faster and glanced back over his shoulder while the cold air scraped his lungs. The Chorus rose again, and the grocer broke into a run.

192

CHAPTER TWENTY-FOUR

F. Millard dropped the last box just inside the front door of his grocery and flipped off the main lights. In the pale wash of a street lamp he made his way past dim counters and shelves to the lighted back room.

The night watchman had just left. On his next round, in another hour, he would let the expressman in to pick up the things for the airfield. Now all F. Millard had to do was make out his bill and write a short letter before dashing down to Bonanza to see for himself what was going on at Klondike's.

The nearer he came to the little back room the slower he took each step. What was the matter with him tonight? First he wanted to see the marshal's trap close, and then he didn't. Now he didn't even want to go into the back room. He shook himself, walked briskly through the door and shut it.

Of course the room was as empty as he'd left it, with his flat-topped desk and swivel chair, the clerk's apron hanging, limp and lank, from a nail, F. Millard's overcoat covering his. No one could have come in. There was just one door, and he'd been working near it all evening. The only outside window was high in the wall, nailed down, with the old blackout shade drawn. His eyes stopped at the square of linoleum on the floor—stopped and stared. Dingy, no bigger than a large bath mat, it covered a trap door. . . . But the old cellar hadn't been used since before Blaine bought the store when local steam was piped in. Laying the cement sidewalk had blocked off the coal chute, which was the only outside entrance. So no one could come up through the trap door. Anyway, it was Klondike whom someone wanted to get at, not F. Millard.

He gave himself another shake, pulled the typewriter forward, and opened a ledger.

One short letter and a bill didn't take long to write. And here he was, back in his quandary again. Ten minutes ago he'd been all for flying to Bonanza; now he wanted to stay away.

He gave a big stretch that carried him back in the swivel chair till his fingers grazed the light switch on the wall. Righting the chair with a clatter, he pulled out his watch. Nothing could have happened yet. Jeff had agreed to let him know if he didn't get home in time. It was one a.m., and the telephone on the other side of the partition was as quiet as the shelf-lined store. How creepy it was to think that his watch—that every watch in the world—was ticking off the last minutes of freedom for someone—whoever sprang the trap set at Klondike's. F. Millard tried unsuccessfully to stop a shiver.

The street noises, muffled back here, had now ceased altogether. The sound of the watch still in his hand accented the hush of the room—the metallically nervous *tick-tick-tick,* and the hoarse rasp of his breathing.

On such a cold night no one would be out but those who must be, like the men from the marshal's office—and the killer.

A feeling of smother, of walls closing in, swept suddenly over F. Millard. He shoved the watch back in his pocket, ready to jump up for his coat and run before it was too late. But the smooth gold case had hardly left his fingers when he heard the sound: the click of the front door—closing.

The part of his brain that wasn't benumbed said it couldn't happen, said he'd locked the door himself, and the key was in his pocket. The clerk had no key. It was far too early for the watchman. The only other key to that door had been on the ring that was lost.

On the other side of the partition, steps crossed the store. Steps too light to be made by shoes—the unmistakable slither of mukluks.

The little grocer sat paralyzed. The steps came on. Whoever made them was attempting no concealment. They came quickly and firmly, louder as they approached.

Then the door knob turned, and F. Millard couldn't breathe.

A figure in a muskrat parka and reindeer mukluks entered. A scarf covered the lower part of the face, tucked into the hood.

A hand in a Siwash mitt came up. F. Millard made an involuntary ducking motion from the waist, numb legs still hugging the chair. But the hand only plucked away the scarf and showed Beulah's three-cornered smile.

He couldn't smile back. If Beulah had his keys . . .

Her bright eyes examined the room, even, he saw, the kneehole under the desk. "Lord, Smitty, it's fifty-five below! Thought I ought to breathe through a scarf, but my lungs feel like raw hamburger anyway. I brought you something I didn't think you'd want to wait for till morn- mg.

She slid both hands out of her mittens, and, still wearing her inner wool gloves, while the mittens dangled from their harness, she fished inside her big handbag.

F. Millard could hear himself inhale with a wheeze like an asthma victim's. Beulah seemed so natural, surely she couldn't—but what was she feeling for?

"I carried this bag yesterday and they weren't in it then. But tonight—look, Smitty!" She brought out a clinking key ring.

"The k-keys I lost two weeks ago!" F. Millard gasped. Surely she'd never produce them or act like this, if she wasn't innocent?

She sat down on the desk, mukluked feet swinging, and settled the big brown handbag more firmly in her lap. "Got your work done, Smitty?"

He tried to sound as casual as she did. Everything *must* be all right. "The order's ready to pick up, and I just finished the letter that goes with it."

"Someone coming for it soon?"

Why did she care? "In—in about an hour," he stammered.

She glanced at her watch.

"Oh, I don't have to wait for him, Beulah." Words came in a rush. How could he suspect Beulah Raymond? "The watchman's going to let him in when he makes the next round. I can take you home right now."

"That wasn't what I was thinking of." Her voice sounded queer.

He looked up quickly. Something like light fingers ran up and down his backbone.

Her bright blue eyes were fixed on him. But she always gave him flattering attention. "All that babbling you did about Klondike—I suppose you wanted—someone to try to stop her remembering. Jeff got big deputies planted all over her cabin?"

"My g-gracious, I hope no one else—"

Her feet stopped swinging. The head inside the parka hood nodded. "Guess he figures it's ending tonight. And he's right. But not like he thinks."

Again the sensation of walls pressing in caught the little grocer. Beulah's hands went to the catch of her bag. In his knuckle-rigid grasp the chair arms were slippery and wet.

She brought out a paper, and F. Millard exhaled. Nothing more than an oblong of paper.

Sliding off the desk she laid it in front of him. Typed words blurred under his eyes.

"Put your John Henry on that, Smitty. Down here at the bottom." She touched the paper with a wool-gloved fingertip, and her perfume made his stomach churn. Her voice was warm and coaxing, eyes harder than Gus Ingersoll's. "Come on, Smitty, you'll be doing more than Jeff to stop the killings—a whole lot more than Jeff."

Shaken by the tocsin in his chest, he still couldn't focus his eyes. He bent nearer the paper and blinked.

"That's right, Smitty. Never sign anything you haven't read." Her sugared voice held all the enforced patience of a ten-year-old coaxing someone else's baby brother to let go of her curls. "You'll find it's all right. I came in one night and used your typewriter. It's typed on your machine, worded the way you'd word it yourself."

Your machine—the way you'd word it. . . . He could read it now. Black letters on the back of his own grocery billhead. Black letters that said he'd killed Tom Blaine and Dwight Archer. Black letters that said when Jeff read them F. Millard would be dead.

Slowly his head turned toward Beulah—and a gaping automatic.

"Yes, it's Blaine's gun," she told him. "I had it and the keys and Klondike's rose cached away for future reference. But there's no time like the present. If Klondike remembers too much tonight, I'll have an ace up my sleeve that'll make anything she has to say look made up."

"B-but, Beulah, it's so hard to believe . .

She smiled—the charming off-center smile that, an hour ago, would have started motors all through him. Now it was like the baring of fangs, the warm chuckle that followed, ghoulish gloating. "I fooled you, didn't I, Smitty? You had no idea till tonight. And even tonight, when I horsed around about the keys and my scarf and asked about your work, I had you guessing again. I had to make sure there was no one here, or coming soon."

His mind pedaled like a bicycle going downhill. If he could keep her talking. … It couldn't be much more than half an hour before the watchman was due again.

"You—you certainly put it over on all of us, Beulah. No one could guess that such a friendly, lovely—" he choked. "Blaine must have done something awful to make you— want to kill him."

The face in the parka hood hardened to match her eyes. Then her smile flashed again. "Thanks for them kind words, Smitty. It wasn't what Tom did. It was what he was going to do."

"Was he trying to kill you, Beulah? You acted in self-defense?"

"You might call it self-defense, though I doubt if a jury would. He didn't pull a gun, but if he told what he said he was going to, I would have landed in the pen, or the noose end of a rope."

"You mean—that sounds like—Beulah, you didn't kill someone else before Blaine?"

Her lips drew up again above her teeth. No one could have called it a smile. "What if I did? What business is it of yours? All you've got to do is sign this letter—and keep still."

"K-keep still? You mean if I sign—a suicide note, you won't shoot me?"

Now her face was all friendliness again—friendliness and warmth and charm. F. Millard held back a shudder. "Of course not, Smitty. Not if you do your part. Jeff's getting too close, dragging up that old talk with Eliot. But he's got a lot of confidence in you, and if I had this"—she gestured toward the note—"I could use it if things got too hot—and you'd be sure to see that they didn't."

With a suicide note in her hands, and the knowledge now in his head—how could he believe she'd let him go? Good gracious, what a low opinion she must have of his intelligence! F. Millard's lashes batted as fast as Mae's. If Beulah thought that of him, maybe he could make her think . . .

"How could I—you—we . . .? You want me to try to steer Jeff in another direction Beulah?"

"Why not? You and the lovely Natalie might railroad Long Ed. It wouldn't be hard to get enough on him. I'll help you."

"Then—then what's the gun for, if you're not going to—make what the note says come true? I wish you'd put it down."

"Not yet, Smitty. You may need a little persuasion if you hesitate too long."

"Won't you—tell me how it all happened, Beulah? You —you've been so clever. . . ."

She pushed back the sleeve of her parka to look at her watch. She mustn't look again and see time running short —it was up to him to keep her from thinking of time.

"How did you know Blaine was going to be in the warehouse that night, Beulah?"

"I delivered the note," she said complacently, "the one you didn't get."

"But it said he'd see me at my place. It didn't mention the warehouse."

She gave a superior smile. "I went to the hotel the night they arrived, and pretended to write letters in the little writing room off the lobby. When Tom passed I beckoned him in. He was just as anxious to see me on the q.t. as I was to see him. I told him about your lodge meeting, so he wrote you he'd come at nine-thirty, but we planned to meet in your warehouse at eight-forty-five."

Eight-forty-five. . . . No wonder Klondike hadn't had to persuade Blaine when she phoned! He must have thought it was Beulah disguising her voice. No wonder he'd said he wouldn't need to see F. Millard later. "You got him to write the note then, Beulah? How on earth . . .?"

"Oh, that was easy. You bought the store right after Dutch Harbor was bombed, and Kiska and Attu taken. Tom wanted to get out of Alaska quick, even if he had to take a loss. But now that the Japs are on the run he wanted to come back and go in for essential minerals, and he needed all the money he could get. I said he might bear down on you harder at home than in the store and offered to take the note to your cabin, in case you didn't look in your post office box."

"So you stuck it under Mae's door, and when she put it under mine, you got it back and put it under Klondike's."

Beulah laughed. "And when *she* took it back, I got it for Gus. I was going to leave it at Whit's door too, but I saw Val Voss bring Klondike home, and figured if he didn't read it, he could have, and could have told Whit. So anyone in the neighborhood could have been involved, and that was what I wanted."

"Anyone but Frank."

"I didn't know then about his connection with the Blaines, or I'd have left it at his door too." In the frame of the brown parka hood Beulah's smile came on again. "It tickled me the way you fell in line when Frank was squawking to Jeff. I didn't even have to tell him to look for cigarette stubs on the roof; you took care of it for me.

"After you'd taken care of the stubs, I suppose?"

"Of course. I slipped down there at two a.m. with a flashlight, after Frank told me, and gathered up all the litter. My mukluk tracks looked just like his; so if Jeff had gone up before the snow came, I'd have said Frank trampled the roof to bear out his story, but forgot about cigarettes."

"And the stuff you told Frank about a soldier?"

"Just a line. The kind of thing he'd fall for."

For a moment quiet hovered over the room—a dangerous, muscle-tensing quiet. F. Millard's mind raced again, and he wet his lips. She mustn't look at her watch. "What—what would you have done for an alibi, if Frank hadn't told you that story?"

"Claim I spent the whole time in the kitchen and Mae couldn't hear me under the drier. She'd never have known I went out. I wore gloves to keep my hands warm and not leave fingerprints—red gloves, of course, since the rest of you had them, too."

"It was lucky for you, Beulah, that Frank gave you a chance at a better alibi.

Because Mae admitted your hands were warm, but she said your skirt was cold, like you'd just come in from outdoors."

"Why, the little fat bitch! After all I've done for her, too."

Beulah dropped her mask of false warmth, and her face looked hard and forbidding. F. Millard jerked out another question.

"You—did you put out the street lights too?"

"Sure I did. You poked your head out of your cabin Tuesday night when I popped the one by the warehouse and I ducked behind your wood pile. I was so damn mad! I'd put them out the night before, and that fool Mae had to get the bulbs replaced Tuesday morning!"

Good gracious, he must ask her something that wasn't connected with Mae—and ask it fast. "It—it was smart of you to wear mukluks so Gus couldn't spot your footprints. Did—did you wear a parky too?"

She nodded. "Sure, everyone looks alike in parkies." The grimness was leaving her face, but she didn't look enough yet like a cat licking cream off its whiskers.

He tried again. "You've been so smart about it all— I'll bet it didn't take you long to decide to fasten it on me. You—you pointed it so cleverly my way."

She began to purr. The mask was in place again. "I thought you'd be the best bet, but I kept an open mind. **I** almost made Klondike take the rap instead of you."

"Why Klondike?"

"Little fool came into the warehouse all togged out like her mother. I'd just dragged Tom's body to one side and piled boxes over the bloodstain when I heard her; so I jerked off the light and ducked. She came in with a flash light and climbed up and tied the light cord out of reach. Then she went out again and up the covered stairs. I watched her light the candles on the balcony. Then you came in, and I saw the whole performance. And after you'd both gone—I got that rose."

"Then—then you gave it to Archer?"

"He gave it to himself. I put it where he—Look here, Smitty, I haven't got all night. Get busy and sign that paper."

Once more the automatic pointed.

F. Millard swallowed. His chair arms were slippery again. He didn't dare look at his watch, but it couldn't be much longer before the watchman was due. She *had* to go on talking. "You've been so smart the way you managed everything I just can't wait to hear it all. Aren't you going to tell me why you killed Blaine? What it was—who it was he knew about?"

Beulah's bright eyes looked levelly back from the hood. One hand moved toward her watch.

"Seems like you could have done wonders in business, Beulah, with a brain like yours. Did you ever think …?"

As he talked, the hard blue gaze above him softened. "What's business, Smitty, but different ways of coming out ahead of someone else? I've done all right for myself as it is."

"You—you certainly have. When I think how you outwitted Jeff—"

Her eyes began to sparkle. "Even from the very first, when he and everyone else thought Eliot killed himself."

"Eliot ki— You don't mean Eliot Malone, do you, Beulah?"

She looked more and more pleased with herself. "Everyone thought it was suicide—because I made them think so.

"You—you shot him with his own gun and put it in his hand?" F. Millard shivered. The parallel was disturbingly close.

She shook her head. "I didn't want to give him ideas by going to the drawer for his gun. I whipped out my own from my handbag. And after I was through I shot his out the open back door and put it in his hand."

"But the shots—didn't anyone hear two shots?"

"Bonanza Road was the other end of nowhere in 1930, Smitty. My gun was the same caliber as his and there was no ballistics expert here. A man who'd just lost both legs and wasn't noted for any more guts than Eliot—no one ever thought of anything but suicide."

"But why?"

"I never could have stood the pen. He was going to send me there for swiping his furs."

"S-swiping . . .?"

Beulah laughed. "I'm sure giving you an earful, Smitty. That's what he must have been telling Tom about when Klondike was a kid. Warning him against me. If Klondike had remembered their mentioning me . . ."

She paused and F. Millard wet his lips again. "But, Beulah, if Blaine knew you stole furs from Klondike's father, didn't he wonder about Malone's death?"

"No more than anyone else. I tell you I did it right!"

"Oh, I—I'm sure you did," he said quickly. "The way you've done everything's just incredible. Do you think Blaine . . .?"

"Bet he didn't even smell a rat till he got my letter. Guess he thought Eliot's fur story was a sickbed hallucination. Or if he did believe it he had a good reason to keep still. He wanted to marry me."

She touched the fur around her face coquettishly. Before F. Millard could ask another question she went on of her own accord. "Guess my letter made him so mad he was willing to believe anything about me. It must have all come in a flash, the way things do when you're mad."

"What letter, Beulah?"

The face in the parka hood turned pink with righteous indignation. "Tom thought I'd still deed him half that cinnabar claim he staked for me. Why, I've been doing the assessment work for fifteen years! He said he didn't want it in the first place—when mercury was too low to pay to work such a faraway claim. Now that it's valuable he expected me to turn it right over to him like a—like a worm! Well, he found out when I answered his letter! Archer was there when it came and told me all about it."

"Archer was there! G-gracious, Beulah, what . . .?"

The anger left her face and smugness returned. "Oh, I have my little ways that reach clear to San Francisco. Archer lived with his sister, you know. He and Tom used the library for an office—neither of them needed one much. They were both there when the maid brought in the Alaska mail and Tom read my letter. He let out a string of cuss words and jammed some paper into the typewriter, and pounded out an answer; then shot right out to mail it, and Archer picked up the sheets Tom had used for a back. He was too cagey to make a carbon of a letter like that, but mad as he was, he remembered to protect his roller. The keys had been hit so hard their impressions went through, and there was my name—Archer didn't pick it up in a bar—and enough information so he thought a trip to Fairbanks'd pay him. At least he might get my cinnabar claim ahead of Tom."

"So that's what brought Archer to Fairbanks," the grocer murmured.

"But the joke was on him in the long run," said Beulah. She smiled again, that charming smile that made F. Millard's flesh crawl. "I named a figure he couldn't meet, and it took too long for Klondike to get her five thousand from Tom's estate. So Archer, knowing what that letter said, thought he could make something on the side. He dropped me a few hints and made a date to come in Sunday night for a talk. Well, I got things ready for him."

"R-ready for him, Beulah? How do you mean?"

"I went over to Klondike's earlier that evening and found she was going out—and I knew where. She may have thought she shut her bedroom door, but you know Klondike. It wasn't quite shut, and I saw Silver Star's dress on the bed. So I made sure the ax was there, and planted the rose in the washtub, and put out the light on the corner of Second where anyone who heard the pop would mistake it for backfiring. Then I watched in my parky and mukluks till I saw Klondike start for the warehouse, and I hit the other street light with a chunk of ice while she was going up the stairs. And then I went home to meet Archer."

"What did—how did you take care of him, Beulah?" F. Millard breathed, eyes round and dazzled.

"He said he left the letter at the hotel, but he recited it word for word—the letter Tom sent me that I'd destroyed. I laughed and said he'd got it all wrong; Tom meant something quite different. I told Archer if he wanted to do a little private detecting I'd show him something to open his eyes right across the street."

"How did you ever get him to go with you? If he really thought you killed Blaine—"

"I told you I had my little ways. I made a game of it. Said if he still didn't trust me—and laughed while I said it—he could find out for himself I wasn't armed. We both made a game of that, and he enjoyed it—patting me here and there—quite as much as I did. Don't you envy him a little, Smitty?"

F. Millard tried to leer, and almost gagged.

She smirked and chattered on. "Archer put on a little act of his own. Took a sock out of his overcoat pocket with something heavy in the toe, and stood sort of absent mindedly twirling it around. So he was armed, and I wasn't. Poor fool San Franciscan—when we got to Klondike's back yard, he never thought to look at the chopping block."

F. Millard rubbed wet hands down his thighs. "So then you—"

"I told him to look in the washtub. He held my flash light and his hat in one hand, so he could get up close to the wall. And as soon as he took out the rose—I let him have it with the ax."

"F-first Malone." The little grocer was hoarse. "Then Blaine. And then Dwight Archer. I wonder . . ." He thought of the blank sheet of paper in the envelope Archer had left. In the wrong light it wouldn't show impressions. It would only look blank.

He glanced up quickly. The room was as hushed as an undertaking parlor, and Beulah's hand was moving toward her watch. "Th-th-then you searched Archer's room to get the letter?" he croaked.

"And didn't find it," she snapped. "There wasn't time to hunt long. And now there's no more time to talk. Hurry up and write your name on that paper, Smitty."

"B-but, Beulah, what good . . .? I can help you pin it on Long Ed without signing this."

"And leave you knowing all about me without my having any comeback? Guess again, brother. I'm sorry, Smitty. I got so I kind of liked you. I'd even let you kiss me if I didn't think you'd grab for the gun."

F. Millard shuddered.

She laughed. "If I'd said that an hour ago, you'd have died of joy." Her voice hardened. "Now it won't be joy you'll die of—if you don't hurry up. Pick up that pen."

"B-but, Beulah, Klondike said one of your location notices was crooked, and Long Ed robbed a clean-up, and Mae—"

"That brat does too much blabbing. I wish it was her instead of you. But it's going to be you in just two minutes—if you don't sign that note."

This time she really meant business. He couldn't put it off any longer. There was no need to go on pretending. Thank goodness, his voice was as steady as hers. "A shot isn't silent, Beulah. Someone on the street may hear it and come in and catch you."

"The door's locked. I'll have time to skin out the back way while they go for help. If anything slips up, I can always say I just came in to bring your keys and you shot yourself as I got here. ... I told you I'd give you two minutes. Half a minute's gone now."

So he had a minute and a half. . . . When he first thought of someone's last minutes ticking by, he hadn't thought they were going to be his own.

He was a man and she was a woman, but a robust woman with a gun, and a finger on the trigger. He could never knock the weapon out of her hand—with the light on.

With the light on. . . . When he'd finished typing and stretched far back in his chair before Beulah came in, his fingers had grazed the light switch. If he pretended to be sleepy now—made out he didn't believe her. . . . She already thought he was dumb. . . .

He forced his jaw to open. One hand came up to pat the hole, and he made a sound like yawning.

"I tell you I'm not kidding," said Beulah tightly.

"I can't—" he patted another yawn—"can't sign that note if I'm dead. . . . My gracious, it's been a full day."

He raised both arms to stretch, and she started forward. Then they went up over his head, away from her, and she straightened.

"You've got guts, Smitty," she admitted with reluctant admiration. "Or else you're a plain damn fool."

F. Millard arched his back, and his arms stretched another few inches. He had to make it the first time. She mustn't see him fumble for the switch. He gave a final surge. The chair slid back. His fingers struck the switch.

Darkness clicked down. Man and chair crashed. A sharp grunt came through the dark. Was it just surprise, or had the chair hit her?

He lunged for the door knob—and touched wool. Wool with steel muscles beneath it—that turned—made a grab. . . .

Jerking back, he ducked beneath the unglazed window into the store. It was too small to climb through. The outside window, nailed. Its heavy shade was drawn, but faint light came through the opening in the partition. As soon as their eyes got used to the darkness, that light would give him away. Now, in the seconds before she could see—

Thank goodness the wooden shutter was fastened on the side away from Beulah. Cautiously he straightened. Left hand found the metal hook. With rigid care he slipped it from the eye.

Bang, and the last bit of light was removed! A bang that wedged the shutter in too hard for Beulah to pull open.

In the blanketing dark he slipped farther away from the door. She would surely wait there so he couldn't escape. That clutching hand that had jumped from the knob. . . . But now was no time to shudder over past encounters —while he was still shut in with a killer.

He crouched in the dark, not breathing. If he used the chair for a shield— picked it up by the arms and covered his head while he tried to knock the gun from her hand. ... Or suppose he used it for attack—brought it down on her head with all his strength. . . .

But how could he find her head in the dark? Or the gun? Unless, of course, she shot. Would a chair deflect a bullet? She was no longer a woman to him, but a murderer, to be dealt with as murderers must be dealt with.

If he waited for the watchman's next round—waited in the dark and silence to yell when he heard the latch— Beulah would shoot when he yelled.

Thank goodness, she had no flashlight. She would have used it before now if she had. Found him first with the light—then a bullet. A flashlight—

He gulped. The one he'd borrowed from Whit was in his overcoat pocket. The coat hanging just a few feet from the door! If Beulah let her hands explore while she waited in the dark. . . .

F. Millard bent to take off his shoes, felt for the desk to put them where they wouldn't get in his way. Crouching, he crept toward the wall where his coat hung. After the splintery floor boards, the linoleum in the middle of the room felt smooth and cold to his nearly bare feet. Then boards again.

Then the wall. Now Beulah was only a few feet away.

Right arm outstretched, he crept closer. Another step, and cloth was rough beneath his fingers. His hand jerked back. But it was cloth, and Beulah wore a fur parka. His hand slid out again, up toward the nail.

As he eased the coat down, it caught—swished against the wall.

Beulah shot. A flash. A boom less than a yard away that sounded like a cannon. The coat in his hand twitched. Something thudded in the wall by his ear. F. Millard bent lower and slipped back.

If she no longer cared about bullet holes all over the room—had given up the suicide plan—if Beulah, too, realized the time was drawing near for the watchman to make his next round—she'd shoot every time she heard him move.

Every time she heard him move. Could he make her run out of ammunition?

Once more F. Millard's foot felt the chill of smooth linoleum. The trap door! Even if he couldn't make her waste her shots—Blaine said he'd never used the furnace. Maybe Beulah didn't know . . .

Quickly, very carefully, F. Millard crossed the smooth place. Feeling boards again beneath his feet, he gently laid his coat, with that death-bringing flashlight, on the floor. Stooped and raised the edge of the linoleum. Could he jerk it up all at once without letting it slide? In this hush it would sound like dive-bombing, and might be as lethal. Across the room death waited to pounce.

Well, he couldn't hesitate forever—or it really might be forever. He gave a big sideways heave. The mat came up. No slide, but it landed with a flap like another gunshot.

Beulah's automatic barked again.

This shot didn't come near him. By the time the linoleum landed, F. Millard was behind the desk. The flash had been near the door, as he'd expected.

Cautiously he crept forward again, and felt along the floor for the trapdoor ring. His fingers slid into the hole that cupped it, and closed around smooth metal. Carefully, standing well to one side, he began to lift.

Up, up the trap door came. Slowly, silently. Up and over. Carefully he let it down on its back, to the floor. He straightened, starting around it—and stubbed his toe.

Another shot crashed across the room. Sang just past his shoulder. The rest of the way to the desk he made on hands and knees.

Squatting in its shelter he tried not to pant. If she thought he was hit. . . . He reached up on the desk, brought down one shoe, and tossed it behind the trapdoor. It landed with a clunk against the wall, as if he'd stubbed his toe again.

Another boom and flash across the room.

Too bad he didn't dare groan. He couldn't risk its coming from the wrong direction. Something to slide, like a dragging leg. . . . He stood up, cautiously feeling on the desk top. Then he chucked a ledger a little to the left of where he'd sent the shoe, careful not to throw too far to the left where she might hear it bumping downstairs.

The book slid along the floor. Beulah shot again. That made five. Six bullets to a clip. If she didn't have another . . . He tossed another book. She fired again—the sixth shot. Its flash came from farther out in the room.

He tossed the last book. But she had another clip. Two quick shots came out of the dark. Then a voice he could hardly recognize as hers:

"You little runt—you bastard—I've got you now!"

He heard the slide of mukluks on the boards. Then a choked-off scream. A loud thud. And a series of bumps.

Springing up, he leaped for the trap door. Slammed it down and hauled furiously at his desk. Just got it on top of the trapdoor when the thumping began on the floor.

F. Millard clicked on the light and ran for the telephone.

CHAPTER TWENTY-FIVE

Deepening midafternoon darkness laid a grayish pall over the marshal's private office and the two men at the desk.

Jeff made no effort to turn on the lights. "I'm glad she's dead," came his gentle old voice, "glad she had that poison and took it when she couldn't get out of the cellar."

Across the desk F. Millard sighed. "Beulah'd take death any day before life imprisonment."

"She cleared up everything, young feller, before she died, when we didn't know she had any poison in her."

The grocer leaned forward in the dusk. "Did you actually have anything on her, Jeff? Wouldn't it have been just her word against mine? She could even have claimed I put her in the cellar and threw down the gun to cover up my own guilt."

"But we had something on her, and she knew it. I kept the bullet that killed Eliot Malone. Don't know why, when I thought it was suicide just like everyone else. But he didn't leave a note, and suicides generally do."

F. Millard shivered. He'd heard all he ever wanted to about suicide notes.

"If we sent it to a ballistics man Outside—" began Jeff.

"But Beulah wouldn't keep her revolver all these years. She knew about ballistics too."

"Told me she was scared to ditch it right after Eliot was shot for fear it'd start folks thinking. Then Long Ed asked to borrow it, and she didn't dare turn him down."

"Don't tell me he borrowed it for fourteen years!"

"Well, you know how some folks are about borrowed stuff. I had quite a talk with him this morning. He said Beulah kept jogging him about it. Finally it began to look funny for her to be in such a hurry to get it back when she wasn't on the creeks any more and already had a rifle in the house. He didn't know what was eating her, but one day he told her he lost it."

"But if she thought he lost it—"

"Long Ed's never lost anything since he was born except the time one of his cabins on the creeks burnt up. She knew almighty well he had it some place—and there wasn't a damn thing she could do." In the deepening dusk Jeff grinned.

"Wonder if those furs she stole could be traced? My gracious, Jeff," the little man burst out, "how anyone could steal from a legless trapper—"

"He wasn't legless then. Remember those furs Eliot claimed he lost gambling the spring before his accident? Well, he didn't; Beulah swiped them."

"*Those* furs?"

"She knew him pretty well, young feller; all his little weaknesses. One of them was herself. He was crazy about her that winter on the Chandalar. So when she met his boat in Seattle she didn't leave him after supper, like she said. She took him to her apartment and kept him there a week. By the time he got back to normal, with bottles and Beulah all over the place—and his furs gone, he didn't have the nerve to prosecute and let Silver Star find out."

"It—it would be kind of embarrassing," F. Millard agreed.

"He figured to make it up next season—but that's when he lost his legs. Poor devil, we all thought he just didn't have the guts to face it. But Beulah told me last night he'd made up his mind to prosecute, and then, I suppose, start a civil suit to get back the value of the furs. That money's what she set up her beauty shop with; we all thought she made it off her claims. Eliot told Blaine first. That's what Klondike heard."

"Why Blaine?"

"To bury the hatchet, like he said—warn Blaine against his pal Beulah. Then Eliot sent Silver Star for the U. S. Attorney. She didn't know why, and made the mistake of telling Beulah. So when the U. S. Attorney got there, Eliot was dead."

"My g-gracious!"

"That's what Blaine was referring to in the letter Archer got hold of. Tom said, 'Some things aren't covered by the statute of limitations,' and meant Malone's death; the fur theft was outlawed by then."

"Was Blaine checking on those furs, Jeff, when his wife saw him go to all those crummy places in Seattle?"

Head outlined against the darkening window, the marshal nodded. "He found out Beulah sold them, all right. So he could build up a murder motive that might pack a big enough threat to make her do what he wanted."

"Then when Mrs. Blaine saw him take that automatic—"

"Damn right, young feller. Beulah said it was to make her deed over the claim, but I think it was for self-protection in case he'd guessed right about murder. He was too almighty fond of money to go to the U. S. Attorney with what he found out—if there was any way to cash in on it."

F. Millard thought of the stiffened figure in the parka with a hatchet in its skull. Presently he asked, "Why did Beulah steal Malone's furs?"

"She began to run short of money. Lived high when she first went Out on what she made off her claims. Then it was gone, and she didn't like being poor in a city. She said someone else would of gypped Eliot if she hadn't. Beulah was as bone-selfish as anyone I ever knew."

The room was still again.

"Wonder if the letter Archer tried to use for a club was the one—" F. Millard began.

"The one in the safe," Jeff nodded. "Gus found it in the paper salvage this morning. Beulah'd of had a hell of **a** time explaining it. Tom bawled her out in it for not giving him a deed, and hinted about stolen furs and murder."

"But, Jeff, didn't the location notice say she'd staked the cinnabar claim herself?"

"That's what it *said*," returned the marshal. "Remember Klondike raving about Beulah's crooked location and Long Ed robbing a clean-up? Ed told me about it this morning. Seems he and Tom found a cinnabar ledge beside a game trail in one of those hell-and-gone places. They talked over staking, and decided, as other prospectors must of before them, that it was too far away. From where they stood they could see a man working down by the creek—old geezer Long Ed had been arguing with."

"The one he told to take better care of clean-ups?"

Jeff nodded. "Long Ed ducked out of ditch-digging next day, and Tom followed. They took the game trail over the ridge. Tom waited at the cinnabar ledge and watched his partner go down and rob the old man's clean up."

"Why didn't Blaine turn him in instead of giving him an alibi?"

"And break up a money-making concern? Not Tom Blaine."

"What's all that got to do with Beulah's location, Jeff?"

"Tom took that way of letting Long Ed know he'd been caught. Couldn't stake in his own name with the real date and hand out a good alibi, and he'd used up his staking rights anyway; so he did it in Beulah's name. She'd already revoked her power of attorney, but he dated it back a couple of months to when he knew she'd been in the country—and left the notice by the trail where Long Ed couldn't miss it. I'll bet Tom made Ed's life hell till the statute of limitations ran."

The room in the gathering dusk was still.

"No wonder Klondike thought she had something," said F. Millard. "Wonder what she meant about Mae's baby?"

"Usual thing, I guess, young feller. Mae was a dumb, pretty little seventeen-year-old first time she went Outside, and Tom took advantage of her. He was on the same boat and made her believe they'd be married in Seattle. Of course he skipped when they docked. Lucky for Mae, Beulah was out there that winter. Her dad had died, and she and her ma were spending his insurance money. They saw Mae through her time, and some Seattle folks adopted the baby. They kept it almighty dark, for a bunch of women. Bet Mae was in a sweat when she found out Tom was coming back."

"That's right, she didn't move to Fairbanks till Blaine left. Was he the reason she lived in Anchorage?"

Jeff nodded. "Lived here till Tom busted up her first marriage, and she wasn't taking any chances on the second. Suppose we don't say anything about her little slip, young feller. There's only you and me and Klondike that know it now. Poor Mae's already bit off more than she can chew trying to keep up with that young husband. Guess her example's what held Beulah back."

"Held Beulah back!"

In the heavy dusk all F. Millard could see of Jeff's grin was a whitish streak. "You don't think her style was cramped? Well, I've got a sneaking notion if it hadn't been for the Trents she'd of glommed onto Frank."

"Glommed onto . . .?"

Jeff chuckled. "Her funds were running low again, but she had a place she liked in the community now, and marriage is more respectable than theft. Had a couple of good prospects, too."

Grateful for the growing dark, F. Millard felt his face begin to sting. "A c-couple of p-prospects?"

"Neither of them was as rich as she'd of liked, though Frank was good-looking, and you had the store. But Beulah could always get a husband. You turned out to be more useful other ways."

The little grocer shivered.

Jeff's easy drawl flowed on. "Leaving your keys on the table when you went to lodge was almighty handy for her. Though she'd of got them some other way if you hadn't. That gal had a head—like she said you told her. Went down and used Long Ed's grindstone to sharpen Klondike's ax the night he spent in your warehouse."

"Spent in my ...?"

"The night you gave her and Mae and Klondike a screen test on the balcony. Remember they stayed at the door while you and Voss searched the place? Long Ed did just what you thought—played ring-around-a-rosy with you. Once Beulah saw his foot and recognized the moccasin— a pair with red beads that she made him. Then you locked the door with him inside, so she knew he'd be there till morning, and after she come home from the dance she took that ax down to sharpen."

"I kind of thought it was him when I saw what was in that old ledger.

Guess he dropped in at Klondike's and found the note she left for Valentine Voss saying we were all at the warehouse. Was it Long Ed the first time too, when someone slipped in while I was fixing the fire?"

Jeff nodded. "Looking for the ledger. We were right about—"

A knock came on the door to the outer office. In the dusk both men jumped. The knock was repeated more sharply. Jeff ambled across the room.

The light behind the door he pulled open outlined a fashionable feminine hat and smartly cut fur coat. "There's no one out here," came Natalie Blaine's mannered voice. "I wanted to see you about my husband's former partner. Even though he didn't prove to be the murderer, isn't there some way to stop his attempt to defraud me? I'm sure *you* can do it, Mr. Peters, after what you accomplished last night."

"Guess you don't know the whole story, Mrs. Blaine; today's paper's not out yet. You've already got the best man on the job."

"The best man?"

"F. Millard Smyth."

"I hope he didn't tell you I employed him. It wasn't at all a matter of employment. There was to be a reward if he succeeded. But that doesn't prevent men better qualified from taking over. After all, that little Mr. Smyth's only a grocer."

"But as good at catching murderers as selling turnips, and that's saying plenty. Come in, and I'll turn on the light."

F. Millard blinked in the overhead glare, blinked into Natalie Blaine's startled face.

"Oh, I didn't know—Mr. Smyth . . ." She almost stammered.

"Mr. Smyth," Jeff drawled, "caught Beulah Raymond last night, and if it hadn't been for him you'd of been almighty out of luck in the Griswold matter."

Natalie's dark eyes came up quickly. "Can you possibly mean . . .?"

Jeff nodded, and his hand went to his inner breast pocket. "We was just talking about it. Smyth dug up what you needed." He pulled out a folded paper and spread a legal-sized document before her. "Here's a carbon copy of the dissolution agreement between your husband and Griswold, with the grocery mentioned as Tom's separate venture."

F. Millard opened his mouth. Behind Natalie, Jeff shook his head.

"Oh, then it's all right—" she began, her still face almost joyful.

"Sit down, Mrs. Blaine." The marshal put her in his chair and stood behind it. "Smyth, here, got everything fixed up, and Long Ed come clean when I sprang that agreement on him. Seems his own copy was burnt up in a fire on the creeks; so when Archer told about Tom losing his papers, and then Tom was killed, Long Ed thought his chance had come."

"Then Dwight really was working with this Griswold person, Mr. Peters? I thought he was at the bottom of it."

"He only supplied the information. Long Ed thinks Archer snitched his mukluks because he wasn't cut in on the deal. Though he might of just seen the advantage of leaving mukluk tracks instead of the kind that could be traced."

"But this information Archer supplied—•" began F. Millard.

Jeff broke in. "He told about the time your safe was robbed, Mrs. Blaine, and Tom's business papers destroyed before the police got back your jewelry and the stocks and bonds."

"Tom didn't tell me anything had been destroyed, and I didn't know this agreement existed." Natalie fondled the paper on the desk.

"Neither did I," said the marshal, "till Smyth ran it down."

"Why, I—" began F. Millard.

Behind the seated woman Jeff shook his head again. "Fine work, young feller. Long Ed didn't have any scheme, Mrs. Blaine, when your brother first went to see him. According to Ed, Archer thought he might get some dope out of Tom's ex-partner to help him put over a deal with Beulah. Anyhow, Smyth's got everything fixed up now."

Natalie folded the paper and stood up. "That's just splendid, Mr. Peters— and Mr. Smyth." She nodded graciously toward F. Millard also, as she slipped the agreement in her handbag.

Politely but sadly F. Millard rose too. An extra five years to make his back payments would have been a tremendous help. Oh, well, if he'd been six feet tall or J. Edgar Hoover it would have been nice too. Jeff was the one who found the paper.

The marshal took another sheet from his pocket. "Here's a little thing I typed out for you to sign, Mrs. Blaine. I'm no lawyer, so it may not be the usual thing, but with a couple of witnesses, it ought to hold. . . . Hey, Gus!"

"A receipt for this?" Natalie touched the alligator hand bag into which the first paper had gone.

"It's a five-year extension on Smyth's back payments, in return for services rendered."

The other two gasped. Gus strode in from the little room where the suspects had been interviewed. Natalie looked from the two big men to the small one, then abruptly picked up Jeff's pen, ran her eyes down the few lines, wrote her name at the bottom, and hurried out.

Gus gave F. Millard a chilly glance, added his own name, and followed Natalie as far as the outer office.

"J-Jeff!" F. Millard gasped. "I didn't get that paper. You did!"

"No one would of if it hadn't been for you. It's the least she can do, considering all you saved her."

In the glow of the overhead light F. Millard sat with a warmer glow in his chest. Across the desk Jeff pulled out his pipe and cupped the bowl in one hand.

The grocer's eyes turned toward the outer office and Gus. "J-Jeff," he stammered, "if you'd come down to the store last night and found me shot, with Blaine's gun in my hand and a signed suicide note in front of me, would you've thought the case was closed?"

"It would of been hard for me to stomach, young feller. I never did think it was you, just made like I did to see if the killer'd relax. Even Gus would of smelled a rat when he turned up Blaine's letter this morning."

The room was still again while F. Millard basked.

Down the hall came a confusion of running steps. Voices clacked in the outer office, and Klondike and Whit burst through Jeff's door.

The girl's gray eyes danced above the smile like her mother's. "The queen and the rabble," she giggled. "Do you feel very rabblish, Whit?"

The soldier's face was as bright as hers. "Poor Aunt Picklepuss, she's a swell-looking dame, honey."

"Whitman Hawley, if you think—"

"Hey," Jeff interrupted, "I didn't let him out of jail to be picked on."

Klondike giggled again. "We just met the lovely Natalie. If I could be mad at anyone today it'd be her for what she did to Frank."

"What's she done now?" the old marshal twinkled.

"Turned him down again, and poor Frank doesn't have sense enough to know he's lucky."

"But Mae knows 'just the right girl for him,' " mimicked Whit.

"What about your arrest, sergeant?" cried F. Millard. "Jeff, you never did explain it."

The two tall men grinned over the others' heads. Whit answered. "Just to make the girl friend talk. Jeff thought if she threatened to tell all, the murderer would start action. He didn't really pinch me."

"And he wasn't as boiled as he let on the other night," added Jeff. "Just putting out a few feelers."

"Having a reporter in the house helped a lot," said the soldier, "till he landed on the suspect list himself. Then I had to do my own scouting."

"Was it something he told you that made you admit being in the warehouse the night your uncle was killed?" asked F. Millard.

Whit shook his tow head, his eyes swung to Klondike. "I could see she was scared, and I didn't know what she'd been up to. I thought she might need—" He stopped, turned red, and cleared his throat.

If she needed a pair of broad shoulders to divert suspicion from her, Whit had been ready to supply them. Thinking of his own near-romance, F. Millard sighed.

"But say, folks"—Whit's flush deepened—"we're looking for a couple of witnesses."

Under the overhead light the old marshal's face broke into a network of lines. "For a wedding?"

"It's your own fault, Jeff," smiled Klondike radiantly, "you brought us together."

Whit fumbled in his pocket. "Here, have a cigar." He held out an awkward handful.

F. Millard shuddered. Pink-shaded lamps and perfume, the radio playing a dance tune . . .

His eyes went to the pipe in Jeff's veiny hand. All the great detectives—Sherlock Holmes, Flatfoot Flannagan, Jeff Peters . . .

A smile brought up the corners of the little grocer's mouth. "No cigars, thank you, Whit. Got a pipe?"

THE END

A Note from the Author

It's great to be back in print (80 years later)!

About the Author

Eunice Mays Boyd (1902-1971) spent twelve years living in Alaska from the late 1920s until the onset of American engagement in World War II. She was born in Oregon, the grand-daughter of George C. Ainsworth and great-granddaughter of John C. Ainsworth, the scion a prominent pioneer family. She was raised in Berkeley and graduated from UC in 1924. She married George Lloyd Boyd, an attorney whose career took them to Alaska. They divorced in the 1940s and she worked for UC President Sproul and later at UCSF in the Department of Preventive Medicine. Her goddaughter, Elizabeth Reed Aden, secured the literary rights to her novels and has published three manuscripts written between 1948 and 1971 (*Dune House, Slay Bells* and *A Vacation to Kill For*). She also secured the rights to Eunice's out-of-print books, which are being republished. She was a co-author with Anthony Boucher, among others, of *The Marble Forest,* which was made into the movie *Macabre*.

You can connect with me on:

- https://elizabethreedaden.com
- https://www.facebook.com/ElizabethReedAden
- https://www.instagram.com/read_aden
- https://www.linkedin.com/in/elizabeth-reed-aden

Also by Elizabeth Reed Aden/Eunice Mays Boyd

Murder Breaks Trail (1943 and 2024)
Doom in the Midnight Sun (1944 and 2024)
Murder Wears Mukluks (1945)
Dune House
Slay Bells
A Vacation to Kill For